"[O]ne of the stars in the ascendant...
poised for the next big step."★

Praise for More Than Fiends . . .

"Maureen Child . . . has a sharp, witty voice that will leave readers begging for more." —Katie MacAlister, *USA Today* bestselling author of *Holy Smokes*

"Megatalented Maureen Child has a patent on her genre. Fun, sexy, and incredibly entertaining . . . guaranteed to delight. Readers will love this fast-paced winner. . . . It's simply exceptional." —Allie Mackay, author of *Highlander in Her Dreams*

...and for Maureen Child's previous novels

"Sassy repartee . . . humor and warmth . . . a frothy delight."
—★*Publishers Weekly*

"Maureen Child infuses her writing with the perfect blend of laughter, tears, and romance. . . . Well-crafted characters. . . . Her novels [are] a treat to be savored."
—Jill Marie Landis, author of *Heartbreak Hotel*

"Maureen Child always writes a guaranteed winner. . . . Sexy and impossible to put down."
—Susan Mallery, author of *Irresistible*

"Absolutely wonderful . . . a delightful blend of humor and emotion . . . this sexy love story will definitely keep readers turning the pages." —Kristin Hannah, author of *Magic Hour*

A Fiend in Need

Need

Maureen Child

A SIGNET ECLIPSE BOOK

SIGNET ECLIPSE
Published by New American Library,
a division of Penguin Group (USA) Inc.,
375 Hudson Street, New York, New York 10014, USA
Penguin Group (Canada), 90 Eglinton Avenue East, Suite 700, Toronto,
Ontario M4P 2Y3, Canada (a division of Pearson Penguin Canada Inc.)
Penguin Books Ltd., 80 Strand, London WC2R 0RL, England
Penguin Ireland, 25 St. Stephen's Green, Dublin 2,
Ireland (a division of Penguin Books Ltd.)
Penguin Group (Australia), 250 Camberwell Road, Camberwell, Victoria 3124,
Australia (a division of Pearson Australia Group Pty. Ltd.)
Penguin Books India Pvt. Ltd., 11 Community Centre,
Panchsheel Park, New Delhi – 110 017, India
Penguin Group (NZ), 67 Apollo Drive, Rosedale, North Shore 0632,
New Zealand (a division of Pearson New Zealand Ltd.)
Penguin Books (South Africa) (Pty.) Ltd., 24 Sturdee Avenue,
Rosebank, Johannesburg 2196, South Africa

Penguin Books Ltd., Registered Offices: 80 Strand, London WC2R 0RL, England

First published by Signet Eclipse, an imprint of New American Library,
a division of Penguin Group (USA) Inc.

First Printing, March 2008
1 3 5 7 9 10 8 6 4 2

SIGNET ECLIPSE and logo are trademarks of Penguin Group (USA) Inc.

LIBRARY OF CONGRESS CATALOGING-IN-PUBLICATION DATA
Child, Maureen.
A fiend in need / Maureen Child.
p. cm.
ISBN: 978-0-451-22307-4
1. Demonology—Fiction. I. Title.
PS3561.A468F54 2008
813'.54—dc22   2007034089

Set in Bembo • Designed by Elke Sigal

Printed in the United States of America

To my husband, Mark—
my one and only *Best Fiend Ever*.
I love you.

Acknowledgments

Thanks to my World-Class Plot Group: Susan Mallery, Christine Rimmer, Terry Southwick and Kate Carlisle. You guys are the best. And when I need a plot fix fast, I know who to call!

Chapter One

My name is Cassidy Burke and I'm a Demon Duster.

Is there a twelve-step program for that?

Anyway, about a month ago I turned thirty-two, I found out demons really exist, my daughter's long-lost father moved back to town, I had sex for the first time in way too long, my daughter got kidnapped by an evil demon and I found out I was a superhero or something.

A full month.

Oh, and did I mention the guy I actually had sex with turned out to be a demon, too? Yeah. Still getting used to that myself.

As a Demon Duster, I'm supposed to rid the world of demons by punching my hand through their chests and ripping out their hearts. I hear you. Ew. But I'm getting used to it. At least, I thought I was. Up until the moment my darling daughter, Thea, turned to me and said, "Uh, Mom?"

Every mother in the world recognizes that those two words, said in that exact tone, are never followed by the statement, *I've got good news.*

I grabbed a brown sugar–and–cinnamon Pop Tart, took a big bite and muttered, "What?"

"I was, um, looking around on the Internet to see if they had any more information about Demon Dusting."

Thea was sitting at the kitchen table in a golden slice of sunlight that was spearing through the wide window behind her. Her long black hair was pulled back in a ponytail, and her eyes looked worried. Not a good thing.

"What's wrong?" I asked. "What'd you find?"

"This." She leaned back in the chair, pointed to the screen of her laptop computer and waited for me to look.

Sugar, our elephant-sized, black-and-white dog of indeterminate breed, was hiding under the table, hoping for crumbs. Me, I was just hoping that whatever Thea had found wasn't going to make me nuts.

I looked at the screen, blinked and looked again. Stunned, I dropped my Pop Tart, and Sugar made a lunge for it. *"What?"*

"Guess that explains all the extra demons lately, huh?"

I didn't even glance at Thea. I was too busy staring at the Web site she had found: www.dollarstokilltheduster.com. Just perfect. I scanned the information quickly, hoping it was all a big joke. No such luck. It was real. Somebody out there was posting a reward for killing me.

"They put it online?"

"Well, at least it's a nice picture of you," Thea said.

Actually, it wasn't bad. My hair looked great in that picture, and, thank God, I was wearing makeup. But that wasn't the point. "Great. I look good on my Wanted poster. Who's doing this?"

"I don't know," Thea answered, though I really hadn't been expecting an answer at all. "But maybe killing the judge last month pissed off the demons."

I glanced at Thea, remembering how that bastard Judge Jenks had kidnapped her, with plans to sell her as a sex slave, and wished I could only go back in time and dust the old demon all over again.

"How much are they offering for me?"

"Right now?" Thea punched a button, the screen scrolled down and numbers flashed in blinking red lights: $10,000, DEAD OR ALIVE BUT PREFERABLY DEAD.

"That's it?" Now I was offended. I'm the scourge of the demon community and all they could come up with was ten thousand lousy bucks? Where were their standards? I was worth at *least* fifty!

"Cheer up, Mom," Thea pointed out as she disconnected and closed the computer lid. "Maybe it'll go up."

"Sure, sure." I glanced at her as she got up, and moved my bare foot when Sugar licked crumbs off of it. "Where're you going?"

"School," she said. "Unless you want to give me the day off?"

"Nice try, but I don't think so." She didn't even look disappointed. No big surprise there. Thea's a math genius. I have no idea where she got it, but the girl's amazing—plus, she actually likes school. Weird, but there you go.

Outside, a car horn honked, and I winced. Thea's father had moved back to La Sombra the month before, and when he discovered that he had a nearly sixteen-year-old daughter he'd never known about, he'd been a little testy. Since then he's been making up for lost time. He takes Thea to school every morning and shows up with food at least twice a week, to wangle an invite to dinner.

I have to hand it to him: He really knows me well. Show up with food and the chances of your getting in my door are really good.

I walked outside with Thea and lifted a hand in a half-hearted wave to Logan. We had a kind of weird relationship. There was a lot of sizzle and heat, but so far I'd managed to resist. Because at the moment I was getting plenty of sizzle and heat from a different guy: Devlin, the demon I mentioned earlier.

Needless to say, Logan and Devlin hated each other's guts, which, while entertaining, was sometimes a pain in the ass.

"Hey, Cassie!" Logan leaned out of the driver's-side window

and grinned at me. He's the only person in my life who calls me Cassie. Irritating and yet somehow endearing. God, I'm a sap.

"Morning, Logan."

"Wanted to tell you the deal went through."

"What deal?"

He rolled his eyes. "You never actually listen to me when I talk, do you?"

"Not really."

Thea climbed in the passenger side, but Logan didn't put the car in gear. Instead, he leaned further out the window and said, "I bought the house."

"What house?"

He jerked a thumb over his shoulder. I glanced in that direction and spotted the SOLD sign on the house across the street. *No way.*

"You bought the Johnsons' house?"

"Just yesterday, *neighbor.*"

Oh, crap.

Logan was grinning, and even Thea looked pleased. I sighed. How could I resist something that made my girl so damn happy? She was glad to have a father. Glad to have *two* parents to torture. And to be honest, Logan was really getting into the whole father thing.

So, it was only me thinking that this was a bad idea. Only me realizing that having Logan across the street was going to make me crazy in no time at all.

"I'll bring dinner tonight," Logan was saying. "Tell you guys all about it."

Whatever.

When they were gone, I turned and headed back into the house. I hadn't even shut the door yet when a *gorgeous* man was standing on my porch.

And I mean seriously, orgasm-inducing-just-by-looking-at-him gorgeous. He had to be at least six-foot-five, with shoulder-length, dark blond hair and eyes so pale a blue they looked almost silver. His chest was broad, only barely covered by a wispy white shirt that opened his pecs to glorious view— those muscles of his looked like they'd been carved out of bronze. His jaw was square, his lips full and parted in a worried smile, and his legs were about a mile and a half long.

But I already knew that a pretty face could be hiding horns and a tail. So I grabbed the bottle of demon spray I kept beside the front door and gave him a squirt right between those beautiful eyes.

No smoke.

No screams.

So, he wasn't a demon. This mixture, given to me by my "trainer," Jasmine, a tiny woman who looked a couple of hundred years old, reacted like acid on demons. Made them cranky and distracted them enough that I could dust 'em before they could dust me.

He swiped one big hand across his face to wipe off the greenish brown liquid, then looked at me and said, "Sanctuary."

"What?"

"Just say yes," the great-looking guy ordered, and flipped a quick look over his shoulder.

"Are you selling something?" I asked. "Because if you are, you should know I'm really not in the mood. Can't afford to buy anything, and I don't have enough time to be 'saved.' So better luck at the next house—"

"I'm not selling anything." He looked over his shoulder again and this time I looked, too. Nothing out there but that damned SOLD sign on the house across the street.

Sugar came up behind me, bumped the back of my knees with her head and almost toppled me out the door. The dog was whining, Mr. Gorgeous was practically dancing in place and I was fresh out of patience. "Bye."

"Sanctuary," he repeated, like I should know what the hell he was talking about.

Ah, God. Another escapee from the local Nutso Hotel. La Sombra's got one of the biggest mental-health facilities in the state. Every once in a while, though, somebody wandered away from their Jell-O cups. Wouldn't you know he'd find his way to *my* door?

"Okay then, sanctuary to you, too," I said. No point in upsetting the crazy people.

"Just say yes," he implored, and he looked just a touch more frantic this time.

"Why would I say yes?" I asked.

"Good enough!" He pushed past me into the house, and Sugar howled when he tripped on her.

"Hey!" I didn't even have time to grab him and toss his ass back outside before a demon appeared on the porch.

Yeah, this one I *knew* was a demon. His red eyes were pretty much the big tip-off. And then there was the drool. *Ew.* He was furious and made a grab for Gorgeous George. The big guy jumped back, Sugar's howl went up a notch and I gave ol' demon boy a good long squirt. While he was shrieking in pain and the smoke was lifting off the top of his head, I reached into his chest and grabbed his heart.

Just before he died, though, the demon yelled, "Sanctuary won't save you!"

Then he was just dust on my freshly swept porch.

I turned around to look at the guy behind me. He grinned at me and said, "Thanks. I owe you one."

"That about sums it up. Who the hell are you?"

"The name's Brady," he said, leaning down to stroke his hand over Sugar's head. She'd stopped howling and was staring up at him like he was a big bowl of buttered popcorn (her favorite).

"Nice to meet you, Brady. Now get out."

"Oh," he said, grinning again, and his smile was so bright I nearly squinted. "Can't do that. You granted me Sanctuary."

"When did I do that?"

"When you said yes."

Damn it.

"Fine. Why do you need Sanctuary?"

"I'm a Faery," he said, lifting his chin like he was posing for a statue.

I blinked at him. Not what I was expecting—and frankly, from a purely female point of view, a damn waste. Not really the point, though.

"It's great that you're so up-front about it, but you might want to try being a little more politically correct."

He frowned and was just as pretty as when he smiled. "Not *that* kind of Faery," he said, and grabbed me.

He kissed me so hard, so long and so deep, that by the time he let me go my knees were shaking and my brain had shut down. I stared up at him, and a small corner of my mind worried that my expression looked a lot like Sugar's.

Brady gave me another brilliant smile and said, "You are the Duster. *You* are Sanctuary. You're the only one who can keep me alive."

But no pressure.

Chapter Two

The buzz of that kiss was starting to wear off, damn it, and now I was left with one major question rattling through my brain.

Since when was I bodyguard to the weird?

Seriously, I didn't remember signing up for this. Demons, okay, fine. I was beginning to deal with the whole "destiny" issue and was more than willing to rip out hearts. (How disgusting does *that* sound?) But come on. Couldn't the other weirdos in the universe find somebody else to lead their parade?

What was I supposed to do with a Faery, for God's sake? Besides, weren't Faeries tiny, cute little buglike things? You know, Tinkerbellish? (Not a word, I know.)

Brady the Faery was standing there looking around my living room as if he were planning to settle in and get comfy. Me, I was trying to figure out what to do next.

"You got anything to eat?" he asked. "I'm starving."

Was he serious? In my house, there was *always* junk food. "In the kitchen."

"Right." He headed off, Sugar hot on his heels like he was her new hero or something.

The rear view of the Faery was just as impressive as the frontal. He had a very nice butt, I'm forced to admit, and his long legs looked great in those dark blue pants and knee-high black leather boots. Not many men could pull off that outfit without looking like they were chorus dancers in *Peter Pan* or something.

And it's back to Tinkerbell.

You know, I had my first sexual dream after my mother took me to see the play *Peter Pan* at the Pantages in LA when I was eight. I was madly in love with Peter and was truly bummed when I found out later that Peter was being played by a girl gymnast, for Pete's sake. Had a weird moment or two after that, wondering if maybe I was gay. Hey, give me a break. I was eight.

Now, though, I knew exactly what I liked, and to be honest, I was giving my hormones a stern talking-to while a freaking *Faery* strode with long steps toward my refrigerator.

This is not entirely my fault. I'd been pretty much sex-starved for years—and then last month my life all of a sudden picked up speed. Serious speed. Devlin the demon was an amazing lover, although, gotta admit, the whole demon thing was still creeping me out. Especially since I found out from my trainer/mentor/pain-in-the-ass Jasmine that demons and humans could actually make *babies*, and I've been worried that Devlin might have supersperm or something. The thought of giving birth to some red-faced, horned demonette would keep you up at night, too.

Not worried enough to deprive myself of a little hoo-hah happy time, though.

But I digress.

I tend to do that a lot.

While I was on a mental rant, I went back to wondering why the hell I was suddenly the person otherworlders came to for help. Didn't I have enough going on? I had a teenage daughter! Trust me when I say that's more than enough trouble for anybody. Not to mention Logan Miller dropping back into my life, and all the demons, and, hey, let's not forget I'm the star of my very own Web Wanted poster. More than enough going on in my life already, thanks very much.

Yet there was a big damn Faery rummaging through my

cupboards and acting like I was supposed to be glad to see him or something.

So with all of these thoughts racing around in my brain, I headed into the kitchen, poured myself another cup of coffee (mainly because with enough caffeine, anything is survivable) and said, "You wanna explain this Sanctuary thing to me, and just why I shouldn't toss you out the back door?"

The gorgeous, bare-chested Faery grinned at me from behind the open refrigerator door. Pretty impressive grin, too. "You're the Duster. You're the one who can save me."

"Got that much. Save you from what?"

"Who."

"Huh?"

"Save me from *who* not *what*."

"Oh, pardon the hell outta me. Okay," I said, and reached for another Pop Tart. *Hmm. Running low. Mental note: Replace staples.* "*Who* am I supposed to be saving you from?"

He shrugged. "Vanessa."

I took a bite and rolled my eyes. "Oooh. Sounds scary."

Brady pulled out a Tupperware container, pried off the lid and took a sniff. He approved and bit into a slice of cold pizza before I could stop him. I mean, come on. I'll maybe . . . possibly . . . perhaps think about saving his life, but that didn't mean I was willing to give up the pizza I'd been saving for my own damn lunch.

"This is good," he mumbled around a huge bite of cold pepperoni and cheese. (Hey, the pizza was from Tully's—best in the state, so at least he had good taste.)

"Duh." I took another bite of my Pop Tart and tried not to resent the fact that a stranger was eating my leftovers. "Who's Vanessa?"

He shivered at the woman's name and swallowed hard. "Vanessa is the Queen of the Demons."

Queen? My Pop Tart hit the floor. I staggered, sloshed coffee over the rim of my mug and burned my hand. In reflex I dropped the cup; it splashed coffee across the linoleum, slapped against Sugar's big behind, and the dog shot straight up and spun around in midair, looking wildly for her attacker. She landed on her hind feet, planted her front feet on Brady's back and looked like she was in a conga line while she tried to escape the river of coffee.

Brady took Sugar's nearly hundred pounds slamming into his back in stride—his chewing didn't even slow. "There, there," he muttered around yet another bite of my pizza.

I shook my hand, blew on the red spot where the coffee'd burned me, then groped on the counter for the roll of paper towels. *Damn it.* No coffee, no Pop Tart and a damn *queen* to worry about. Dropping to the floor, I wiped up the mess while demanding, "A *queen*? Demons have *queens*?"

"I escaped from her this morning and came right to you."

"Wow, thanks." Just last month I'd dusted Judge Jenks, the head demon around these parts. I'd thought getting rid of him would make life a little easier—not so much. Now I've got my own Web site, and there's a new queen in town. How do these things keep happening to me?

Sugar woofed, dropped to the floor and trotted through the river of coffee. I thought for a moment there that she was going to give me a big kiss to comfort me. But no. She was after the Pop Tart.

While the dog ate my breakfast, Brady finished off my lunch, tossed the empty container onto the kitchen table and dipped back inside the fridge. He came back up holding a KFC box and helped himself.

"Do you have a tapeworm or something?" I pushed myself to my feet, tossed the paper towels into the trash and glared at him.

"It's been a long time since I ate."

Color me curious. "How long?"

He tipped his head back, took a bite of a chicken leg and thought about that for a moment. "Must be fifty years or so?"

I clutched at my heart. *Jesus.* I got faint when I skipped *lunch.* No wonder he was hungry.

"Oh, I don't *have* to eat," he said, as if reading my mind. "I just like it."

"Well, if you don't *have* to eat, stop mowing through my supplies."

He sniffed and had the balls to look offended. Amazing.

Sugar whined for another treat, leaned against me and looked up at me through the tangle of black-and-white hair that hid, I assumed, eyes. Hard to be sure. I hadn't seen her eyes since she was a puppy. "Forget it. Next Pop Tart's mine.

"Okay, look," I said, "you seem like a nice Faery—"

He beamed at me.

"But," I added, "what'm I supposed to do for you? I kill demons. I'm not a bodyguard, you know."

Brady polished off the chicken leg, then waved the bone at me like a magic wand. "Vanessa's a demon. Kill her."

"She's a queen," I reminded him, and as I said it I was thinking that maybe I wasn't really up for queen fighting just yet. Hey, I was new at this. And I just got a manicure and I thought I was getting a cold.

"Yes, she's a queen," he said, tossing the naked chicken bone at the trash can, "but you're legendary."

Hmm. I liked the sound of that. Then a second later I gave myself a mental slap in the head. *Dummy. He's flattering you into helping him.*

And he was good at it.

"Why's this queen after you?" Not that I really cared. I just wanted to know how determined she was going to be to get him back.

The morning sun spearing through the kitchen window gilded him in a brilliant outline. Sugar dropped to her belly and slunk over to him, hoping for crumbs now that she'd finished my Pop Tart. When Brady tore off another piece of chicken and gave it to her, he made a friend for life.

My dog, much like me, can be won over with food.

"If you don't mind breaking your chewing stride there, big guy, maybe you could explain a little?"

Licking his lips, Brady said, "She's held me for more than two hundred years."

"Why?" Seriously? It wasn't this hard to get information out of Thea, and teenagers are notoriously closemouthed.

He shrugged, took another piece of chicken and said, "I was her sex slave."

Oh, boy.

My hoo-hah lit up.

I mean, over the last month it had gotten used to seeing some action, and now it seemed the party was always on down there and ready to go at a moment's notice. My brain filled with images that I would probably go to Hell for, but since I was already headed in that direction, I wasn't too worried. Instead I enjoyed myself a little.

Brady in chains against a gray brick wall. Brady tied to a huge four-poster bed. Brady coming at me wearing nothing but a smile.

I took a breath, blew it out and looked at him. His eyebrows wiggled, like he knew exactly what I'd been thinking.

"I have waited," he said, polishing off the chicken and closing the fridge door with a nudge from his hip, "for centuries. I've served the queen and waited for the time when a strong enough Duster would be called. A Duster with strength enough to protect me."

Uh-oh.

"You are that Duster."

"Lucky me."

"*You* are Sanctuary." Brady came around the kitchen table with Sugar practically attached to his leg while she licked the

Colonel's grease and secret spices from Brady's fingertips. (She really liked chicken.) He stopped right in front of me, looked into my eyes and said, "As long as I'm with you, or here in your house, I'm safe. No demon can harm me."

"Fabulous," I said, wondering why I was still talking to him. Sure, he was gorgeous and all, but I was sooo not looking for another male in my life. Even a sex slave seemed like too much trouble at the moment. "And I get no say in this?"

He shrugged, and that amazing chest of his sort of rippled. Major distraction.

"You are Sanctuary."

"Hell," I argued, "I *need* a sanctuary. I don't think I can be one."

Behind him a face appeared in the window; then in a flash it was gone again. I blinked, sure I'd hallucinated. I sniffed at my empty coffee cup, thinking maybe he'd slipped me something, but there was nothing. Shaking my head, I looked past the Faery, and sure enough a head popped up in the window again.

An ugly head.

One with red eyes, horns sprouting out of its forehead and a really nasty set of teeth. The head was gone a second later, and I knew the demon was jumping up and down. *Good God.* Could this morning go any further downhill?

"Who's that?" I pointed at the window.

Brady the Faery frowned, turned and glanced behind him. An instant later the demon head appeared again, and this time it was snarling.

"DEMON!"

"I *knew* that."

The next time the demon yo-yo made an appearance, Brady stuck out his tongue and laughed. Sort of a nah-nah-nah-nah-nah thing. Very mature. The demon hissed, waved its scaly fists and disappeared again.

Well, I was pissed.

I'd lost a Pop Tart and a cup of coffee, had a Faery burst into my house uninvited and apparently I was going to war against a demon queen, for Pete's sake. "Just stay in the house," I muttered, and grabbed a handy-dandy bottle of my demon spray before opening the back door.

The demon was waiting for me.

He was short, but he was mean.

"You harbor the slave!"

"Wasn't my idea!" I shouted right back. "He just showed up!"

"You die and the slave returns," it shouted.

Die? I didn't think so. I had way too much to do.

It took a swing at me. Short, remember? Its arms were short too and missed me by a mile. Good thing, since those claws of his could have made quite the tear in my last clean T-shirt. I leaped out of range (impressive jumping skills are just part of the whole Duster package), and when I landed I squeezed the pump spray on the bottle, sending a long, graceful arc of brownish liquid right at his head.

It hit the demon on the left horn, and the damn thing started melting even as the demon screamed and flapped its hands at its own head, trying to wipe off the acid. Of course, all it managed to do was spread the acid to its hands. Demons. Not exactly Mensa material.

While it was screeching I heard Sugar howl in harmony; then I slapped my hand through the demon's dirty shirt and into its chest and ripped out its heart. It gaped at me in disbelief just before it poofed.

They never seem to believe the dusting will happen to them. It's always some other demon who gets turned into soup mix.

Sugar was still howling when I turned around and looked at Brady, now standing at the threshold, though safely *inside* the house. He was giving me a proud smile, and when he started applauding, damned if I didn't feel like taking a bow. Hey, I'd just killed a demon on half a cup of coffee.

Not bad, if I did say so myself.

"You are the Duster," Brady said with just a touch of awe that did a lot for my ego. "Your strength, your power will protect me from the queen."

"Yeah, well . . ." I glanced around the yard, just to make sure there were no more scabby little surprises hidden out there; then I headed for the house. I got past Brady and stepped into the kitchen. Then he closed the door and backed me up against the pantry.

He was way too close, and there must have been some kind of Faery pheromone at work, because my brain was going a little foggy and my knees all of a sudden felt slippery.

"I'm *very* handy to have around," Brady said, leaning down to sniff my hair.

Sniff my hair? *Oh, boy.* This could be trouble. Especially since I was sniffing right back at him, and he sort of smelled like cookies. Cinnamon cookies. *Whoa.* Good thing it wasn't chocolate-chip.

Was that *attraction* I was feeling? Or just pure feminine appreciation of an excellent male? Please, not attraction. I just didn't have time for one more guy!

He lifted one hand and stroked the side of my breast, and I jolted out of my stupor, smacking his hand away. It's one thing to let an escaped prisoner eat my leftovers, but I like to get to know a guy a little better before he goes feeling me up.

He shrugged and smiled. "I *am* a sex slave, remember."

Hmmm.

Stop it, Cassidy, I told myself, hoping myself was listening. *You've already got a demon lover and a human ex-lover . . . do you really need a Faery to top everything off?*

Okay, I was better.

For the moment.

"Look," I said, trying to let him down easy. After all, I could see the guy had some problems, but no way was I going to let him move into my house. I had a kid to think about. Keeping Thea safe was the one all-important motivator in my life. "I don't mind taking out the demon for you or anything, but—"

"You will free me."

He looked at me out of those silvery blue eyes, and the unspoken plea in them really got to me. *What* was I thinking?

He couldn't stay in my house.

Thea lived in my house.

Not to mention the fact that Logan was moving in across the street. He's a cop and a little territorial (despite the fact that he broke up with me to marry some rich girl named Busty or Spunky or some damn thing). Of course, he didn't know about Thea at the time, but that's not the important part.

Anyway, the point was that Logan Miller would be living across the street, and he was at my house all the damn time *now*, trying to get in good with the daughter he'd just discovered. He probably wasn't going to like the fact that a gorgeous giant had moved in. Yet, as appealing as it was to think about irritating Logan, I just didn't want to deal with it all.

"I'm really sorry, but you can't stay in my house. My kid lives here, and I don't want your demon queen sending her fangy (was that a word?) minions over here or, God help me, hanging out here herself, trying to get to you through Thea!"

He frowned. Disappointed that his sex-slave tactics weren't working on me? Had he been expecting me to flop over onto my back like Sugar, desperate for a tummy rub? I must have a rotten reputation in Otherworld Town. Did all the demons and such think I was *that* easy? Were my name and phone number on the wall of a demon bathroom: FOR A GOOD TIME, CALL DUSTER SEX BUNNY?

"Did I mention I can cook?" he said.

Hmmm.

Fine. I admit it: I like food. Shoot me now.

Sex was tempting, sure. But if you had to you could live without sex. God knows I had for too long to think about. But you had to have food, and to me the promise of actual home-cooked meals was like a fifty-percent-off sale in Nordie's purse department—too alluring to pass up.

Besides, it's not like I was willing to risk my daughter's safety just for the sake of my *own* stomach. Thea liked to eat too, you know. Plus, with Logan here all the damn time, there was extra protection, even if he didn't actually know about the danger he would be protecting us from. Did that make sense? It didn't matter. It wasn't like I couldn't protect the Faery myself, anyway. I was getting pretty good at the whole dusting thing, and I was bound to get better and better, right?

Whatever.

"Okay. You can stay," I said, and his face lit up like a kid's on Christmas morning. "For now."

"You won't be sorry."

"I'm already sorry," I told him. "Just don't make me sorrier."

"Right." He turned away and started rummaging through the freezer. "What do you want for dinner?"

After the morning I'd already had? "Surprise me," I said.

With Brady busy in the kitchen, I put on my favorite pair of sneakers, brushed crumbs off my red T-shirt with the words CLEAN SWEEP emblazoned across the boobs, and hit the bathroom. I glanced in the mirror, swiped some mascara on and ran a brush through my dark blond hair. I needed new highlights badly, but I was thankful my hair was curly enough that it looked pretty good even when I didn't have time to do the whole product thing.

My reflection didn't look too happy with me, but I didn't even have the time to argue with myself. If that woman in the mirror wanted to rag on me for letting the Faery hang around, she'd just have to wait her turn.

I had places to go. Places to clean.

I run my own business cleaning houses, and now, thanks to the contract to clean Magic Nights, Devlin Cole's exclusive sex club, I'd even picked up a few new business office clients. Clean Sweep was really starting to make good money—partially thanks to the demon spray.

Not only did it act like acid on demons, but the damn stuff made windows sparkle. Apparently the scent of the stuff even convinced ghosts to pack up and move on from their haunts. Me, I like the smell of oregano. Makes me think of pizza and other good stuff. But it seems like oregano is a big turnoff in the otherworld.

I was thinking there weren't too many Italian demons.

I had two houses scheduled for cleaning that morning, and thanks to my currently-in-residence Faery, I was already running late. I had my supplies loaded up in my bright yellow VW Bug and I headed down my street.

I made it to the stop sign at the first cross street before my cell phone rang.

I glanced at the screen, sighed and snapped it open. "Hi, Carmen."

Carmen Mendoza is a short bulldozer of a woman in her fifties who supposedly works for me. The truth is, Carmen really runs things, hiring her cousins when we need the extra help, firing them when they piss her off, and I don't have to do a thing but sign the checks.

The only downside is Carmen's love of clichés. She has one for every conversation.

"My cousin Yolanda is at the Stevenson house," she said, jumping directly into the conversation. "Rosario is going to the Danielses', and I myself am going to be working at Mr. Hawthorn's."

"I'm heading over to the Lopez house now. Busy day for all of us."

"Idle hands are the devil's workshop."

First cliché of the morning.

"Do you have enough of the demon spray?"

"*Sí*. Yolanda isn't comfortable using it, but I told her to wear gloves."

Yolanda wasn't comfortable around the demon spray/ window cleaner because Yolanda was half-demon. Yep. Demons, demons everywhere.

It had been a big surprise to me when I first found out about the whole demon population. Apparently I'd been living in a fugue state all my life, because soon after the truth had smacked me in the face, I found out that practically everyone else in town already knew about the demon thing.

Carmen knew about them because her family was riddled with 'em, but it turned out even my *kid* knew about the demon world operating in La Sombra. Of course, the little half-demon Thea'd had a crush on was the very creep who'd handed her over to the head demon, so Thea'd stopped talking about demon rights. At least for now.

"Before I forget," I said as I made a left on Cedar and headed out to PCH (Pacific Coast Highway to those not living in California), "we've got a shot at the cleaning contract at the clinic on Fifth Street. I'll be heading over there tomorrow to look it over so we can work up a bid."

"This is good. I will tell my cousin Olympia, who also needs a job, that you have hired her."

I grinned. Carmen has an inexhaustible supply of cousins. "Okay by me," I said, "though you didn't bother to ask me. Is Olympia half-demon too?"

"*Sí*," Carmen said. "But she is part Cirio demon. They like things tidy. She will work well for us, or I will tell you to fire her."

"Boy, I'm a tough boss."

"Life is hard and then you die."

Cliché number two.

"That's sunshiny and bright so early in the morning."

"Same shit, different day," Carmen said, and hung up.

Wow. Three clichés in a five-minute conversation. She's *good*.

I drove down PCH, naturally hitting every red light along the way. Have you ever noticed that when you hit one red light, you hit 'em all? I think they set them up like that on purpose. Anyway, I had plenty of time while sitting still to think about the route my life was taking.

To be honest, it was pretty chilling.

I never asked to be this legendary Demon Duster. Turns out the women in my family just become the Duster on their thirty-second birthday. My mom died in a traffic accident before she could take up her powers. Of course, a month ago I'd found out for the first time that the car crash hadn't been an accident, after all. The head demon in town had had my mom killed to protect himself.

Made me want to dust him all over again, just for the hell of it.

Anyway . . . now I had this full-time demon-killing job, along with trying to run my own business, raise my kid, have the occasional orgasm with an incredibly endowed demon and survive the training that Jasmine the Wicked insisted on.

Seriously, this was *not* how I'd imagined my life going.

I turned right onto Birchcrest Road and pulled up at the Lopez house. It was, like most of the other houses in La Sombra, an old California bungalow: wide front porch with stone pillars, big rooms and lots of windows. I figured I'd be here a good two hours, after which I had to hit a small apartment for a quickie cleaning; then I'd be heading down to St. Paul High School for a meeting with Thea's math teacher.

Was it wrong of me to look forward more to cleaning toilets than facing down a nun who wanted to talk math?

Chapter Three

𝒮

𝒺ven if I hadn't known for a fact that Tommy Canter lived in the apartment I was cleaning, I would have guessed a single guy lived there.

I'd just left the Lopez house after an hour of vacuuming, washing windows and bathroom cleaning. Though the house had been way bigger than this one-bedroom apartment, it hadn't taken as long as this place would to clean.

The Lopez house was an easier job because Mrs. Lopez, like women everywhere, always cleaned her house before I came to clean it. We don't want maids thinking we're slobs, after all.

But guys couldn't care less.

The grungier the better in their little worlds. Which made for a lot of work for my company but some pretty disgusting moments while knee-deep in the sludge. I'd been cleaning Tommy's place for only a couple of months, and boy, was I ready to cut him loose.

"What a pig," I muttered, glancing around the narrow living room. Even without the mess the apartment was pretty unimpressive. Beige walls, beige carpet—not counting the stains—galley-style kitchen and a tiny bathroom and bedroom.

Even the sunlight slanting in through the partially opened blinds looked grungy. Dust motes danced in the still air, and the smell of old food and sweaty socks made breathing an adventure.

Dirty clothes were everywhere. Pizza boxes had been tossed on the floor, empty beer bottles were on bookshelves that held more DVDs than books. I didn't even want to think about the state of the bathroom, and made a mental note to have Carmen turn Tommy Canter's apartment over to Olympia from now on. Let the new girl deal with the true slobs of the universe.

I set my cleaning caddy down onto the coffee table and went into the kitchen for one of those giant trash bags most people use for lawn clippings. Tommy used them in the kitchen trash can, and *still* there was spillover. Empty frozen-food trays toppled over the edge of the can, and a mountain of dirty dishes lined the counter.

"God, I'm gonna be here for years."

I could feel cooties jumping up from the floor to cling to me, and I wanted to scratch. Yes, I own a cleaning business because I'm good at it, and I'd wanted a job where I could make my own hours and raise my kid myself. But sometimes, like *now*, for instance, I really wanted to rethink the whole thing.

I was halfway through gathering up the crap in the living room when the front door opened. A tall guy with muscles, a beard and a huge set of keys hanging from his index finger stood in the doorway and smiled at me. Not a good smile. It was more one of those Big Bad Wolf–to–Little Red Riding Hood smiles.

"Hi?" I said.

"I'm the building super," he said as he stepped inside and closed the door behind him.

"Okay . . ." That explained who he was. It did not explain why he was there. The apartment suddenly felt a whole lot smaller and a *lot* more cramped. This guy took up a lot of room.

"Saw you come in."

"Uh-huh." I was *mega* creeped out. As the building super

he had keys to all of the apartments, but why was he using Tommy's key? While *I* was there? Was this just your normal, everyday kind of bad guy? You know, a drooling rapist or a psycho killer? Or was he a demon? Either way, I didn't feel good about it.

"I'm here to kill you."

Now I felt worse.

"Oh." Well, cut me a break. What would *you* say to a statement like that? I still didn't know if he was man or demon, but did it really matter at this point? Dead was dead, and I really didn't want to be dead.

I was just getting orgasms again on a nearly regular basis. And, hey, there was Thea to torture and Jasmine to ignore, and maybe there was a little bit of something with Logan to look into . . . Nope. Too many plans to be dead today.

So I braced myself, hoped I remembered half of what Jasmine had been trying to teach me over the last month and waited.

I didn't have to wait long.

He shot across the room in a blink of motion, and I barely had time to shout, "YIKES!"

Demon, then.

Grabbing me by the throat, he stopped me from reaching for the spray by lifting me off the floor until my feet were kicking out wildly, looking for something to stand on. So not good. My fingers clawed at his grip, but apparently my strength alone wasn't going to be enough to pry myself loose. He was big, and he was clearly determined.

My eyes were bugging, and air was clogged in the throat he was squeezing with a meaty hand. His fingers were curled all the way around my neck, and I stabbed at his hand with my fresh manicure and didn't make a dent.

Acrylic nails are *not* good weapons.

Damn, that demon queen moved fast, I thought, even

while my vision was beginning to narrow down to a tunnel-like scope where all I could see was his beady eyes flashing at me. Brady hadn't even been with me a full day yet, and already three of her minions had attacked me.

My life really sucked.

"You're worth ten thousand dollars, Duster," the demon said. "Easiest money I've ever made."

Great.

If I could have rolled my eyes, I would have.

So this wasn't a queenly hit man. This was a self-starter. This guy'd obviously seen the Web site and was looking to make himself a little nest egg.

Just fabulous.

He laughed and shook me like a big ugly dog with a very attractive bone, and I was getting a little frantic. Damned if I'd let this nasty-ass demon kill me and collect more money than *I* had in the bank. What kind of justice was that? I swept out one hand, jabbing at his eyes, but he pulled his head back. I kicked again, aiming wild, hoping for a miracle. Then I got one. The toe of my sneaker slammed into his nuts, and he let me go with a shriek of pain (his pain, not my pain) just before dropping to the floor and cradling his favorite part of himself.

Apparently some demons keep their jewels in the same place as a human guy. Lucky me.

Oh, yeah, real lucky.

I was gasping like a landed trout and trying not to fall on Tommy's dirty laundry. I *so* didn't want to have to boil my whole body when I got home.

I gave the big demon moaning in front of me another kick just on principle. Then I grabbed my bottle of demon spray and gave him a squirt right between the eyes. Okay, I didn't have to squirt him. Hello? Already identified. But it made me feel better to see his skin start smoking and to hear his screams hitting higher notes.

"Nice try," I croaked, and winced at the pain in my throat. I jabbed my hand through the big guy's chest, ripped out his heart and held my breath when he poofed. No way was I inhaling any of this guy.

Just from being in Tommy Canter's apartment, I needed a hazmat suit. Sucking in demon dust on top of that? I didn't think so. Adrenaline pumped through me in a tidal wave, making me shake so hard I could hear my teeth chatter. Close one. But hey, score another big one for me.

I blew out a breath and looked around, half expecting to see more demons coming out of the walls or something. This was really getting old fast. Apparently the Web site was already getting attention. Perfect. Web sites. Queens. Faeries.

I needed to sit down. I needed sugar. I needed a new life. But I couldn't sit down in Tommy's apartment. God knew what might crawl onto me.

So once the demon had added to the dust-bunny population, I got out the vacuum cleaner and went to work.

_&_

Three hours later I was in sad shape. And it wasn't just Tommy's apartment and my near-death experience that had me feeling like a squashed bug.

Nope, that's what a half-hour meeting with Sister Mary Merciless could do for you. Squirming under that nun's iron glare had sapped every ounce of strength from me. I needed a nap. And chocolate.

Just walking through the halls of St. Paul made me feel like the pregnant sixteen-year-old leper I'd once been. Back then the nuns had done everything they could to either ignore my presence entirely or point me out as a cautionary tale to the remaining "good" (read: luckier) girls in my class.

The School Sisters of Notre Dame ran a tight ship at St. Paul. And even now that they didn't wear the black-and-white habits, they hadn't lightened up any. Still, St. Paul was still the best school in the district. Heck, even Rachel Cohen sent her daughter, Zoe, to the Catholic school. And really, Rachel felt like I did: If we survived the nuns, so could our daughters.

Of course, these days there were far fewer nuns and brothers and priests running the school.

Sister Mary Mercy (Merciless the Evil) was still running the math department, even though she'd been made dean of girls. She was in charge of all detentions, God help all the little mistake makers everywhere. But she was also top dog in the honors math program, where Thea was the star student.

I swear Sister Mercy was half convinced that I'd somehow switched babies in the hospital. The truth is, I sometimes wonder where Thea got her brain, too. I'm not saying I'm stupid or anything, but math is just beyond me. And I like it that way. The only reason I ever got out of algebra class was that the teacher was so beaten down and demoralized by the end of the year, he passed me for the sake of his own mental health.

The upshot of this little meeting was, Sister Mercy was concerned that Thea's concentration in math would be splintered, since she'd decided to try out for the cheerleading squad.

My response to that probably hadn't helped the situation any, either.

"Woo-hoo!" I'd cried.

Hey, just knowing that Thea was thinking about something besides school and/or the demon boy she'd had a crush on was good news to me. Sure, I'm proud that my baby girl is so smart. But I wanted her to have a whole life, not one devoted solely to working out math problems on chalkboards.

Sister Mercy's mouth froze up into that lemon-sucking pout I remembered so well. "I expected nothing less from you, Cassidy. This is why I called this meeting. You must see that for the sake of Thea's future she should be focusing her energies on applied physics and advanced calculus."

Why anyone would want to concentrate on those things was beyond me, but beside the point.

"But she wants to be a cheerleader," I argued, though this was a news flash for me. Thea hadn't even told me about it yet. My guess, Sister Mercy had seen Thea's name on the try-out list and had made a move to ambush my baby girl. "Look, traditionally everybody hates the cheerleaders; I know. But this is the first time Thea's wanted to join anything other than the Math Club. This is a good thing."

"Her focus will be splintered."

How did she talk through that pruny mouth?

"Good. She's a kid. She *should* have splintered focus."

"You owe it to your child to see to it that she takes all the steps necessary to ensure her success in future endeavors," Sister told me with an audible sniff.

"Come on, Sister." I tried a smile that fell flat. "Thea's grades are great. They'll stay that way." I picked up my second-best Coach bag off the desktop. (I couldn't actually carry my best Coach bag around to clean houses, could I?)

Sister Merciless stood up and looked down at me from the podium her desk sat on. I'd always believed she liked the feeling of looking down on us. And since I was only five-five and hadn't grown a bit since high school, she still had a long way to look down.

But times were different now. I wasn't a kid worried about going to Hell if I backtalked a nun. Now I was going to Hell for way bigger sins.

Funny—Sister Merciless could still give me stomach-aches, but I wasn't worried about standing up to her anymore. Duster power? I didn't think so. It was more like I was willing to take on anybody in defense of my kid. "If Thea wants to be a cheerleader, then Thea gets to be a cheerleader. End of discussion."

That mouth pruned up even further, and she drew breath

in through a long, pointy nose. "I will speak to Thea myself, since it's clear you won't uphold your parental obligations."

"Good luck with that," I said, knowing darn well that Thea had her own mind, and not even a nun was going to make a dent if she didn't allow it.

I left the classroom with the sister's dark eyes boring a hole in my back, and it was all I could do not to go get my demon spray and give her a squirt. Probably she wasn't a demon—I mean, a demon *nun*? What were the chances? Anyway, I got out of there as fast as I could and practically ran down the long, empty hallway.

Classes were over, but I could swear that the locker-lined hallways still echoed with the misery of generations of students. The scent of desperation and chalk dust hung in the air, and the sound of a nun's heels clipping on linoleum could still give me cold chills.

I stomped out to the parking lot (where the few remaining students' cars were *way* more impressive than mine, and how pitiful a statement is that?). I leaned against the hood of my car, tipped my face up to the October sunlight and let the warmth ease away the last of the cold Sister Mercy had filled me with.

I needed chocolate.

Or sex.

Hmm. That thought immediately brought to mind my current boyfriend. (I needed a new word for Devlin, because it really felt lame for a thirty-two-year-old woman to call her who-knew-how-old-he-really-was demon lover a *boy* anything.) But just thinking about him made my hoo-hah sit up and beg. Devlin was pure charm, with amazing dark eyes, broad shoulders and a truly talented mouth. He also had some seriously magical fingers and a Mr. Happy that, when at full alert, was big enough to saddle.

As I daydreamed for a minute or two about my last Devlin-induced orgasm—on the terrace of his apartment over Magic

Nights—I wondered if I could go to hell for having sexual thoughts on the campus of a Catholic high school. If I did, it'd be worth it, I told myself with a smile.

But I wasn't really sure just where my "relationship"—God, I hated that word—with Devlin stood in the grand scheme of things. Sure, we'd killed a bad demon together and shared a few of our own magical nights at his sex club. But what did that really mean?

I liked Devlin a lot, but were we a couple? Or just bed buddies? The truth was, Devlin and I lived in such wildly different worlds that even if he hadn't been a demon, we wouldn't have had much in common. So what kind of connection could there ever really be between us?

Was I going to totally overthink this and make myself crazy? Oh, yeah.

Bottom line, though, I couldn't go to Devlin's at the moment, anyway. I had to beat Thea home to explain Brady's being there. Which should be interesting, since I didn't really understand it yet myself.

"Don't think about it," I told myself, and myself really appreciated the advice. Cassidy Burke, master of oblivion. Plus, there was plenty of time to come up with a good lie later. I'm an excellent liar. Not about important stuff, you understand, but the little things in life go much easier on everyone with a little creative embellishment.

"Besides, if I stress now," I reasoned, "that's just wasted stress. Better to wait and do all the stressing when I absolutely have to."

There. I felt better.

Yes, I know it didn't make any sense, but it worked for me.

Standing in the crisp October sunshine, I speed-dialed Thea and waited. The sun felt warm, a nice ocean breeze was sweeping in off the sea, and from a distance I could hear the smack of football players practicing in full gear.

By the time Thea answered, I was half-asleep.

"Hi, Mom."

I straightened up, pushed my hair out of my eyes and said, "Hi, baby girl. You at Zoe's?"

"Yeeeessss, MOTHER."

Ah, there was that tone I'd come to know and loathe. When making a point—as in, "of course I'm at Zoe's—where else would I be after school?"—she spoke in what sounded like capital letters. I think all teenagers do it—the better for me to understand just what a trying parent I was. Guess I was doing the job!

After school Thea always went to Zoe Cohen's house so the two of them could do homework together. Zoe was Thea's best friend and the daughter of *my* best friend, Rachel. Good to see traditions carried on. Anyway, I wanted to make sure Thea didn't go home until I was there. Walking in and finding a Faery might be a little traumatic. Especially finding *that* Faery.

Wow, I was seriously wishing I could go find Devlin, after all. An orgasm would have helped me through what was coming.

"Homework?" I asked, not because I had to, but more as a matter of form. Homework to Thea was like a mani/pedi to other girls. What can I say? My daughter's a genius.

"Almost done," she said. "Where are you?"

"At the school."

"*My* school?"

"No, my other daughter's school."

"Funny. WHY are you there?"

Again with the capital letters. "Sister Merciless was worried about your math concentration, now that you've decided to join one of the world's most hated in-group clubs."

There was a long pause, then, "I CAN'T BELIEVE SHE TOLD YOU."

At least she was mad at somebody else for a change. "I couldn't believe it either," I said. "When were you going to tell me?"

"Soon. I was just . . . I don't know; it felt kind of weird, you know?"

My eyes rolled up in my head. Trust Thea to think something normal was weird and that scoring a perfect score on the SAT as an eighth grader was normal. "It's not weird. You'll be great."

"No, I won't. I suck. I tried to do one of those high kicks with Zoe and I think I pulled something."

I winced. "It'll probably get easier."

"Maybe I should rethink this," Thea said.

"Don't give up so fast." Digging my car keys out of my bag, I opened the car door, climbed inside and shut the door after me. "We'll talk about it when I get home. And, um, stay at Zoe's till I come and get you, okay?"

"Sure, I'll be here."

Great. Potential problem avoided.

"Mom?"

"Yeah?"

"Why's there a Faery in our house?"

~

Interestingly enough, it was much easier getting Thea to accept having a Faery houseguest than I thought it would be. Especially when Brady offered to teach her to cook. Hey, this could only work to my benefit. I mean, I *can* cook if starvation is the only other option. But my talents don't really lie in the kitchen.

It turned out it was Jasmine who took the news of Brady's presence a touch too unenthusiastically.

"You are the Duster. You do not have time to guard a Faery." Jasmine, my trainer/pain-in-the-ass, looked about two hundred years old. Her steel gray hair was cut short and curled close to her skull. She had icy blue eyes, gnarled hands, a bosom that long ago gave up the fight against gravity, and she wore orthopedic shoes tied with double knots. She always wore a dress and habitually carried one of the ugliest vinyl purses I'd ever seen.

"You know," I said, lunging around the backyard, looking like a complete idiot, "I totally agree."

Every evening and most mornings you could find me out in my backyard doing stupid squats and lunges and jumps. When this "training" had first started it had nearly killed me. Now it was just way annoying.

"You agree?" She was stunned, and who could blame her? She hadn't had an easy time of it since turning up on my back porch the month before. She claimed that I was the most irritating Demon Duster ever born, and I was willing to claim that crown. Hey, I didn't ask for this gig.

"Sure. But what was I supposed to do? Make him leave? Let the demons kill him?"

"He is not your responsibility."

"But he's making stroganoff!"

She muttered something I didn't quite catch, but I think it was something along the lines of, "Food. It's always food with you."

"He's harmless," I said, and really hoped I was right. If he wasn't, then I'd just reach right into his chest and rip out his heart. Wait, though. Could I reach through a chest that wasn't a demon chest? Did I *want* to?

I stopped dead, made a face and worried for a second or two about just how easy this whole dusting thing was getting for me. Then I caught a whiff of mushrooms and sour cream on the air and shrugged the worry off.

"The demon queen wants him, and you are not prepared to do battle with her." Jasmine laid one knobby hand on Sugar's head, and the dog sighed with pleasure. My dog's easy. Feed her, pet her, she's yours forever.

Needless to say, she'd come to the right house.

"I'm really not worried about the queen at the moment." I pointed to the base of my throat, where a lovely handprint was still evident. "I've got other worries—like that Web site offering cold, hard cash for my head."

"The queen will win in a battle between you."

"So I won't battle her," I said on a groan as I lunged again. Seriously, all this exercise couldn't be good for a person. I was still operating under the theory that exercise was a dangerous fad and would soon be replaced by something more civilized. Marathon chocolate eating, for instance.

"You will have to face the queen eventually if the Faery remains." Jasmine speared me with one of those infuriating disappointed/angry/resigned glares.

"Well," I said, finally coming to a grateful stop when I reached her side, "let's just worry about that then, okay?"

"Cassidy"—her sigh was a windy one—"you must make plans. You must be prepared for whatever comes against you."

"I'm training, aren't I?"

"Halfheartedly."

I did a little glaring of my own. "I'm standing here sweating—actual *sweat* is pouring down my back as we speak. I've got grass stains on my jeans and a cramp in my thigh. I call that *whole*heartedly."

Her mouth pinched, and I had to notice just how much Jasmine sort of resembled Sister Mary Merciless. What was it with skinny old women and the lemon-mouth look?

"Practice your jumps."

"You jump. I'm jumped out," I said, slumping down onto one of the Adirondack chairs that my dad had made ten years ago.

"You haven't even been training for an hour."

"Yeah, but I've had a full day."

"Fine." Jasmine's teeth ground together, and I glanced at Sugar to see if the dog was growling or if it was Jasmine. Sugar dropped her head onto my lap and blew hot-dog breath against my stomach. The growling wasn't coming from her.

Oh. Did I mention that along with training me how to *kill* demons that Jasmine actually *is* a demon? I know. Weird. But she insists that not all demons are evil, and I've got to say I kind of see her point. Seems that demons are no different from everybody else: Some are cool; some are nightmares.

I still wasn't totally sure of where Jasmine fit on that scale.

"The demon queen will be sending others out after the Faery."

"His name's Brady."

Jasmine sniffed.

I opened one eye and looked up at her. "You have a problem with Faeries?"

"They're not to be trusted."

"Said the demon."

She took the chair opposite me, perched uneasily on the edge of the seat, and folded her hands in her lap. "Cassidy, you are new to the ways of the otherworlders."

"And?"

"And there is much for you to learn."

"I get that. But first," I said, pushing Sugar off my lap and staggering to my feet, "I'm going to eat dinner. A real cooked dinner. Made in my kitchen. By a Faery." I took a step toward the kitchen, biting my lip against the cramp in my thigh. Then I looked at her. "You hungry?"

Chapter Four

Outside twilight dropped over the yard like a cool blue blanket. The days were getting shorter, the sea breeze a little nippier, and trees were just starting to think about maybe, someday-really-soon-perhaps-but-don't-count-on-it, turning green leaves into splashes of autumn color. (This is Southern California, remember? We don't actually *do* seasons. We pretty much have summer and summer light. And the rainy season that lasts for about twenty minutes.)

Yep, outside, it was cold and dark.

Inside the house it was heaven.

Steam covered the windows, and drops of condensation streamed down the glass panes in tiny rivers. Unfamiliar scents filled the kitchen, and I took a second to simply stand there and *smell*. (Fine, I know how that sentence sounds, and no, *I* wasn't personally smelling; I was doing some serious deep breathing to drag every atom of the fabulous aromas deep into my lungs.)

As much as we like to eat, Thea and I don't really cook. In fact, my best friend, Rachel, says my stove is more of a piece of art than an appliance. But, boy howdy, the old four-burner was getting a workout now.

"Stir the pasta once in a while," Brady was telling Thea. "Otherwise it'll stick to the pan like concrete."

"Right." Thea nodded and moved in so close she was stuck to Brady's side like a dryer sheet on a sweater. "This is so cool. I mean, you, like, made this from nothing and everything."

My girl. So poetic.

"Cooking's fun, and I don't get much chance to do it," Brady said with a shrug.

As far as I was concerned, if he could make my kitchen smell like this every day, he could stay as long as he wanted. Okay, maybe not *that* long, but still.

Just as that thought popped into my head, Brady turned at the stove and gave me a smile and a wink. "Duster."

"Call me Cass."

"As you wish."

I don't know about you, but I *love* it when men say stuff like that. Even if it *was* from a Faery who'd pretty much forced his way into my life and refrigerator.

"Brady says he's moving in, Mom."

I glanced at Thea. "Not forever."

"Hmmph." Jasmine snorted from right behind me, leaving no doubt where she stood on the whole Faery-in-the-house thing.

Sugar ambled inside, planted her big, furry butt on Brady's foot and gave him the I'm-so-cute-I-should-get-a-treat look.

Brady didn't notice. Instead he was looking past me at Jasmine, and the twinkle in his eye did a quick disintegration. That gorgeous face of his froze up, and I thought today was really my day for the whole lemon-sucking expression.

"I have no quarrel with you," he said solemnly.

"You shouldn't be here," Jasmine countered.

"I claimed Sanctuary."

"By trickery."

Voices were raising, pasta was boiling and even Sugar was starting to pick up on the tension in the room. This could turn ugly in a second. And I didn't want ugly. I wanted dinner.

"She is the Duster. It is my right to come to her for Sanctuary."

"She is not capable of fighting the queen."

"*She* is standing right here!" I glared at both of them. Neither of them looked impressed.

"You're gonna fight a queen?" Thea asked in the humming silence.

"Not if I can help it," I admitted, and staggered back as Sugar ran to Mommy for comfort. A one-hundred-pound dog leaning on you will have you toppling over if you don't lock your knees and lean back.

"You have to!" Brady argued.

"Ha!" Jasmine snorted again after that one short bark of laughter. Guess she was thinking that he wasn't going to have any better luck ordering me around than she did. And, hey, she was right.

"I'm not fighting anybody." I bent down, rubbed my hand over Sugar's head, then moved away. The dog did a slow slide to the floor without support. Grabbing a bottle of water off the counter I took a long drink and wished it was a beer.

Brady looked disappointed. Jasmine looked like she always did: disapproving. I blew my hair out of my eyes and said, "Look, Brady can stay here for a while"—I held up one hand to shut him up when he looked like he was going to say something—"and if that keeps him safe from the queen, great. I'm not going out looking for this bitch; I've got other things to do."

"Good," Jasmine said. "Your patrolling should take precedence over—"

"I'm not talking about patrolling," I said, lifting my voice to carry over everybody else's. "I'm talking about Halloween. It's almost here. Thea and I've got to get busy decorating—"

"True," Thea said. "We're way behind schedule on that."

"Foolish," Jasmine snarled.

"But the queen," Brady whined.

"Jeez . . . can we all cut Cassidy a break? It's been a long day, what with the work and the nuns and, hey, the big-ass demon who was looking to kill me for the reward."

"Oh," Thea said, smiling. "I forgot to tell you: The money went up this afternoon, too. I checked."

"What's it up to now?"

"Fifteen."

"Huh." Good news or bad news? More money offered for my dead-or-alive-but-preferably-dead body was certainly less insulting. But more money meant more greedy demons looking to score that retirement fund.

"What is she talking about?" Jasmine demanded.

"Later. I need food." And time to stop thinking about all of this stuff for a while. Yeah, I know: denial. Sue me. I need a break sometimes.

Brady nodded bravely. "Fine. Dinner's ready. Sit while I strain the noodles."

"Excellent." Worked for me. Sit down. Be waited on. Eat. In fact, this was the best part of my day. I ignored Sugar, Jasmine and even my own child in my excitement over someone else cooking for me.

When the doorbell rang I waited expectantly for one of the others to go answer it. But they all sat down at the table, comfortable ignoring the chime repeating itself over and over. Sugar lay down under the table, not even bothering to bark because it could distract her from possible spillage.

Which left *me* to go get rid of whoever or whatever stood between me and my stroganoff.

I stalked through the living room, grumbling when the doorbell rang yet again, and since I was crabby about the interruption I threw the door open, ready to send whatever demon might be out there straight to Hell.

"I brought meatball subs." Logan stepped past me into the house.

CRAP.

I forgot he was coming over to tell me all about how he

was planning on ruining what was left of my life by moving in across the street.

CRAP.

I had a Faery and a tiny, mean old demon in the house.

"Uh, Logan . . ."

"Where's Thea?"

"Kitchen."

"Great." He took a step, stopped dead and sniffed the air. Then he looked at me, one black eyebrow arched. "What's that smell?"

I sniffed too. Stroganoff and—yum—the meat sauce on the meatball subs. Then I lied my ass off. (If only that were literal, not figurative. If I could actually *lie* my way to a better figure, I'd be a supermodel.) "I don't smell anything. Um, Logan, tonight's not good for us. . . ."

"I smell stroganoff," he said.

Damn. "I have a cooking show on TV." Fine. My spur-of-the-moment lies are less than spectacular.

Logan stared at me as if I were nuts, and pointed to the silent, dark television. "It's not on. And besides, they don't have *Smell-O-Vision*, Cassie."

"Wouldn't it be great if there was, though? I mean, except for, like, *CSI*—that'd be gross."

Thea laughed, and the sound swept from the kitchen like a song.

"Uh-huh," Logan said, slanting a look toward the kitchen before giving me a curious look. "So, how come you're trying to get rid of me?"

The best defense is a good offense. Worked for football; must be true about life.

"Why is it always about you, Logan? Maybe this is about me. Maybe I just want my house to myself for tonight, huh? I mean, you just show up and expect me to let you in because you've got subs? What's up with that?"

I was starting to ramble and, worse, run out of things to say when he cut me off cold.

"Are you on your period?"

"Aaaarrrrggghhh . . ." What is it with men? How do they know the one absolutely most stupid thing to say and then blurt it out? And why don't they get it when we want to beat them to death afterward?

"Hey." He held up one hand and took a step back. I may have looked a little scary. "No problem. I'll leave the subs—we can talk tomorrow. When you're calmer."

Gonna take a lot longer than twenty-four hours, I thought, but at least he was leaving.

"Cass?" Brady's deep voice rumbled out from the kitchen. "Dinner's getting cold."

Both of Logan's black eyebrows rose up in twin arches. "Company?" he asked.

"Sort of."

"Who?"

"No one you know."

"So it's not Cole."

Logan had a problem with Devlin Cole. It started out because he really wanted to shut down Devlin's exclusive sex club. Now it was more that he hated Devlin because *I* didn't. Logan had the idea that he and I were going to hook up again now that he was back home in La Sombra and divorced from Musty or Twisty or whatever.

To be honest, Logan could still make my toes curl just by walking into a room. Plus, he had been my first love. The echoes of that love were still with me, whether I wanted to admit it or not. Not to mention that he still had great hands and a terrific mouth. But there were issues keeping him out of my bed. Not the least of which was that our daughter would be so grossed out she'd probably never speak to either one of us again. And when Thea wasn't talking to me, she was so loud I got headaches.

"Nope," I said. "Not Devlin."

"Hey, Mom," Thea shouted, "this is really amazing. Brady's a great cook. Come on, already!"

"Brady?" Logan gave me the death stare, and I crumbled. Fine. I admit it: I'm not good at confrontations. This is exactly why Thea was fifteen years old before Logan ever knew of her existence. I'd planned to tell him all about his brand-new baby daughter at his college graduation. Then he'd introduced me to his new fiancée, Spiffy or Sparky or something, and I'd avoided the whole thing.

"You're not leaving, are you?" I asked, more for form than anything else.

"Not a chance."

"Didn't think so." I shrugged and walked past him, headed for the kitchen. "Come on then."

We walked into the kitchen. Logan dropped the grease-stained white bag of subs onto the kitchen counter, then turned to face the table. He was wearing his cop face: all stern and nonexpressional. His gaze slipped over Jasmine, settled on Thea for an instant or two, then shifted to Brady. Then his eyes narrowed and a muscle in his jaw twitched.

"Hi, Logan," Thea said around a mouthful of noodles. (She liked having a dad, but she wasn't really comfortable *calling* him Dad just yet. Logan was waiting impatiently for that happy day.)

"Thea." He never took his gaze from Brady.

Slowly Brady stood up to his full, impressive height, and he and Logan were at eye level. Logan looked dark and dangerous. Brady looked a little uneasy and a lot gorgeous. Probably not to Logan, though.

I tried to see the situation through Logan's eyes, but frankly I was too hungry to be really sympathetic. I knew this could really degenerate into a nasty situation, what with Logan acting like a guard dog, and Brady standing there looking all comfy and right at home.

Then Logan spoke up and I braced myself.

"Who're you?" Logan asked.

"I'm Brady the Faery."

Just like that, situation defused.

Yep. Every muscle in Logan's body relaxed. I watched it happen. The coiled tension in his body slowly dribbled away, and he actually found a smile. Of course. I looked at Brady the way Logan was and saw a tall, really built guy dressed like a professional dancer. And after that introduction there was only one conclusion to draw. At least for Logan.

But why would I correct him? What am I, stupid?

"Nice to meet you."

Brady was delighted. He held out one hand, and Logan reluctantly shook it. I'm not saying he's a homophobe or anything—it was more like he was really hoping he wasn't Brady's type or something. Didn't really matter to me. All I could think was, *Hey, no war and still time to eat.*

"Want some dinner, Logan?" I was already sitting down, letting him make up his own mind.

"Sure. Smells great."

"Thank you, I love to cook," Brady said.

"Uh-huh. Of course you do." Logan winked at me as he grabbed a plate from the cupboard and sat down at the table next to Jasmine. He frowned when he saw her, and I knew he was remembering the night he'd met the old woman. The night I turned Judge Jenks into a towering pile of demon dust right in front of him and Logan *still* wasn't able to believe in demons.

So not my problem.

There we were: the cop, the demon, the teenager, the Faery and the Demon Duster. All of us sitting down to share a meal together.

Is this America or what?

The next morning I woke up to tingles all over my body and a slow, burning throb between my thighs. I was having the great dream to beat *all* great dreams. There were warm hands rubbing my skin, long fingers dipping into hot, soft places, whispered words promising me enough to make me arch my hips and whimper.

Morning sunlight was streaming through my bedroom windows, beating against my closed eyelids, and I knew the dream was going to be ending soon, damn it. I twitched a little on my sheets and sighed wistfully, wishing that really good throbbing would pick up speed and push me into Orgasmland (like Disneyland, only for grown-ups).

Sadly, nothing happened, so I opened my eyes and— "YIKES!"

Brady was leaning over me, smiling. His hands were moving under the baseball jersey I wore for a nightgown, and parts of my body were jolting to attention.

"Hey, hey, HEY!" I pushed his hands out from under my nightie and scrambled to a sitting position, dragging my sheets and blankets up to my chin like some Victorian maiden and wondering wildly where my panties were. Give me a break; I was just a little surprised. It's not every morning you wake up to find a Faery giving you a hand job.

"Good morning," he said, and his voice was like melted chocolate. WOW. How'd he do that—squeeze all that sexy innuendo and promises into two little words?

"Yeah. Good morning, all right," I said, trying to quiet the tingles still happening inside. "Um, what do you think you were doing?"

"Pleasuring you," he said with a shrug. Muscles shifted in a tantalizing display that made my mouth turn dry and my tingles go even more tingly.

"Why?" I asked, still gripping my blankie to my boobs like a thermal chastity belt.

"It's what I do."

"Not to me, you don't."

I have standards. Sure, maybe you think they aren't very *high* standards, but I have 'em just the same. Right then I was sort of involved with a demon, and while I was riding his impressive love stick, I wasn't looking for extra doodling on the side. I'm a one-lover-at-a-time kind of woman.

Why?

At that moment, I wasn't able to think of a good reason, but I was sure it'd come to me.

"As you wish."

Hmm. He was saying that a lot, and yet I had the feeling that Brady did more of what *he* wished than anything else. Gorgeous men had a way of getting what they wanted no matter what. He reluctantly pushed off the bed and stood up. My eyes bugged out. Let's just say that those skintight pants let me see firsthand that Devlin wasn't the *only* otherworlder carrying around a telephone pole in his pants.

All of a sudden it got *really* hot in my bedroom.

"Look," I said, steering my eyes away from Mr. Eager up to Brady's eyes. "No offense or anything, but get out."

"What?" His eyes went wide. "But . . . but . . . you are Sanctuary."

"I didn't mean get out of the house," I hedged, though I knew I'd probably regret that later. "Just out of my room. You shouldn't be here, and I have to get dressed and go to an interview about a new job and—"

"Yes." He nodded sagely. "Work. I've heard of that."

Wow. He's *heard* of work. Next incarnation I was thinking I'd come back as a Faery. Sex all the time, and apparently you don't have to work. If there was chocolate involved, that would pretty much be the perfect life.

"I will have your breakfast ready for you."

He was nearly out the bedroom door when I shouted, "Pop Tart! And coffee. Lots of it!"

When he was gone I slumped down in my bed again. My tingles were slowly petering out, and I had to deal with my body's disappointment before I could convince it to get into the shower.

By the time I was showered and dressed I was feeling better. I have two words for you: Shower Massage. Sure, it's not the same as a demon woody, but it'll do in a pinch.

I was wearing my second-best, I'm-a-businesswoman-take-me-seriously outfit: black skirt, white shirt, fitted red jacket and black open-toed high-heeled shoes. My hair still needed highlights—mental note to call Sandy and offer a liter of blood in exchange for an appointment sometime in the next millennium.

Then there was my bag. I'd even bought my new red jacket just to match the purse: a multipocket Marc Jacobs hobo bag in a deep, dark red. In short, it was perfect. I had my mini squirt bottle filled with demon fluid tucked inside, so I was ready to roll. Maybe I'd even go see Devlin later.

Fine. The Shower Massage thing was already wearing off, and I was ready for a real *male*-inspired orgasm.

Downstairs Thea and Brady were laughing it up in the kitchen, and I shook my head at the bizarro turn my life had taken only a month ago. Back then, in the good ol' days, my only worries had been about supporting both Thea and my purse habit. Now I had demons to worry about, a Faery diddling me in my sleep and an ex-boyfriend I still cared too much about moving in across the street.

Man, could life go to crap in a heartbeat or not?

I walked into the kitchen in time to see Brady demonstrate a high kick for Thea. And those long legs of his made the Rockettes look like clog dancers.

"That's AWESOME," Thea said, applauding for good measure. "And you can teach me how to do that without killing myself?"

"Absolutely." Brady spotted me, poured me a cup of coffee, then took my arm and steered me to a kitchen chair. He set a plate of eggs and bacon down in front of me, and I was suddenly so hungry I didn't even wonder how he'd managed to get groceries into the house.

"And," Brady told Thea, "I'll help you come up with a wonderful routine guaranteed to get you onto the cheerleader squad."

Thea *beamed* at him. Her face held a smile she usually reserved for those surprise physics quizzes she enjoyed so much. "Isn't that great?" she asked nobody in particular. "Mom, he's great; isn't he great?"

"Great," I mumbled while biting into a crisp strip of bacon. "So you never told me. When'd you decide to become a cheerleader?"

Brady sat down beside me, and Thea shrugged. "One of the girls on the squad fell off the top of the pyramid and broke her leg, so they need somebody new and I just thought . . ." Her voice dwindled off, and my Mom radar lit up.

There was more here than she was saying; I just didn't have a clue what it was. But she was avoiding looking directly at me, so I had the feeling that a guy was involved somehow. This was *not* good. The last boy Thea'd had a thing for had turned out to be a half-demon thug who had turned her over to the bad guys.

"Thea . . ."

"WOW!" She looked at her watch and leaped up from her chair, snagging another piece of bacon as she went. Sugar lurched toward her from under the table, making a play for the bacon, but came up empty. "Look at the time. I'm gonna be late."

"Your dad's not even here to pick you up yet," I said, giving the last of my breakfast a wistful look as I stood up too. I wanted a couple of answers before she hustled off.

"Is there something wrong with the food?" Brady asked.

"Thea . . ." I followed her into the living room, and Brady was right behind me.

There was a pounding on the door, and a second later Thea was throwing it open and Logan was standing there looking at us. "Ready?" he asked.

"You bet." Thea grabbed her backpack, slung it onto her shoulder and bolted. "Gotta go, Mom. Talk to you later, okay? Don't wanna be late!"

"Who is he?" I hollered. (Screw tact. If I was worried about being nosy I'd never find out anything.)

"He who?" Logan asked.

"Good-bye, Thea," Brady called.

"Nobody, Mom," Thea hissed.

Logan draped one arm over Thea's shoulders, holding her in place while he looked at Brady. "What're you doing here so early?"

"I live here," Brady said, dropping one arm around *my* shoulders.

Logan noticed, and his eyes went all squinty. Just imagine the look on his face if he had seen my wake-up call that morning!

"You *live* here?"

"Temporarily," I put in, but Logan wasn't looking at me. He was too busy watching Brady stroking my arm. I did a quick sidestep away.

"Cassidy has been *very* generous," Brady said.

Logan's jaw twitched. "I thought you said you were a fairy?"

"I am."

"Then why're you all over Cassie?" Logan's gaze landed on me as if Brady were still holding me.

Brady frowned for a minute, then seemed to get what Logan was talking about. Typical male—he scowled even more fiercely and said, "I'm not *that* kind of fairy. I'm a *real* Faery."

"Real?"

Brady folded his arms over his chest, lifted his chin and narrowed his eyes. "Magical. I've come to Cassidy for Sanctuary. She's protecting me from the demon queen—"

"Brady . . ." *Oh, man.* I so didn't have time for this.

"Magical," Logan repeated like a man in the grips of an extremely weird hallucination.

"And he's teaching me how to be a cheerleader," Thea piped up, then shot a glance at me, noted my don't-talk-about-this-now expression and immediately shut up, trying to look invisible.

Logan let go of his daughter, planted his hands on his hips and pushed the edges of his flannel shirt back far enough to display the gun hooked to his belt. "Will *somebody* tell me what's going on here?"

Chapter Five

The thing is, Logan doesn't really want to know about demons.

I tried telling him the truth about just what was going on a month ago, and he'd laughed himself sick. So no way was I getting into it again. Especially when I had a meeting to get to, a daughter to interrogate and a Faery to keep off of me.

"Logan, why don't you just get Thea to school and we'll talk about this later?" See? I can be reasonable when I absolutely have to.

"Yes," Brady said. "Thea will be late."

"Who the hell—"

"Logan," Thea interrupted, tugging at his arm, "I really need to go."

He glanced at his newfound daughter, and the smile he couldn't give me bloomed on his face. "Fine. We'll go. Get in the car, Thea. I'll be right there."

Brady moved toward me and I batted him away. I was really uncomfortable with Brady being so touchy-feely with Logan standing right there.

There were certain things left undefined in this new relationship with Logan. For example, he was my past. Did I really want to go back and risk making another mistake that would not only hurt me this time, but Thea, too?

Besides, I already had this thing going with Devlin Cole, and I just didn't think I was up to juggling a cop and a demon.

The Faery wasn't helping the situation any.

"This isn't over," Logan said, shifting his gaze from me to Brady and back again. "We'll talk about this tonight."

"I might be busy," I said, thinking that I could find a way to be busy. Maybe I'd actually do the patrolling that Jasmine was always on me about. Heck, dusting demons sounded like way more fun than discussing anything with Logan.

"Get *un*busy."

I bristled. Yes, I have issues. Start bossing me around and I dig in my heels and go the opposite way just to spite you. Which is why Jasmine finds me so irritating, no doubt.

"Sounds like an order."

"Good call," Logan ground out. "And I don't want this guy around when we talk."

"I live here," Brady said.

I ignored Brady and gave Logan the death glare. "Wait. Maybe I should go get some paper. I can make notes to make sure everything in my life is just the way *you* want it."

"Of course I'll be here. Where else would I be?" Brady said to no one in particular.

Anywhere, I wanted to say, but that would have seemed too much like being on Logan's side, so I didn't.

"Anywhere," Logan said, and I gave myself a mental pat on the back for restraint.

His car horn honked, and we all looked out to see Thea waving at her father, trying to make him get a move on. Teenage type-A personality to the rescue.

"See ya, Logan."

He looked like he wanted to say something else, but then decided against it. "Later, Cassie."

"Right."

When he was gone, Brady looked at me. "You should not let him come over tonight."

"Just what I need. Another guy giving me orders."

"He's not worthy of you."

I blinked at him. "You've known me for what? Five minutes? Who are you to say Logan's not worthy?" And *why* was I defending Logan to Brady?

"Cassidy . . ."

Enough already. "I gotta go," I said, completely unwilling to keep this conversation going. "So, um, don't let any demons in the house while I'm gone."

"As you wish."

Huh. If anything in my life was as I wished it, I'd be a bazillionaire living on a tropical island with hot and cold running cabana boys.

Not likely.

I hugged my new Marc Jacobs closer to my body for comfort, then headed out.

&

The clinic on Fifth Street was small and tucked between the Sand Dollar Diner and Beryl's House of Wax. The diner served great food at really cheap prices, so Thea and I usually spent a lot of time there. But I tended to avoid even looking at Beryl's.

Old Vincent Price movie connotations aside, Beryl's place had a superhigh creep-out factor. Her list of waxing services was painted on the front window—eyebrows, facial waxing (something to look forward to, I guess—growing a beard), legs and, God help me . . . *Brazilian* waxes. Just my reading the word made my hoo-hah cringe. Hot wax next to party central? I didn't think so. Plus, I'd heard that the clinic deliberately opened up shop next door to Beryl's to take advantage of customers needing "accidental" burn treatments. Oh, yeah. Sign me up.

I shuddered when I parked my car and climbed out. The whole walk to the clinic I was squeezing those internal muscles as if I could pull my hoo-hah higher up inside just to protect it.

The clinic's waiting room was empty and smelled like alcohol and old people. Ten vacant chairs sat in a circle around a low table with out-of-date magazines scattered across the surface. I knew at a glance that they were out-of-date, because there was a picture of Brad and Jennifer on the cover of *People* with the tagline BABY ON THE WAY?

"Can I help you?" A fortyish woman with small eyes and a mole the size of a quarter on her chin spoke up from behind the reception desk. She was wearing pink polyester and had her graying brown hair done up in a braid wrapped around her head like Heidi Hits Middle Age. But nothing took away from that mole.

"Yeah," I said, trying desperately not to look at the mole. "I'm here to see Dr. Forest about the cleaning contract."

"Right." She sort of froze up, then forced a smile. "She said you'd be coming today and that I should show you around."

"Okay." I walked through the door, and the receptionist was doing her best to keep some distance between us. I didn't take it personally. If I worked in a clinic I'd be wearing a mask and gloves all the time just to keep myself cootie-free. "It's bigger than it looks from the outside," I said, mentally ticking off examination rooms and loving the sound of mental calculator keys clackety-clacking along.

"There are six exam rooms," she said, talking as fast as she was walking. Big hurry to get this over and done with. "And then the break room and the medicine room, and then that's the whole thing—well, except for the lobby, which you already saw, so if that's all you need . . ."

Things started adding up in my head. Mole Woman looked like she wanted to be anywhere but there, and since she actually worked there, I was beginning to think that I was the one giving her the heebie-jeebies. Since I'm a nice person and she'd never met me before, the only reason she'd be trying to ditch me was because she knew I was the Duster and she must be a demon.

"You seem nervous," I said.

"Who? Me?"

Only one way to find out if she was the kind of demon who needed dusting or not. I smiled at her and reached into my purse for my mini squirt bottle. I brought it out and hit the trigger, and a stream of green-flecked dark brown liquid shot at her.

"Yow!" She leaped back, hit a file cabinet, toppled a stack of manila folders off its precarious perch and sent piles of papers flying through the air. She danced in place, trying to find a way past me and out of this mess. But she slipped on one of the papers, landed on her ass and smacked the back of her head into that cabinet.

"Oopsie." She was climbing to her feet, hissing a little, but smiling anyway, like this was no big deal. Smoke was lifting off the top of her head, and she winced as she tried to stud it out.

"You okay?" I asked. That was me: considerate Duster.

"Fine, fine," she said. "Um, that's interesting. A new perfume?" Beads of sweat glittered on her upper lip, and even the mole sort of looked like it was shrinking.

"Give it up. Your head's smoking."

"I don't know what you're talking about." She smoothed one hand over the top of her head and then wiped her now-smoking palm on the side of her pink polyester uniform pants.

"You're a demon."

"Demon?" She laughed, but it was more like the sound of coins jingling together: sort of flat and tuneless. "No such thing as demons."

Okay, see, I'm a reasonable Duster. In the last month I've figured out that the best way to know if a demon needs its heart removed is if I squirt it and it tries to kill me. The ones like Nurse Mole, who just stand there and cringe, aren't really in the threat-to-mankind category, so I leave 'em alone.

Look at me: One month on the job and I've already got priorities.

"Relax," I said, tucking the spray back into my purse. "I'm not going to dust you."

"Thank God." She slumped in relief, then instantly turned around to the mountain-springwater fountain and cupped her hand under the spigot. Then she slapped the water on top of her head and sighed in relief. "Good. Thanks." She glanced down at her palm, then held it up accusingly. "Look what that stuff did! Man, it really burns."

Her skin was blistered, but, hey, I refused to jump onto the guilt train. *Demon.*

"So they tell me." I leaned against the doorjamb, inhaled the tempting scent of oregano and asked, "So, is the doc a demon, too?"

"Uh . . . uh . . ."

"So that's a yes," I said, and shook my head. I mean, come on. A *demon* wants to hire a Demon Duster to clean her clinic? What was this? Suicide by Duster?

"Look, the doc's really great." The nurse was still acting like she wanted to sprint for her life, but she kept smiling like we were friends. "She's really into this whole karmic attitude. You know, live and let live? Plus, she figured since you clean for Devlin Cole and you haven't dusted him yet . . ."

See what happens? You sleep with a demon and bingo! There goes your reputation.

"Anyway, she's only half-demon, so it'd be like killing a human, and you don't kill humans, right?"

"Not so far." Boy, could I talk tough or what? The truth was, I was still having trouble killing demons. Killing a human?

So not gonna happen. Although now that Nurse Mole had said that, I had something to think about. Killing a half-demon was actually like killing a half-human. Right? How did that figure into my own karmic scale?

Oh, God. This gig just kept getting more confusing.

"She's half-demon?"

"Uh-huh. Half Tarrana demon. They're demonic healers."

"Yeah?" You learn something new every day. I'd have to remember to ask Jasmine about Tarrana demons, because if Mole Woman was lying to me, I'd have to come back.

She frowned and asked, "You're not going to dust her, are you? I really need this job."

"Probably not," I conceded. "But if she's a healer you ought to have her look at that mole."

Magic Nights gleamed like a white palace in the early afternoon sunlight.

It took up practically the whole block, and at night it was lit up like a wedding cake under a spotlight. Devlin's club was almost impossible to get into. You had to be rich, famous or infamous to get a table in the club. And to get to the real club, upstairs in one of the private fantasy-sex rooms, you practically had to donate a kidney.

Or, I thought, be sleeping with the owner.

Yep, for the last month I'd been having semiregular sex with a semi-irregular demon. Hey, nobody's perfect. Besides, Devlin had really helped me out when I needed it.

These days, though my life kept getting weirder, my hoo-hah had never been happier. And with a happy hoo-hah, all things are possible. (Now *that's* a bumper sticker!)

Ever since that morning I'd been thinking it was time Devlin and I had a little talk. You know the one—to see where we were headed, if anywhere. What we were feeling, if anything, beyond mind-expanding sex. And what kind of relationship we actually had, if we had one.

I'm pretty sure we did. I liked him. He liked me. And we both liked the sex. I wasn't looking for promises of forever or white picket fences. But I guess I just wasn't the whoopee-easy-sex-no-strings kind of Duster. It might have been easier if I were, but what could you do? I guess I needed some actual caring with my fling.

So I parked behind Magic Nights, walked into the office and faced down Devlin Cole's assistant/secretary/pit bull.

Serena Sands and I had taken an instant dislike to each other when we first met, and nothing had happened to warm us up any. Personally, I think she wanted Devlin to herself and sort of figured that it was just too twisted for a demon and a Duster to be slapping the sheets together.

So whenever I had to face her, I kept my hand on my squirt bottle just in case she ever decided to go against Devlin's orders to leave me alone and clear out the field for herself.

"Hi, Serena." Big smile. Lots of teeth. Never let a demon know she makes you crazy.

"Cassidy." A bow of her head, very queen-to-peasant. Of course, to be honest, she looked pretty damned royal. Which made me wonder what the *actual* demon queen looked like.

Serena stood at least six feet tall *without* the three-inch spike heels she consistently wore. Her legs were about five feet of her height, and her long, silvery blond hair fell in fairy-tale ripples down her back. I told myself that this was just her human costume. That no doubt in her real demon skin she was troll-like and had spinach permanently wedged into her fangs.

I spun my squirt bottle like a gunfighter with a .45 and gave her a smile when she eyed me warily. "I'm just here to see Devlin. He available?"

She smiled too.

See how nicely we both lied?

"Sure. He's in the penthouse; just go on up."

Hmm. That was easy. Too easy, really. Usually she liked to make me cool my heels for a while before letting me through the gates to Good-time City. *Whatever.* Maybe she'd had an epiphany. Maybe I was starting to worry her. Maybe . . . I didn't care what the reason was.

I headed for the elevator, still swinging my Duster liquid, just in case she changed her mind and got a little feisty. The elevator opened with a silent swish, and then I was inside and hitting the button for Devlin's private apartment at the top of the building. He also had a huge house on the point overlooking the ocean, but I'd never seen it. Hey, why drive out of town when you've got all of these nice, comfy beds right here where they're handy?

Just for a moment or two, I remembered our last night together. A week ago we'd used the swing room, and let me just say that a man with good balance is worth his weight in condoms.

The doors opened on Devlin's suite, and I came up out of my memories to stop for a second or two just to admire it. The room looked as though it belonged in a mountain cabin. Lots of wood, leather and big, overstuffed furniture. The drapes were closed, making the room dark, but a couple of the lamps were on, showing me the way across the floor in a stream of pale light.

Not that I needed a road map. Heck, we'd been all over the room together. Terrace, couch, tabletop (my back hurt for days, but it had been worth it). My hoo-hah trembled and started lighting candles, readying for the party that was soon to begin. I was already hot, and I hadn't even *seen* Devlin yet. Regular sex can really spoil a girl.

Still absently swinging my squirt bottle, I wandered through the apartment toward the bedroom. There were noises coming from inside and I figured Devlin was relaxing with a some TV, so I sneaked up, wanting to surprise him with a little afternoon game of hide-the-demon-part. *After* our heart-to-heart chat, of course.

I opened his door and stopped dead.

My jaw dropped and my stomach pitched. I knew I was breathing because my head was getting light due to the hyper-ventilation going on.

There was definitely a game of hide-the-demon-weenie going on, but I hadn't been invited.

In the wash of golden lamplight I watched Devlin—*my* demon—balance a naked, three-boobed freak of nature on his dick and give her a spin. Okay, maybe she wasn't spinning, but I'm pretty sure my head was.

"WHAT THE HELL?"

Everybody stopped and looked at me. The demon babe on Devlin's lap was smiling. Easy to understand why, since I'd been in her position often enough to know there was plenty to smile about.

Devlin looked uncomfortable, though. Small consolation. "Cassidy . . ."

"Who's she?" I demanded.

"Excuse me?" Three Boob demanded right back. "You're the one barging in."

Her boobs—all three of 'em—were *perfect*: Big and bouncy and making my measly two seem even smaller than they actually were in comparison. And they looked real, too. *Damn it*.

"Okay, let's not get excited," Devlin said, and tried to disentangle himself from Three Boob. She wasn't having any of that, though. She locked her long legs around his middle and clung to him like melted chocolate on Saran Wrap.

"EXCITED? WHO'S EXCITED?" I heard myself screech-ing, and couldn't care. For God's sake, you couldn't trust any-body anymore.

So much for our chat about our relationship.

Pain shot through me, surprising me with its strength. It wasn't the wounded-till-you-bled feeling you get over losing the love of your life, though. This was more like sheer humiliation. Damn it, I'd really liked him. Now that I knew he was a lying, cheating dick of a demon, I was seriously pissed off.

"Get rid of her, Dev," the demon cling-on whispered, rubbing all three of her boobs against his chest like she was trying to start a fire. Maybe she was.

"Get rid of me?" I shot Devlin a look that should have sizzled his ass to the sheets. Hey, when I'm hurt, I make sure everyone *else* in the room is hurt, too. "Yeah, let's see you try that, Dev."

He was still trying to pry his babe from his body. "Cassidy, you're overreacting. . . ."

"Really? Cuz I don't think I am." I waved one hand and noticed that I was still holding my squirt bottle. Funny. I'd forgotten all about it.

What I wanted to do was reach into Devlin Cole's amazingly broad and tanned chest and rip out his shriveled, wormlike heart. I wanted to cry, too. But I wasn't about to do that in front of Three Boob. My fingers were itching to reach into that chest of his, but I'd probably regret it later, so instead I pointed my bottle and took aim.

"Cass, don't!"

A gentleman demon to the last, he tried to shield Three Boob from the spray, but I was way too thorough for that. I sent so many streams of liquid shooting at the two of them, they had as much chance of drowning as they did of being burned. I was mad and hurt and feeling a little outboobed.

The demon babe was howling and screaming and trying to wipe herself off, using Devlin as a towel. Devlin was trying to peel a hysterical female off of him and wipe himself down with the silk sheets at the same time. Me, I just stood there squirting the two of them. I watched them roll off the bed, crash onto the floor and drag the quilt up over their heads, and still I squirted 'em.

Demon babe's screams were piercing, and Devlin's shouts were getting more frantic. All good. Finally, though, I'd had enough. There was only an inch or so of fluid left, and I might need that for emergency dustage. So I turned around, stomped back to the private elevator and jumped inside.

I felt like I didn't even need the elevator. I was so damned mad I could have jumped out the window. I could have stood in front of a speeding train and had it bounce right off me. I could have—The elevator dinged and let me off in the lobby, and I stepped out to face Serena's broad smile.

Made me glad I'd saved some demon spray.

"Leaving so soon?" Her voice was a croon that stabbed at me. She'd set me up, knowing full well what I'd find when I went up to Devlin's place. Fine. She wanted to play games— let's see how good *she* was at 'em.

I gave her a squirt right between the eyes, and she hissed in a breath while her skin bubbled and smoked. Serena leaped up, jumped across her desk and snarled at me. Her human costume slipped a little, and I caught a glimpse of red eyes and yellow skin. *Hmm.* Not quite so pretty when the makeup was off, were we?

She charged me, six feet of furious demon, and I was more than ready to hit somebody. I could have just dusted her and let it go at that, but the truth was, with the mood I was in, it would be way more satisfying just to beat the crap out of her.

She hit me hard, and we toppled over backward. She was pretty strong, and I felt the heel of my shoe snap as I went down, and that only made me madder. Serena hissed at me again, blinked, and her mask dropped completely: yellow skin, red eyes and raised ridges along her cheekbones. Her silvery hair looked even better against her real complexion than the phony one she normally wore, and that really pissed me off.

I slugged her hard and felt satisfaction when her nose broke. Blood spurted over both of us, and when she howled I pitched her off me, jumped to my feet and swung my Marc Jacobs tote in a wide enough arc that it slapped into the side of her head and knocked her off balance again just as she was looking for her footing.

"You stupid bitch," she said, shaking that hair back out of her face and sending droplets of pink blood flying around the room. "You never should have come here. Never should have started up with Devlin."

"I didn't start with *him*," I told her. "*He* started with *me!*"

She wiped her face with the back of her hand, smearing that ugly pink blood across both cheeks. "You were just a bump in the road. A diversion."

She really knew how to throw a punch. Even the psychological ones.

"Yeah, well," I sniped, "that's over. Your boss is just a pile of lint."

"You DUSTED him?" Her voice hit a note that only dogs should have been able to hear.

"What'd you *think* I'd do to him?" I countered, letting her believe Devlin's being toast crumbs was all her fault. What the hell? Why should *I* be the only one in pain here?

"You . . . you . . ." She looked from me to the elevator as if she were going to run upstairs and try to piece her boss back together again.

"Back at you, babe." I stepped in close, swung my right arm back to get full power and gave her one more punch just for the hell of it. She took off like she was shot from a cannon, and I watched her fly backward through the air. (Duster strength? Pretty impressive.) Serena landed hard, legs splayed, eyes practically jittering in their sockets. When she could focus again,

I leaned in and said, "Just so we're clear? Next time I see you, I'll dust your ass."

Then I was out of there.

Magic Nights, my ass.

Tears stung my eyes, but damned if I'd cry over a two-timing demon. I should have known better. Shouldn't have been steered down the road of sin by such a skilled driver. Shouldn't already be missing the big jerk.

I stepped out the office door into a patch of sunlight, and another damned demon jumped at me. This one had pointy ears, ragged hair and liver spots all over his green face. Two red horns curved up from his forehead, there was another horn dead center in his chest and yet one more a little lower that looked suspiciously like— Never mind; I didn't want to know.

Chapter Six

"The money is mine, Duster!" The demon's voice roared out around me just before its big freaking fist slammed into my jaw.

Suddenly I knew what it felt like to fly. I sailed through the crisp autumn air. My heelless pump flew off, my brand-new Marc Jacobs tote skidded across the pavement and my skirt hiked up so high, I let La Sombra know I was wearing my best ivory thong. I landed on the sidewalk, thunking the back of my head so hard, my eyeballs rolled up into my skull. I felt my bones rattle and took a second to shake my head enough so that my eyeballs would settle into place. Just in time to see the demon charging me again.

Well, damn it.

As if this day weren't crappy enough.

The demon was practically drooling, and *all* of its horns were vibrating.

Nasty.

"Ohmigod!"

Somebody screamed, and it wasn't me.

CRAP.

This was new. I was fighting a demon right out in the open. Half of my still-pissed-off-and-slightly-scared brain noted that there were a few people watching this little show. A woman walking to her car (probably the screamer). A kid on a skateboard. An old guy on a bus bench.

Great, I had an audience watching me get my ass kicked.

It didn't seem to bother the demon any. It ran at me, hands outstretched, long fingers clicking together as if it could already feel my neck snapping. Well, audience or not, I wasn't going to just lie there and die. My own fingers curled around the bottle of demon spray I'd somehow managed to hang on to, and when Horny got close enough I gave him a good squirt.

The demon howled, stopped dead and wiped at its eyes with those nasty fingers. While it was busy sizzling from the demon acid, I did one of those great, swing-your-legs-out-and-flip-to-your-feet moves. (Hey, all that training with Jasmine was starting to pay off. Not that I'd admit that to *her*.)

Then I spun into a half circle and slammed my now-shoeless foot into the demon's belly. He flew back like he was yanked on a rope, and I was so damn mad by this point that I was on the demon almost before he landed.

"You seriously picked the wrong day to screw with me!" I shouted.

He scrabbled back on the gravel-dusted cement, still trying to clear his vision enough to kill me.

"Do you *know* what I've been through?"

"You bitch!"

"*That's* the best you can do?"

He screamed at me then and made a grab for my leg, but I leaped straight up in the air and landed on the other side of him.

So there I was, standing in a parking lot with my skirt hiked up to my waist, my hair studded with gravel from my landing, and bloody scrapes on my hands and knees. I had one shoe, and my new purse was totally ruined. I was pissed. Hurt. Disappointed.

Tears were starting to form, but I choked them back. No way was I crying. Not yet anyway.

"I am *not* a bitch!" I reached into his chest. He was still staring at me—stunned, confused and a little ticked off, when I ripped his heart out and sent him blowing into the wind.

"Cool!" the kid on the skateboard shouted.

Funny: I'd forgotten about the audience. Quickly I yanked my skirt down—barn door open, horse gone—and turned around in time to see the old guy on the bus bench drop his mouth open so that his lit cigar fell into his lap. He leaped up, beating at his crotch, then ran for it like I was some kind of deranged killer or something.

Hmm.

Maybe that's how it had looked to the casual observer.

I heard sirens getting closer and knew my day was about to get worse. I glanced over at the woman who had been walking to her car. She was already behind the wheel, and her tires squealed as she peeled out of the lot.

Good move, Cass, I told myself. So much for the whole secret-identity thing. Although Buffy never had been able to keep her slayer status a secret, and she'd done all right. But then, Buffy's demon lover had never cheated on *her*!

Great. Plan your life on the workings of a TV show.

I was all alone in the sun-drenched parking lot, looking like I'd been dragged behind a trash truck, when Logan wheeled into the parking lot, a flashing red light on the roof of his black SUV. He slammed to a stop three feet away, and his eyes bugged out at the sight of me.

Perfect.

All of the cops in La Sombra and I got my *ex*.

"Cassie?" He left the car door open and walked toward me. "You all right? We got some nine-one-one calls about a fight. Some woman getting beaten up by a big guy. I was close, so I responded, and . . ." His gaze moved over me, apparently those catlike cop responses kicking in, and he noticed the bloody knees, the ratty hair and the tears in my skirt. "It was *you*? Are you okay?"

He grabbed me and pulled me into a hard hug, and just for a second or two I let myself enjoy it. His strength felt good, and the fact that he cared enough about me to be worried was like a soothing balm. Logan was the first guy who'd slept with me and then hurt me. Was it weird that now I was willing to accept comfort from him?

Pulling back a little, he caught my chin in his hand and turned my face from one side to the other. He winced and said, "Damn, honey. You don't look so good."

Just what I needed to hear.

"I'm fine, Logan." Not really, but fine enough. The bruises weren't even painful anymore, and I knew from firsthand experience that most of them would be healed by tomorrow. The whole Demon Duster package could really work to your advantage when it came to physical injuries. What really hurt was my insides.

And nobody could do anything about that.

Least of all Logan.

"Where'd the guy go?" he asked, scanning the lot, looking for the assailant and/or witnesses.

He was fresh out of luck, though. The demon was long gone, and my audience had faded away almost as quickly. Guess nobody wanted to stick around once they saw a guy dissolve into dust bunnies.

"Can you give me a description?" he asked, even while two squad cars rolled up.

"Doesn't matter," I said, glancing at the other cops and wishing they'd go away. Heck, I wanted *everybody* to go away. Me most of all. I wanted me to be in a bar, a margarita in my hand and nachos in front of me.

"Of course it matters," Logan argued, then turned and shouted to the other cops, "Spread out. Look for witnesses."

They moved off, and he turned back to me. "Do you know who the guy was?"

"Just some demon," I said, shaking my head. "He didn't give me a name."

Logan's face froze up, and I did an inward mental head thunk. Why had I even bothered?

"Don't start that again, Cassie," he warned.

I looked up at him, squinting into the afternoon sunlight, and suddenly all the warm fuzzies I'd been feeling for him evaporated. I was completely out of patience. It had been the day from Hell, and Logan wasn't making it any easier. Yes, he'd been right there with me a month ago when I'd dusted Judge Jenks, but even seeing it for himself, Logan had made excuses, unwilling to admit that there actually *were* demons living happily in his cozy hometown. Looked like nothing had changed. Well, I was done making nice. I wasn't going to make up some comfortable lie for him. He could believe me or not.

"Wake up, Logan," I snapped, and limped off on one shoe to pick up my Marc Jacobs tote. I grimaced at the long scrape on the formerly pristine red leather and wished I could dust that damn demon all over again. I turned to face Logan and said, "Look around. Do you see any attackers? Do you see any witnesses? No. Know why?"

I bent down, scooped up some dust and let it dribble through my fingers to be caught by the ocean wind. As it streamed out behind me on a current of air, I said, "*This* is why. I dusted him. He poofed in front of witnesses, and it scared the crap out of them." I paused. "Well, I don't think it scared the kid. He seemed to enjoy it—but the others were freaked out, so they ran. *That's* why we're all alone here, Logan. That's why you won't be finding my attacker anytime soon."

Logan's blue eyes narrowed, and that muscle in his jaw started to twitch, so I knew he was grinding his teeth together. He shoved the edges of his dark green flannel shirt back, planted both fists on his hips and glared at me. "This demon shit is getting old, Cassie."

"You're telling *me*?" I brushed the dirt off my red leather bag and wondered if a shoemaker could do something about that scrape. "You think I *like* dealing with demons? You can't trust 'em, you know. Not even the ones who pretend you can. They lie to you just like humans, and then they turn on you like rabid snakes and—"

"Will you knock it off with the demon crap already?" Logan demanded.

"Cass."

A deep voice spoke up, and whatever I would have said to Logan died unuttered.

I whipped around to watch Devlin step out of Magic Nights. He was wearing a shirt, but it was unbuttoned, giving me an unobstructed view of his burned and still-smoking chest. Small satisfaction.

He glanced at Logan and dismissed him before turning his gaze back to me. "We have to talk."

Riiiiigggghhhhttt . . . I'd said all I was going to say to Devlin Cole.

"Yeah," I muttered, "that's gonna happen."

"Cass," he said on a long sigh, "you're making too big a thing out of this."

Logan piped up. "Butt out, Cole. I'm talking to Cassie."

Devlin didn't even acknowledge that. Instead he took a step toward me, and damned if I didn't back up a step or two to compensate. I so didn't want to be anywhere near him at the moment. I could still see him balancing Three Boob on his lap while filling his hands with two of her boobs.

Two and a spare. Any man's wet dream.

"I know you're angry," he said.

"Good catch," I told him.

"You're mad at him?" Logan said, clearly enjoying the thought.

"We need to talk about this, Cass," Devlin said, and shoved

one hand through his long, thick black hair. His nearly black eyes fixed on me, and I thought for a second that I saw color swirl in them. Something reddish. His demon nature poking through?

"*We* don't have to do anything," I told him. "*I* am going home."

"Hold on. You can't leave," Logan argued. "You were attacked. We have to fill out reports—"

That was Logan. When in doubt, fall back on what you could count on. Paperwork. Logic. Reason. Well, all of those things had zero to do with my life.

"No reports," I snapped. "I'm not pressing charges against anybody, so forget it."

"Attacked?" Devlin echoed.

"Hello?" I countered, waving both hands up and down my body. "Did I look like this a few minutes ago?"

"Are you all right?" Devlin asked.

"None of your business," Logan said.

"No, I'm not, and you know why," I told Devlin, ignoring Logan myself, since I really didn't want to deal with either one of them.

"This is a misunderstanding," Devlin said.

"Oh, I understood plenty. Where's Three Boob?" I looked behind him at the door, half expecting his cleavage-gifted honey to make an appearance.

"She's gone."

"Too bad for you."

"Three Boob?" Logan asked.

"You know what?" I asked nobody in particular. "I'm done. I need a drink. And some chocolate. Maybe a chocolate drink. And then I need a bath. And maybe another drink. What I *don't* need is you guys."

I dug in my ruined purse for my car keys, curled my fingers around them and headed for my trusty VW. I was limping, of

course, since I had only the one shoe, and the bits of gravel in
the lot bit at the bare sole of my foot. Wind zipped in off the
ocean and made me shiver. At least, I think it was the wind. It
could have been a reaction to everything that had happened in
the last fifteen minutes.

I couldn't hope for dignity, but I had a little pride left, so
I just kicked my other shoe off to get rid of the limp and left
that pump lying abandoned in the lot.

"Damn it, Cass." Devlin.

"Cassie . . ." Logan.

"Screw you guys." Me.

Then I was in the Bug and driving off. I checked my rearview mirror once and saw both men staring after me, still
looking furious.

Maybe I'd get lucky and they'd kill each other.

E

"Cohen Dental."

The familiar voice on the phone didn't sound happy to be
at work. "Men suck," I said.

"Too true," Rachel agreed.

That was the best thing about having the same best friend
your whole freaking life: She immediately knew what she was
supposed to say. And she was always on your side.

"Can you leave the office?" I asked, and steered my car
down PCH toward the La Sombra pier.

"Sure, where am I going?"

"Tully's. It's a margarita emergency."

"Excellent," Rachel said. "Give me twenty minutes. I'll get
Simon's mom to come in and answer the phones. She just *loves*
getting a chance to worm her way into the business. Then she
can tell me what a lousy wife I am and how Simon deserves
better."

"Sorry."

"No biggie. I let her harass me once in a while. Makes her feel better."

Simon was Rachel's husband, and an orthodontist. I'd just recently discovered that he was also the dentist of choice for the demon population in town. It was comforting that I could talk to Rachel about the weirdness. Although I still hadn't gotten around to telling her about me being the Demon Duster. Don't ask me why, 'cause I don't know. It just never seemed like the right time, and, hey, I'd known myself for only a month!

"Thanks, Rach."

"Cass," she said, clearly picking up on something in my voice, "you okay?"

"Not really."

"Make it fifteen minutes."

I had a head start on Rachel. I was halfway through my first margarita by the time she got to Tully's. The bar/pizza place sat at the end of the pier and boasted glass walls, so you could get a great view of the ocean. About twenty years ago Tully slapped some of that do-it-yourself window tinting on the glass, so the only time you got hit with a little sun blindness was when you got a seat in the direct line of some of the peeling-off tint.

Tully's wasn't long on ambience, but Tully also didn't care if you came in barefoot—a real plus for a restaurant right on the beach. It worked out well for me that day, too. Surfers crowded most of the tables, with a sprinkling of fall tourists just for atmosphere. There was sand on the floor, music pumping through ancient speakers and plastic ivy in brown baskets hanging on silver chains from the ceiling.

"Wow," Rachel said, sliding onto the blue Naugahyde seat opposite me. "You look even worse than you sounded on the phone."

"And feel worse than *that*," I said, and grabbed one of the pepperoni pizza sticks from the plate in front of me.

Rachel grabbed one too and picked up the trailing thread

of mozzarella to pile on top. She took a bite, then lifted one hand to the bartender and pointed at my margarita. Then she took another bite of pizza stick, looked at me and said, "Spill it."

I slumped against the seat back, sipped at my drink and enjoyed the icy slide down my throat. "All men are dogs."

"Good start," Rachel said. "Is this a general man bashing, or is there one in particular we're gonna kick around?"

"Devlin."

She frowned, but probably no one but me would have known that. Rachel was a big fan of Botox.

"Damn," she said when the bartender brought her margarita. "What'd the bastard do?"

"Better question is, *Who'd* the bastard do?"

"Oh, man." Rachel took a long drink, set the glass down and grabbed another pizza stick. "That sucks. I thought he was a good demon."

Yep, Rachel knew all about Devlin being a demon, too. Hey, she's my best friend, remember?

"Me too."

"So, who'd he do?"

"I caught him with a demon. She had *three* boobs! All of 'em bigger than my measly two."

"Show-off."

"Exactly." I finished off my margarita, signaled for another one and idly spun the empty glass in its damp circle on the tabletop.

"Did you dust him?"

I blinked at her. Apparently I really stank at the whole having-a-secret-identity thing. "What?"

She shrugged. "You know. Did you kill him?"

"How did—"

"Thea told Zoe; Zoe told me." Clearly there was a downside to this friendship-next-generation thing.

Rachel took a long sip of her drink and said, "But *you* should've told me."

"I was going to." Well, that didn't sound too lame. "It's just such a long story, and—"

"Women in your family become Demon Dusters on their thirty-second birthdays?"

"Okay, not that long."

"You should've told me," Rachel said again, and took another sip.

"You're right. I should've. It was just weird, you know? I mean, it's not every day you find out something like that, and things have just gotten crazier, and— Why didn't you tell me you knew?"

"Because I didn't want you to know I knew until I knew you wanted me to know, you know?"

"Terrifying to admit I actually understood that," I said, then handed off my empty glass for a fresh one when the bartender strolled over. Strange, but I didn't even have a buzz from the alcohol. Was this another piece of the Demon Duster package? Was I destined to go buzz-free the rest of my life?

"So did you? Dust him?"

"No," I admitted, remembering my urge to do just that. "But I squirted him and made him sizzle like a steak on a hot grill."

"That's something, I guess." She shook her head, and her dark brown hair swung out into a smooth arc at chin level, then fell back into its perfectly cut style. Rachel always had had good hair karma. "What'd he say?"

"You mean after the screaming stopped?"

"Yeah."

"Not much. But then, I didn't want to listen. I pretty much stomped out while he and Three Boob were still smoking." All of this talking about it wasn't helping. I'd thought it would.

You know, spill your guts, immediately feel that cathartic rush and become a new person. Not so much.

I was still hurt and pissed off, and every time the hurt started getting bigger, I just concentrated on the mad and let that take over. I liked mad way better than hurt. "Plus, when I left the club another demon tried to kill me, and it ruined my new bag—"

Rachel gasped. "The Marc Jacobs?"

This is why Rachel is my best friend.

"Yes." I lifted the bag, showed her the scrape and appreciated the wince of sympathy. I dropped my purse onto the bench seat again. "Then Logan showed up, because some people saw me dust that demon, and somebody called the cops, and then Devlin came out and they were both yelling at me, so I left."

"Who could blame you?"

I took another long gulp of frozen tequila, and an ice-cream headache throbbed into life. *Perfect.* No buzz, but I still got the pain. That was starting to feel like my motto. I rubbed my forehead, looked at Rachel and said, "I hate men."

"Of course you do. You're female."

I smiled at her and felt a little better. It was good to be able to talk to somebody who so clearly understood. Who knew that all I wanted was somebody to agree with me. To let me rant and piss and moan.

Rachel grinned. "So, no more Devlin the demon. You gonna let Logan in to play?"

"No. Been there, done him." I shook my head and remembered how I'd let Logan comfort me. His arms were strong and he smelled good and he could make my insides light up like a tiki torch with a single look. But he also made me a little nuts. Especially because I was pretty sure I still felt a *lot* for Logan—which couldn't be good. Right?

"Besides," I said, trying to talk myself off the mental ledge, "even if I *was* interested, Thea would go ballistic. She's just getting used to having a father. I don't think she's ready to have a mom and a dad *dating*. Plus, still hating men, remember?"

"Uh-huh."

"So, I'm going to forget about men entirely. Demon and human. I'm going to concentrate on Thea."

"Oh, that'll make her happy," Rachel said. "Nothing an almost-sixteen-year-old likes better than having her mother focused on her."

"And," I said, talking louder to drown Rachel out, "I'm going to go out there and kill demons. I'm going to make so much dust, people will think they're living in Oklahoma!"

"Uh-huh."

"And I'm gonna go on a diet. And maybe work out more. And stop eating so much junk. And help Thea make cheerleader."

"Then maybe you could work on world peace and find a new fuel source and—"

I cut her off. "You're not being supporto-friend."

"Yeah, I am. I'm talking you down off the roof. You can't let one demon do this to you, Cass."

I pushed my margarita away. No point in drinking it if there wasn't going to be a buzz.

"I'm just so damn mad," I said.

"Now *that*, I get."

"Devlin made me feel like an idiot."

"He's the idiot."

"Okay," I said, smiling at her. "There's support gal back again."

"I do what I can."

"I appreciate it."

"Enough to tell me about the new guy you've got stashed at your house?"

I just stared at her. "Is there *anything* you don't know?"

She laughed.

"Are you trying to take my mind off of that dirty, cheating demon?"

"Depends. Is it working?"

I thought about it. "Yeah. Really is."

"Good," Rachel said, leaning her forearms on the tabletop. "So spill. Who is the mystery Faery?"

"How'd you know about the Faery thing?"

"He told me."

"He told you he's a Faery?"

"First thing he said," Rachel told me. "Of course, I knew right away he wasn't *that* kind of fairy."

"How?"

"Because God would never do that to women everywhere. Too big a waste."

Good point."

"How'd you find out about him?"

"It was so great." Rachel grabbed up one of the last two pizza sticks and took a bite. "I had to run back home after I dropped Zoe off at school, and there was a FedEx truck outside your house. I wondered what you were getting, and then this amazing-looking man opened your front door and signed for the package. When the truck drove off I went over, because"—she shrugged a little—"I wanted to make sure he wasn't a burglar or something—"

"A burglar who signs for packages?"

"Fine. Shoot me. I'm nosy. Big revelation. Anyway, Brady introduced himself, and I swear, Cass, that man should be illegal or something. He says he's living with you, and why didn't you tell me THAT?"

I sighed. "I'm really scoring low on the best-friend test, aren't I?"

"So far? Bottom third."

"Fine, fine. He's not *living*-with-me living with me. He's just staying with me for a while."

"Uh-huh."

She didn't roll her eyes, but it was implied. If she had known about the wake-up call I'd had that morning, she'd have been drooling into what was left of her margarita. The upside of this conversation was that I had stopped thinking about Devlin and Three Boob. The downside was, "What was in the package Brady signed for?"

Rachel drained her margarita. "He said it was a new set of pots and pans. Said he couldn't cook with what you had. Which was kind of surprising, since your old pans have hardly been used at all."

"New—"

"He also said he'd give me cooking lessons."

"How do you know he can cook?"

"He made me breakfast. Belgian waffles."

"I don't have a Belgian waffle–maker."

"You do now."

Chapter Seven

I had more than a Belgian waffle-maker.

After leaving Tully's, I went home and found boxes in the living room. Lots of boxes. Some empty, some still unopened, they littered the floor and formed a path into the kitchen. I only glanced at the names on the boxes, since I was really wanting to talk to the shopping Faery.

In passing, I caught a couple names I recognized—high-end kitchen goodies. Then there were the boxes from Pottery Barn and Macy's. Intriguing.

But first things first. I hit the kitchen and, for a minute or two, thought I might be in the wrong house. The lights were bright against the coming night outside and shone down on counters crowded with . . . let me just tell you. I had a Belgian waffle maker, omelet pans, grilling pans, sautéing pans, saucepans, stockpots, Crock-Pots and griddles. I had more spoons, knives, spatulas and forks than I'd ever seen in one place before. *And* I had my own personal Faery busily cooking away at the stove. Poor stove. Probably wondering how it had landed in a strange house. The most I'd ever used the thing for was to heat up pizza.

Having a six-foot-five, muscular, gorgeous Faery working in her kitchen was enough to take a woman's mind off her problems, anyway. Hard to sit and mope about Devlin or fret over Logan while I watched silvery bits of what I guessed was Faery dust sparkle in the air around Brady as he moved from stove to table and back again.

It turned out that even though Brady'd been a demon queen's captive for a hundred years, he still knew his way around the Internet.

And he'd been busy.

Not only did we have a new set of pans, he'd figured out how to grocery shop online. Hard to argue with a Faery who stocked your house with food.

Sugar had OD'd on dog treats and was now flat on her back, tongue lolling out, all four paws extended, and snoring like a hairy drunk. Thea was acting like it was Christmas morning.

"Mom!" She pulled her head out of the fridge long enough to give me a wide smile. "Brady bought stuff for *sandwiches*. I mean, meat and cheese, and did you know there's more than one kind of mustard? And there's chicken and salad stuff and Snapple iced tea and—"

"I get it," I said, cutting her off before she started giving me a shelf-by-shelf description. "We have food."

Thea finally took a good look at me, and apparently the sight was enough to distract her even from the glories of food. "What happened to you?"

Thea's eyes bugged out, and heck, even Brady looked sort of concerned. I glanced down at the front of me and noted my torn red blazer, the rip in my skirt that went halfway up my thigh and, oh, let's not forget the bloody gashes on my knees. I looked back at Thea. "Bad demon day."

"Are you okay?"

Hmm. Physically, I didn't hurt as much anymore. Emotionally, I was still pretty much a train wreck. But no way do you tell your teenage daughter that you just caught your demon lover slipping it to a three-boobed wonder. So I sucked it all up and said, "Yeah. I'm fine."

"Oh, good." She flipped her long black hair behind her shoulder. "This is so cool. I don't think the fridge has ever been this full."

Fine. I admit it. Thea and I went through life buying what we needed when we needed it. We're big on preservatives in our house. Cheetos have an eternal shelf life, for instance, so we've always got them and Pop Tarts. And coffee. And chocolate. And salad in a bag. It's not like we're food-deprived. We just weren't used to seeing the kind of food you had to *cook.*

Brady was back at the stove stirring a gigantic, gleaming stainless-steel pot bubbling with something delicious and smiling at Thea like a benevolent uncle. "I'm making beef-and-barley soup for tonight."

"MAKING soup?" Thea asked, slamming the refrigerator. "You mean it's not from a can?"

Horrified, Brady sniffed. "Please."

"Mom, are you getting this?"

"Traitor," I muttered, then walked over to Brady's side. Okay, fine. The soup smelled good. Great, even. But what I wanted to know was how he'd bought all this stuff. If he'd used my Visa card, he'd have had enough to buy maybe a soup ladle. If it was on sale. Not that I have bad credit or anything; it's just that my Visa hovers pretty close to maxed-out most of the time.

Just the thought of that sent me on a search for chocolate.

I stepped over Sugar, walked to the table, pulled out a chair directly opposite Thea and dropped into it. I was feeling pretty pooped until I looked at the stack of food on the table and saw that Brady had also bought me Pop Tarts. There was a family-sized box on the table in front of me. Brown sugar and cinnamon. All for me.

Thea curled up in her chair, lifted her Snapple in salute and grinned. "Brady is so cool."

The Faery in question shivered with pleasure, and even more of that Faery dust sparkled out all around him. But maybe not. Maybe I was just so wiped out from my totally crappy day that I was seeing things. Hallucinations. Fabulous.

I sighed and said, "So, Brady. Not that I don't appreciate the soup and the Pop Tarts—"

"And chocolate, Mom," Thea crowed, holding up a bag of Hershey's Caramel Kisses. Just what I needed. He'd managed to get our favorite kind. Could Faeries read minds, too?

Scary thought.

"And chocolate," I added, reaching for the bag and tearing it open. Don't judge me. If ever a woman needed chocolate, it was me. Actually, I thought I was doing pretty well. After a day like I'd had, most people would have needed therapy.

"So," I said, still chewing as I turned back to Brady, who was chopping carrots with an excellent—and new—knife. "How'd you buy all this stuff?"

He glanced at me, and those big blue eyes of his twinkled. Actually twinkled. "I used your computer. Online shopping is very easy."

Tell me about it.

"I couldn't very well leave Sanctuary without you," he said. "Too dangerous. So I had them bring everything here. Amazing what you can buy online."

"Uh-huh. I got that much. *How* did you buy it?"

"Hmm?"

"You know, how'd you pay for everything?"

He stopped, knife poised above the chopping block, and gave me a confused look. *"Pay?"*

Oh, boy.

I reached for more chocolate. "Brady, you had to use a credit card or something to order all this stuff. People don't just give things away free. I mean, it'd be great if they did, but they just don't."

"They give things to Faeries."

"Uh-oh," Thea said, looking at the Snapple in her hand as if it were contraband. And, hey, it was. It was stolen Snapple and, being the superior human being she was, Thea couldn't drink it. Being less superior, I had no problem eating stolen chocolate. In fact, I unwrapped three more, threw them in my mouth and lost myself in the glory of caramel.

I didn't steal 'em.

"Faeries don't have money," Brady said with a shrug, slicing through the rest of the carrots in front of him with the touch of a master chef. "We don't need it."

"You just STEAL things?" Thea asked, and I could see that in her eyes, Brady was losing his cool factor pretty quickly.

He scooped up the carrots, tossed them into the bubbling pot, then gave his soup another stir. Instantly clouds of amazingly scented steam lifted into the air, and I had to remind myself that I should be mad at him. After all, he was a felon Faery.

Or Faery felon.

Whatever.

"Brady, you can't just steal stuff from people."

"I don't steal." He straightened up to his full, pretty impressive height. Lifting his chin, he gathered dignity around him like a cloak and said, "Faeries have always lived this way. We do not steal. We take only what we need. And we give those we take from a sense of well-being, of having done something noble and good. They feel as though they have helped the less fortunate and gained much in their karmic souls. Many go on to donate to other worthy causes."

A headache jolted behind my eyes. "When you get stuff online you have to use a credit card number, Brady," I said, really striving for some calm. "Whose did you use?"

He looked appalled at the suggestion. "I would not do that. I made up the number and used magic."

"Magic?"

He shrugged. "It was not difficult."

So my overworked Visa was off the hook, and he hadn't

exactly stuck anyone else with the bill. Still, he had to be stopped.

I picked caramel off my back teeth with my tongue and studied the affronted Faery. "So you think that by taking stuff from people without paying for it, you're actually doing them a favor."

He absolutely *beamed*, pleased that I understood. "Exactly."

I shot a look at Thea and knew she wasn't buying this either. In fact, she was looking a little sick.

I shook my head and sighed. "You can't keep doing this, Brady."

"It's the Faery way."

"Not while you're living with me. We can buy our own groceries."

He frowned. "This is a rule?"

"Sure. A rule." Because I always have such excellent luck laying down rules.

"I see." He studied me for a moment, then nodded. "You do this to set a good example for Thea?"

"Partly," I said, as fatigue weighed down on me like a sack of rocks. "But mostly because you just shouldn't be stealing from people, Brady."

He inclined his head briefly. "Then it will be so."

"Mom?"

I looked at Thea.

"Is it okay for us to eat this stuff?"

I took another chocolate, balanced the shiny brass-colored blob in the palm of my hand and thought about it for a moment. "Yeah. It's okay. We didn't know how he bought it. And it's already here. It'd be worse to waste food, wouldn't it?"

Thea considered that, her genius brain working over tricky things like ethics versus greed. Then she picked up her Snapple and took a drink. "You're right."

(Like I said—Thea goes for the rules she likes.)

"But no more felonious Faery shopping," I said, giving Brady a stern look.

"This seems foolish," he said, "but it will be as you wish."

*

I woke up tingling again, and if a part of my brain knew it was Brady and I should stop him, a bigger part of my brain didn't care. Give me a break. I'd had a crappy day and a couple of long hours of feeling sorry for myself.

So when I felt those magic fingers dancing across my skin, I kept my eyes closed and enjoyed it. Yes, I may have some slut issues, but I'm planning on working on them.

Someday.

I shifted on the sheets and realized something.

I was naked.

Hmm. Now, I usually sleep in an extra-large T-shirt and panties—you know, in case of fire I wanted to be able to grab Thea and run outside. No way in hell would I want to face a truckful of firefighters stark naked.

So I had to wonder what happened to my nightie. Had Brady taken it off me? Apparently. Then how'd I sleep through *that*? More Faery magic?

His fingers slid across my body, and I told myself not to worry about it. I mean, really. Weren't there bigger things to think about at the moment?

The bed dipped, and I knew Brady was getting comfy. I should probably have said something. You know, *stopped* him. But my hoo-hah was all stirred up, and there's something to be said for an orgasmic wake-up call.

His hand slid across my belly, and the heat he put out was really amazing. Just the touch of his skin to mine sent tiny bursts of electrical energy buzzing through me, and let me tell you, I was ready for it. I'd been cheated on and dumped. I'd been humiliated.

Now, here was Brady, a really nice guy, who'd been nothing but sweet and helpful and nice to my kid. Why shouldn't I be able just to enjoy what he offered?

Why shouldn't I get a nice little Faery-driven good time?

"Beautiful," he whispered close to my ear, and I ate that up. Let's face it, none of us are beauties first thing in the morning, but hearing a gorgeous man lie about it was kind of comforting.

"Why're you here, Brady?" I whispered, arching into his touch as his fingers slid lower and lower down my body.

"To give you pleasure," he said, his voice deep and quiet, a hush in the air. "To share with you."

He really was good at the pleasure thing, and for a second or two I told myself that I should get up. Get out of that bed and remind him that I'd told him he shouldn't be doing this. Then I heard him say, "You are the Duster, strong, brave. It is my honor to touch you."

I gasped when his fingers dipped low enough to touch the good stuff. Let's face it: No way was I going to tell him to stop *now.*

One stroke. Two.

I was quivering and more than ready for this. Boy, was I ready. He must have been lying beside me for hours, stroking and petting me, to get me this churned up. I wished I'd been awake for more of it.

He bent over me.

I still didn't have my eyes open; I could just *feel* what he was doing. Then his mouth closed over one of my nipples. His lips, his tongue, even his teeth moved over that hard tip, and let me tell you, the man had a great mouth.

While he was sucking on me, his fingers dipped inside and stroked me hard, inside and out. My hips were rocking, my eyes were squeezed shut and a buildup of something incredible was mounting fast. *God.*

There was something more going on than just an orgasm, though. My whole body felt like it was shimmering, glowing. Every time he touched me that sensation got bigger.

And he was touching me *a lot*.

Before I could figure out what was going on, my hoo-hah sat up and shouted. It felt like every cell in my body was splintering and, boy, was it fun! The ripples went on for, like, *ever*, and I was happy to ride them. But finally, of course, that incredible orgasm ended.

"Whoa." I opened my eyes, looked up into his steady blue gaze and thought about surrendering to the slut within. The man was just too gorgeous for words, you know? And he wanted *me*. But that would only complicate my life even further, and was it really fair of me to sleep with a guy who was depending on me to keep him alive?

"That is just the beginning," he promised, and I believed him. The man had some serious talent.

But dawn was starting to lighten the night outside, and pretty soon Thea would be up. I couldn't let her catch Brady in bed with me.

So reluctantly I lifted his hand away from party time and said, "You've *got* to stop doing this."

Points for me.

"You didn't like it?"

"Oh, I liked it fine," I said, and noticed that he was sparkling again. Faery dust surrounded him like a silver aura. He was covered in magic. "I really like you, Brady."

He smiled at me, and I have to say the man was truly amazing-looking.

"It's just," I said, "we shouldn't be doing this."

"Another rule?" He frowned.

"Yeah, a rule."

Brady sighed and pushed himself around to lean against the headboard. "You have many rules."

"I know it must seem that way." Suddenly I felt a little too naked. I tugged the sheet out from under him and draped it over myself. "Look, I really appreciate the attention." I swept one hand through my hair, scooted up beside him and looked at him. "Especially this morning, since after yesterday I so needed it, but you don't owe me anything, Brady. You can have sanctuary with no strings. You don't have to do this . . ." I waved a hand at the bed.

"But this is pleasurable," he countered, looking more confused than ever.

"Right there with ya, sparky," I said, still enjoying the remaining buzz lighting up my insides and wishing I could go again. Boy howdy, I felt *great*. Seriously great. Like my batteries had just gotten a fresh charge. Rachel swears an orgasm is the best sedative she's ever tried. But for me it's the opposite. And this orgasm was like a lithium battery or something.

"I wish to touch you."

Hmm.

I shook my head. "Like I said, I appreciate it, but not necessary."

"But you were unhappy and now you are not."

"True."

"And it is better to be happy, yes?"

"You bet."

"So . . . ?"

Convoluted logic designed to give me orgasms. *Hmm.* He really was a dream guy.

"Look, Brady. This was fun, but I'm not looking for another guy in my life, okay?"

"Because of the demon."

I narrowed my eyes at him. "What do you know about it?"

"Only what I pulled from your mind."

"Only what you *what* from my *what*?"

"Pulled. Mind."

"You *can* read minds?" I yelped that last sentence, and why not? Instantly I tried to go back over everything I'd been thinking since I first saw him. *Right.* My thoughts were usually like a shotgun blast—you know, wide and scattered. I do know I had spent a lot of time thinking he was pretty yummy.

God. Embarrassing much?

"He should not have done that to you."

Great. Now he knew about the humiliation, too. "Yeah, I know."

"But he was a fool. I am not."

"Brady . . ."

"Fine." He bowed his head. "As you wish. I will touch you no more this morning."

Hmm.

Had he built himself a loophole there? Did I care? A problem for later.

"Look, Thea will be up soon. Gotta get her ready for school and—"

"Yes," he said, bounding off the bed with more energy than I had *ever* had. He sent me a flashing grin. "I will make the breakfast and talk to her about the cheerleading. I have many plans for her success."

"Great."

He turned to the door, and then I thought of something. "Brady?"

"Yes?" He spun around again. "You have changed your mind about the touching?"

"Yes. No. I mean . . ." Hey, *you* try to think clearly when you're faced with a sweetheart of a god who only wants to give you orgasms. "Look. No more touching." (Boy, it hurt to say that.) "What I want to know is, you said you read minds?"

"Yes."

"Have you, um, read Thea's?" (Yes, I'm a terrible human

being. But if you have a teenage daughter, you'll understand this.)

He cocked his head and looked at me. "Why?"

"Um, has she been thinking about a guy at all?"

"Ah . . ." He nodded solemnly.

I gripped the sheet up tight over my boobs and said, "It's not like I want to spy on her or anything (okay, sometimes I did); it's just that I want to know if she's thinking about this one little half-demon, because she used to have a thing for him and it got really ugly really fast, and if he's back in town I want to know about it so I can go dust the little thug before he worms his way back into Thea's life."

Can I cram a long thought into one sentence or what?

"She does not think of a demon," Brady said with a wink. "She thinks of someone called Ryan. He plays a game called ball foot."

"You mean football?"

"Yes!"

Interesting. Brady knew his way around the Internet but didn't know the word *football? Beside the point here, Cass!* A football player? I slumped and my chin hit my chest. Thea had a crush on a football player named Ryan? *Oh, man.* This was not good. See, Thea's a genius, and the jocks of the world almost never look at a girl who's smarter than they are. No wonder she wanted to try out for cheerleader.

There is just nothing harder than sitting by and watching your kid set herself up for a letdown. Even if she made the cheerleading squad, there was no guarantee this guy would ever consider her more than tutor material. (Oh, come on; football players aren't exactly known as Rhodes scholars.)

Okay, I'd talk to Thea as soon as she got home from school. Well, I'd talk, and maybe Thea would listen. Teenagers. You do what you can.

Brady left, closing my door quietly behind him, and I lay

there for a few minutes, trying to figure out what to do next. I mean, sure, shower, get dressed, go to work. But what to do *next*. Did I go find Devlin and dust him? Did I forget all about him and move on? Did I set fire to the house Logan just bought to keep him out of the neighborhood? Never mind on that last one. I was kidding. Sort of.

I slid down flat on the bed, pulled the sheet over my head and tried to make the world disappear. Didn't work. The phone on my bedside table rang, and I ripped the sheet off my head to glare at it. Maybe Faery powers were contagious, because all of a sudden I was feeling a little like now *I* could read minds. The point is, I just *knew* who was calling. On the second ring I grabbed it only because I didn't want it waking Thea up.

"Cassidy, don't hang up."

I knew it. "Devlin, don't call here ever again. In your whole long, hopefully miserable, disease-ridden, poverty-stricken life, never call here."

"I can explain."

"HAH!" I sat straight up and shook the phone receiver like it was actually Devlin's neck, before I slapped it back to my head again. "Explain? You can explain? What happened then? You were lying in bed naked and Three Boob *fell* on you? Did she accidentally *impale* herself? Poor you. It must have been a terrifying experience."

"Damn it, Cassidy, I didn't know you were coming over, and—"

"Oh! So this is MY fault!?!"

"I didn't say that; all I said was—"

I was so damn mad I couldn't just lie there for this conversation. I jumped out of bed, hooked my foot in the sheet and fell face-first onto the rug. "Ow!"

"What happened?"

I slammed the receiver against the floor a couple times just for the hell of it. Maybe I'd break his rotten stinking demon eardrums. My bruises from the day before were almost gone. Lucky me—I had new ones blooming and it wasn't even *dawn* yet! Pain ratcheted across my face, and my ears were ringing as I kicked free of the stupid sheet.

"Damn it, Cassidy, are you all right?"

"No!" I hung up as hard as I could and then stared at the phone receiver, snapped cleanly in two.

Hmm. This Duster-strength thing could get expensive.

Chapter Eight

Jasmine was all over me that morning.

And I wasn't really feeling like jumping and running in the stupid yard. The battery charge I'd gotten earlier? Long gone. Besides, I believe I've mentioned that I hate exercise of any kind. Well, exercising after a breakfast of Belgian waffles with whipped cream and sliced peaches was even worse.

"That's it," I said, dropping to the grass and sprawling, spread-eagled. It was still early enough that the dampness of the grass soaked into my T-shirt, but I so didn't care. "I don't care if minions from Hell jump over my fence to kill me; I'm not moving."

"If you are going to fight the demon queen, you must be prepared."

I pried open one eye and lifted my head to look up at my nemesis. Every gray hair was sprayed into place. Her gnarled hands were clasped at the waist of a blue paisley dress, and her orthopedic shoes were shined to such a high gloss, I could see my reflection in them. At that moment, not a good thing.

"If the queen's so damn scary, why hasn't she come after me herself already?" I closed that eye and studied the blackness behind my eyelids. "All she's done so far is offer a cash reward that's got all the dweeb demons after me."

Jasmine sighed. I didn't have to see her to know her eyes were rolling. "For now, the queen isn't worried enough about you to come after you herself. She's content to let her legion of followers try to take you out."

"Content," I mused aloud. "Wonder what that's like?"

"But sooner or later she will become impatient," Jasmine nearly shouted, clearly irritated by me. Again. "Your fight will come and you have to be ready for it."

"I'll be ready," I said, and yawned.

"You're not taking this seriously, Cassidy. It is your duty—"

"Jasmine," I said, interrupting her before she could get into another of her long-winded speeches about what a crappy Duster I was turning out to be. "I had a bad day yesterday, and this one's not looking any better."

"You shouldn't have trusted Devlin."

I lifted my head off the grass and glared at her. "EXCUSE ME?"

"Demon lovers are notoriously capricious."

"Capricious?"

"They are not known for their monogamous tendencies."

"How the hell did you find out about it, anyway?" I was shouting now, still lying flat on my back on the grass. Mad, yes, but still too pooped to get up.

Sugar hurried over to me—upset by the shouting and worried about all this exercise Mommy was doing—and dropped across my middle. Hundred-pound dog, trying to save Mommy from herself and now smashing Mommy. "God, Sugar . . ."

She whined, so I petted her and took shallow breaths.

Could this get any worse? Now Jasmine knew about how Devlin had treated me. Wasn't it enough that I knew? That Rachel and Brady and Three Boob knew? Did the whole world have to know that I got dumped?

"News travels fast in the demon community."

I sneered. "They have bulletin boards, do they?"

Jasmine sniffed, unimpressed by my lame attempt at humor. "The demon woman had to be treated for severe acid burns."

"Aw, poor booby."

What might almost have been a smile twitched at the corners of Jasmine's mouth for a heartbeat; then it was gone. "You've made an enemy there."

"She'll have to get in line," I said, and dropped my head back to the grass. Staring up at the sky, I watched as thick gray clouds scudded in from the ocean. The wind picked up and tossed the leaves of the trees into a wild dance. Sugar shivered on top of me, and I took another cautious, shallow breath. "He called me this morning. Said he could explain."

"Hmmph."

"Yeah, that's what I said." More or less.

"You have more important things to think about than—"

"Sex?"

"For example."

"It's not like I always think about sex," I argued. In fact, up until last month I hadn't thought about sex much at all. Because there hadn't been any in my life *to* think about. But then Devlin stormed into my world and woo-hoo! Now I was sort of accustomed to the orgasm-filled lifestyle, and it really pissed me off that it was all over.

Of course, I still had Brady. . . .

Stop it! I needed help. Demons Anonymous, maybe.

"No," Jasmine agreed. "Mostly you think about food."

Good point.

"You should also be wary of the Faery."

"Ha! You made a rhyme." Jeez, I was really beat. "His name is Brady, by the way. But why wary of the Faery?"

She frowned. "There is a reason the demon queen held him as a sex slave."

Yeah, and I could guess what it was. The man had some

serious skills. But probably that wasn't what Jasmine meant. "What reason?"

Jasmine scowled again, and the heavy lines on her face fell into that oh, so familiar expression as easily as Cinderella's foot slid into the glass slipper. "Sex with a Faery enhances one's own powers."

"Huh?" My eyes were bugged out. I was thinking about the too-excellent finger orgasm I'd had that morning and wondering if that counted as sex in the Faery world. I had felt pretty good afterward. Until Jasmine got hold of me and sucked every drop of energy out of my body like a Hoover on bread crumbs.

Jasmine's mouth pursed like she had another lemon slice clamped between her teeth. "Vanessa, the queen, has been using Brady for centuries to increase her strength. To maintain a stranglehold on her dominion."

My brain was sifting through all this at a pretty slow rate. Exercise? Not my friend. Makes me so tired the whole world seems to move in slow motion.

"Without the Faery, Vanessa's strength fades every day. This is why she is so frantic to get him back."

Hmm. "So the sex must be great."

When Jasmine's gray eyebrows shot straight up, I realized I'd said that out loud.

Ignoring me, she said, "Vanessa has been so busy with Brady, she hadn't noticed that a new Duster had been called."

"So when Brady escaped and came to me—"

"Yes. She was alerted to your presence. Hence the Wanted poster on the Internet. She wants to reclaim Brady and will eventually do so."

"Fabulous."

Have I mentioned lately that my life *sucks*?

"You must beware of the Faery." Jasmine's blue eyes drilled into mine like she was trying to *force* me to listen. She knows me pretty well. "Sex with him will increase your power, but the strength is fleeting and will leave you weakened for a time after that enhancement ends."

"So without Brady, Vanessa's weak now?" *Hmm*. Maybe it was time to pay her a visit, after all. The way I was feeling at the moment, a weak demon was my favorite kind.

"Weaker than she was. She is still many times stronger than the average demon."

Average demons. Who knew there *was* such a thing? Naturally, the queen had to be an overachiever or something. *Swell.* Now I had to beat off a Faery—perhaps I should rephrase that—and keep from getting stomped on by a jealous queen looking for a battery charge.

Okay, maybe I should train a little harder. Not a lot. But a little wouldn't hurt.

"Vanessa will not give up easily," Jasmine said. "And she won't be as easily defeated as Judge Jenks."

"Easily?" I echoed, remembering that fight in the beach caves with the head demon in La Sombra. "You thought that was *easy?"*

She sighed and rolled her eyes so far back in her head, all I saw was solid white. Fairly creepy. When she looked at me again she said, "The judge was strong. Vanessa is in a category all her own."

Now *I* wanted to roll my eyes. Just what I needed to hear. My spanking-new enemy was Super Demon. Was it too late to take a vacation? Someplace far away. Maybe I could take Thea to Florida to visit my grandmother. Grams had promised to visit us, but she hadn't yet. I was thinking it was because she so didn't want to get into the whole Demon Duster thing, and how she hadn't told me a thing about it for my *entire* life.

Jasmine had been *Gram's* trainer when she started out. She would have trained my mom too, I guess, if Mom hadn't died in a car accident when I was twelve. Anyway, Gram never said a word about me being a hereditary Demon Duster—suppose I couldn't really blame her. After all, I inherited more than Duster powers from the women in my family. I also got their propensity for procrastination. (Say *that* three times!)

"Now," Jasmine said, "if you're entirely rested, perhaps you would like to continue the training that will one day save your life?"

"Snippy . . ." I shoved Sugar off my chest, ignored her piti-ful whimper and pushed myself to my feet.

There was actual sweat sliding down my back—not the best feeling in the world—and my legs were trembling. I might have mentioned before that I'm not really into the whole ex-ercise thing, and my body was *not* happy about this training business. But better trained than dead, right?

"Okay, what now?" I looked at Jasmine. "Leaping tall build-ings in a single bound? Stopping a speeding bullet?" God, I hoped not. I had a feeling Duster strength wouldn't be enough to protect me from a gun. But then, so far the demons I'd come up against had pretty much seemed to be traditionalists, in the way that they preferred trying to kill me with their bare hands rather than gunning me down with an Uzi. Hey, let's hear it for tradition.

Jasmine cocked her head, stared off blindly into the distance and listened so hard I'm pretty sure I saw her ears twitch.

"Sensing a disturbance in the Force, master?" (Yes, I quote movies and TV shows. *Some* people think I spend too much time watching these things. I think it's more fun to sit and watch TV than it is to fight demons or get ordered around by a tiny demon, but then, that's just me.)

Jasmine didn't even acknowledge me. She was off in her own little world, listening for God knew what. As the seconds ticked past, I got a little creeped out.

"What? What is it?" I looked around the yard, half expect-ing a demon from Hell to appear out of nowhere. But all I saw was grass that needed mowing, dead flowers that needed to be pulled out, and a jacaranda tree that was bent over at a weird angle. It grew that way because the wind blew it over when it was a baby tree and I never bothered to straighten it. I kinda liked it. It had character.

"Listen." Jasmine's voice was a thin hush.

"To what?" I whispered back.

She turned that glare on me. "When I say *listen*, I mean, do not speak."

"FINE." I planted both hands on my hips and listened. What did I hear? My neighbor Harlan Cates humming out in his backyard—probably going over his beloved grass with a tweezer. The old goat had an unnatural love for his lawn and was roundly hated by every kid on the block. He had a collection of Frisbees, baseballs and basketballs that he'd confiscated and never returned.

I also heard the Marchetti boys across the street. Who could miss 'em? At the moment they had Metallica blasting from the speakers in the garage while they worked on their latest dog of a car. Down the street, the Sanchez's dog, Rosie, was barking like a loon, but that was her hobby. She pretty much barked all the damn time. Sugar was whining, but then, that was *her* hobby, and I could hear my own heartbeat thundering in my chest and getting louder the longer Jasmine stood there like a damn sentinel.

She looked eerie, sort of like a gray-haired statue carved by a sculptor with a twisted sense of humor. That gray hair was stuck close to her skull. Her nose was twitching as she scented the air, and her blue eyes were sharp and narrowed.

"You're creepin' me out," I whispered, and got another glare.

"There is something . . ."

"Some*thing*?" Well, that didn't sound good. *Damn it*. I hated this. How come *I* was born under the lucky Demon Duster star? Why couldn't I have been born under the incredibly-wealthy-princess star?

"Wait for it." She braced herself, every scrawny bone in her body going on full alert.

Fabulous.

The back door flew open, and I jumped out of my tennies and shrieked. (Demon Duster, always prepared.) It was Brady. I slapped one hand to my chest to hold my heart in place. He was standing there on the threshold, and he looked as weirded out as Jasmine. Probably not a good sign.

His gaze darted around the yard. Jasmine glanced at him and frowned. Brady shouted, "Cria!"

"Cria to you, too!" I shouted. "What the hell is Cria?"

"Die!" somebody else shouted, and instantly snagged my attention.

"*That* is Cria!" Brady called.

I whirled around again, my heart in my throat, and watched a demon vault the fence into my backyard. A woman this time, she was wearing black leather pants, a black leather jacket zipped up to her throat and black boots with a spiked heel.

Demon Barbie.

Her eyes were blue with a tinge of red fire. Her hair was blond with dark roots (tacky). And then she came at me, teeth gleaming in the early morning sunlight—and those teeth were pretty impressive. Her canines had to be two inches long. Instantly I flashed to Buffy and Angel, 'cause this babe looked like a vampire, and I was sure Jasmine had told me that vampires weren't real. Okay, fine. Vampirelike demon then. She still had to go.

She was running full-bore at me while these stupid thoughts were flashing through my mind. But even while I was distracting myself, my body was getting ready for the attack. I crouched down, held my arms out, fists clenched, and waited for it. She hit me like a freight train and bowled me over. I hit the ground hard and felt my teeth rattle. But I kept a grip on her leather jacket while we went down and used her own momentum to toss her over my head. (And good for me!) I got up pretty fast, but Barbie was already on her feet. Her blond hair was in a long braid that hung down over her left shoulder. She had a nice tan that really set off the whites of her fangs.

"What's the deal?" I asked, walking in a tight circle, keeping her right in front of me the whole time.

"Don't talk to it," Jasmine shouted from the sidelines. "Kill it!"

"I'm getting there!"

Nothing worse than a backseat Duster.

"She fights for the queen!" Brady shouted, but I didn't care who she was fighting for. The only thing I cared about was the fact that this bitch had hopped into my yard and was making my dog howl in terror. Hell, Thea could have been home. What if she *had* been?

It seriously pissed me off. Bad enough that I had to deal with the whole demon thing. But damned if I wanted my *kid* dragged into the mix.

I blew my hair out of my eyes and focused on the demon dominatrix fixed on me. "What's the deal with coming to my *house*?"

"I go where I will, when I will," she said, and ran the tip of her tongue across her fangs. That had to hurt.

"Yeah, well. Spread the word: No more coming to the house. You want me, get me out on the street somewhere." *Way to go, Cass. Invite the demons to attack you.*

She swiped out one long leg and caught my knee with the spiked heel of her boot.

"OW!" I hopped a little, giving in to the pain, and ignored Jasmine's *tsk* of disgust.

"The queen has sent Cria to steal me away!" Brady was shouting, but I think he was just projecting. See, the demon bitch hadn't even *looked* at him. As far as I could tell she was there to kill me, and if she got the queen's Faery, then she'd call that a bonus.

"I kill you for my own glory," Demon Girl said, letting me know I was right, even while she smiled at the thought of my ugly death. Good to love your work.

I looked around for a bottle of demon spray, but naturally there wasn't any out there. I'd been training. I wasn't really expecting to be attacked in my backyard. Okay, maybe I should have been, since this wasn't the first time it had happened.

"Look, Cria," I said, still limping a little from the heel to my knee. New bruise. "If you take off now, you get to live."

"You won't kill me, Duster. I've been alive for centuries."

"I wasn't going to say anything, but yeah, I can see that. Mostly around your eyes."

She hissed in a breath. *No* woman, demon or human, likes to think she's got wrinkles.

She leaped at me, but this time I was ready. I managed to dodge the sharp fingernails she had aimed at my eyes, felt her hot, rank breath on my cheeks and slapped my hand through her black leather–covered chest. She was still flying when she went to dust and what was left of Cria sprinkled down on top of me like a flurry of brown snow.

Ick.

I held my breath. Secondhand demon dust couldn't be healthy.

"You are a powerful Duster." Brady applauded from the threshold. "You defeated Cria, one of the queen's top warriors."

"Yeah?" *Well, yay, me.*

"You were sloppy." This from Jasmine. *Ooh. Color me surprised.* The woman was *never* satisfied.

"You know," I said, as Brady's applause petered out, "a little appreciation wouldn't be out of line."

"You should have been prepared. She should not have been able to draw you into a prolonged fight."

"That wasn't prolonged. And I won, didn't I?"

"Lucky."

Jeeezzz . . .

"Okay, you know what?" I said, already heading for the house. "Training over. I want a shower; then I've got to go to work."

"Training is not complete."

I looked at her, and Jasmine threw her hands up and hissed out an exasperated sigh. I'd pissed her off. Again. My work here was done.

I limped up the steps to the back door, and when I got close enough Brady brushed demon dust off my shoulder. He shook his head. "At least when Faeries die, we leave behind *sparkling* dust."

⤸

Logan didn't come by that night. Apparently even *he* could figure out that I wouldn't be in the mood to talk to him. By the time dinner was over and the house had quieted down, I knew it was time to talk to Thea. Now, I love my girl. We've been a team since the beginning. The two of us were like the Lone Ranger and Tonto. Mel Gibson and Danny Glover. Bert and Ernie.

So why was I worried about talking to my baby girl about guys? Hello? I'm not the best role model in town. I had Thea when I was sixteen. Although it worked out great for us, it wasn't something I wanted Thea to try out for herself.

But it wasn't just the candle-lighting, pray-like-crazy fear of teenage parenthood that threw me. It was worrying about Thea getting her heart crushed by some jock bozo who wouldn't recognize a great girl until he was probably thirty. High school boys—not really known for looking at a girl's personality.

I knocked on her door and waited. There was some rustling, and I was guessing she was sticking her journal back into her secret hiding place under the loose floorboard. What can I say? I grew up in that house, and Thea's room used to be *my* room. I knew all about the "secrets" in there.

"Come in, Mom."

When I opened the door, she was stretched out on her bed, trying to look casual. I half expected her to whistle.

"So," I said, strolling around the room (I can pretend casual too). The room had changed a lot over the years. At the moment Thea had a blue theme going on. The walls were slate blue and then she'd sponged on a lighter blue so that they looked like cloud-filled skies. There were posters on the wall that changed with her tastes, everything from Taylor Hicks (did *not* get the attraction) to Orlando Bloom (which I totally got). There was a desk, a dresser, a comfy reading chair by the window and clothes scattered all over the floor.

She's a genius.

Not neat.

"What's new?"

"I got an A on my physics test today."

That was *not* news. Thea getting a C would be news. A's? Not so much. "Great, honey. So, who's the football player?"

Her eyes went wide and then narrowed, and if I weren't so sore from the fight with Demon Barbie that morning, I would have kicked myself in the ass. *Way to go, Cass. Real casual.*

"How do you know . . ." She sighed. "Zoe."

"Don't be mad at Zoe," I said really fast. Because if Thea got mad at Zoe, Zoe would yell at her mom, and then Rachel would yell at me—a vicious cycle no one wanted to get started.

"Actually, Brady told me." *There. Throw our Faery to the wolves. He's magical. He'll be fine.*

"How did Brady know?"

"He reads minds."

"Cool," was her first reaction and then a second later she looked worried. Like mother, like daughter. She was probably trying to remember what she'd been thinking around him and if she'd revealed too much. Then I started wondering what else she might have to reveal. *Hmm. Okay, worry about that later.*

"So, who's the guy?"

Thea scowled at me, folded her long legs up Indian-style and said, "His name is Ryan."

"Does Ryan have a last name?" See? Calm. Cool. Collected. I could do this.

"Butler. Happy now?"

"Delirious. So, is he cute?"

"MOTHER."

"I'm guessing cute." I sat down on the edge of her bed and looked at her. Amazing to me that I had this gorgeous, nearly grown-up daughter. I know it's a cliché that Carmen would have loved, but it's really true: Time *does* fly.

Funny, but I could look at Thea and see her both as a girl and a woman. She was beautiful, but then, you'd expect any mom to think her kid was beautiful. There was way more to Thea than that, though. Genius, like I've said before. The kid was balancing my checkbook when she was six, and started doing my quarterly taxes when she was ten. But she's also funny, warm, kind, and so tenderhearted it makes me want to run in front of her with a shield.

I wanted to keep her safe. Make sure she was happy. Give her a life filled with roses and puppies and—

"Mom, you're acting like a big freak here."

Okay, then, hearts-and-flowers time was over. "So, who is this guy?"

"He's a football player."

"That much I know. Is he a demon?"

"MOOOOOMMMMMM . . ."

Outrage, teenage style. "Is that a yes?"

"No, it's an I-can't-believe-this."

"Let's pause to remember the last boy you had a thing for."

She got all huffy, and let me tell you, Thea can do huffy like nobody else. "Jett is ancient history."

"Gee, yeah. A month now."

"MOTHER."

"Is. Ryan. A. Demon?"

"No."

"Okay, good. One problem solved."

"There's another?" Thea asked, reaching out for Einstein, the bedraggled one-eared, one-eyed, three-limbed teddy bear she'd had since she was five. (Sugar ate one of the bear's legs when she was a puppy—our first clue that Sugar was capable of digesting the universe.) Thea wrapped her arms around Einstein, and in that moment she looked about five again. And frankly, life was a lot easier on me when she *was* five. She'd thought boys were yucky and I was great.

The good old days.

"There's the problem where if Ryan breaks your heart I have to kill him."

A smile curved Thea's mouth, and she dipped her head to hide it. "He won't."

I scooted around on the bed until I was sitting beside her, my back against her padded headboard. Then I wrapped one arm around her and dragged her up against me. She tried to hold out for a second. Hey, fifteen-year-olds have standards. But an instant later she sighed and leaned into me, putting her head on my shoulder. Her hair smelled like apples, and I loved her so much my heart hurt with it. "He'd better not."

She hugged her bear and shrugged into me. "Trust me, Mom, he doesn't know I'm alive."

"This is what the cheerleader thing is for then?" I asked. "To make him notice you?"

"Sort of."

"And if you don't make the squad?" I waited, wondering whether she was prepared for disappointment.

"Then I'll find another way."

I had to smile. Nobody stops a Burke woman once she's made up her mind. "That's my girl."

Chapter Nine

𝓛ater that night I was looking for some alone time. Not so easy to find in my house. Even when Thea wasn't speaking to me, she liked to be in the same room *telling* me she wasn't speaking to me. Otherwise there's no torture. And Sugar . . . well, I'm the key to the fridge, so she never wants me far from sight. Not that I think my dog loves me only for my Pup-Peroni, but food's a big motivator in our house.

Anyway, with Brady at the house now, I figured it would be even harder to hide. Nope. Turns out none of them wanted to hang with me. Brady, Thea and Sugar were in the backyard working on routines—yeah, I know, another demon could be right around the corner. But what was I supposed to do, lock Thea in a closet till she was thirty?

Hmm. Actually, I've considered that. But she'd find a way out. Besides, I didn't think demons were going to come back so soon. They probably wanted to give Cria a little time to blow off the yard.

So I was taking a little personal time on my front porch swing. The chains were a bit rusty, and they squeaked every time I gave myself a push off the cold cement porch with my bare toes. But sitting in the dark on the swing my father made always helped me feel better. Almost as if Dad were there giving me a hug, telling me everything was going to be okay and that I was a great person. Denial? Maybe.

But what the hell, it worked.

The street was quiet. Even the Marchetti boys had to keep it down after nine—a year ago most of the block showed up at their house and said, "Shut off the music by nine or die." Their mother agreed she'd rather have the boys alive, so no more noisy nights. Anyway, it was almost ten, and I could hear Brady and Thea chanting in the backyard. I smiled, enjoying the chill air that almost tasted like real autumn. The Sanchez's dog was howling at the moon, and the heavy plop of a basketball carried from a distance like a giant's heartbeat.

Hard to believe there was a bounty on my head when everything seemed so normal. Or that there was a demon queen who was trying to kill me to get her Faery sex slave back. Or that Devlin Cole was a lying, cheating, no good, three-boob-humping . . . Fine. So I was still a little bitter.

A car door slammed, and footsteps started up my walk. I tensed for a second, then relaxed. The footsteps didn't sound sneaky. I listened to the scrape of shoe leather on the sidewalk and wondered which man it might be. The ex? Or the newest ex? And which one did I *want* it to be?

Devlin had been great—for the whole month we'd been together. But so was Logan. And we'd had *two* months. Man, was I a walking poster child for short-term relationships or what?

Logan was a good guy. A cop. Steady. Trying to be a good father to Thea. Trying to worm his way back into my life by inches. He made me think too much and want too much, so it was easier to not think about him at all. Well, not easier, but clearly safer.

Devlin . . . *not* such a good guy, apparently. A cheating demon who could make my toes curl with a kiss. He'd been fun. He'd respected my abilities as a Duster (points for him, since I really wasn't very good at it yet). But then an image of him and Three Boob lurched into my brain, and it was all I could do not to yak up the pot roast Brady had made for dinner.

Hell, I didn't want to see *any* of the men in my life. So I kept swinging. Maybe it wasn't Devlin *or* Logan. Maybe it was a fiend from Hell come to rip my throat out.

Then I saw my mystery visitor. I sighed even as he lifted a white sack and gave it a shake.

"I brought cinnamon rolls."

I had to smile. "That's evil."

"I know."

Damn it. Logan knew me too well. He had my weaknesses (of which there are many, I'm forced to admit) down pat. The biggest one, I need hardly add, is food. Food of any kind. But he'd really hit below the belt now.

The town of La Sombra's known for two things: One, the biggest mental health institution, i.e., Nutcake Hotel, in the state, where Jell-O cups are dessert and joining Popsicle sticks with glue is considered art time; and two, the Sun and Shadow bakery. People drove up the coast from all over for their fancy cookies and cakes.

Me? I was addicted to the cinnamon rolls. Big as Frisbees and drenched in that thick white icing . . . one bite and your worries went away.

Still . . . "I don't really want to talk to you, Logan."

"Okay," he said, all Joe Friendly and Mr. Trustworthy, "we won't talk. We'll just eat."

Hmm. I could use a little worry-going-away time. "Fine. Come on up."

He did, and waited for me to scoot over on the swing before he sat down beside me. The chains really screeched now, sounding like a dying cat.

"You ought to oil this thing," he said.

"I'll put it on the list," I told him, and reached for the bag.

He held it away from me and grinned. "What'll you give me for it?"

"Be more afraid of what I'll give you if you don't hand it

over. Besides, don't toy with me, Logan. You said no talking, only eating."

"Okay. Jeez. Your sense of humor's on vacation, huh?"

I bit into my cinnamon roll, let the taste of it fill me as I chewed and then sighed as I swallowed. "God, these things should be illegal."

"They probably are. The cholesterol alone would be enough to stop a heart."

"Are you determined to ruin this moment?" I had my legs curled up under me, and I was tucked into the corner of the swing so I could keep an eye on Logan. Hey, I let my guard down around him when I was sixteen and I became a mommy!

"Sorry, sorry." He held up one hand in surrender. The other hand was filled with cinnamon roll. Finally—a man who could multitask.

"What're you doing here, Logan?"

One black eyebrow lifted. Thea could do it too. Must be genetic. I've tried, but I gave myself a headache and gave up.

"So we're allowed to talk after all?"

"About you?" I said, feeling more benevolent now with the sugar rush. "Sure. About me? Uh-uh."

"Okay." He tore a hunk of his cinnamon roll off and bit into it. "I wanted to see if you were okay. You looked like you were hurting this afternoon."

"I'm better now."

"I can see that." He leaned in closer, squinting at my face like he was trying to see the freckles I used to have. "In fact, I don't see any bruises at all on you. Good makeup."

I wasn't wearing makeup. But he wouldn't want to hear about the whole demon-and–Demon Duster thing again, so I let it go. Besides, it was nice of him to wonder if I was okay or not. "Thanks for checking on me, but I'm fine. So . . ."

"You could let me finish my cinnnamon roll before throwing me out."

I sighed again. My nice, private swing time was shattering around me. God, he smelled good. That cologne he wore was sort of spicy/musky delicious, and the wind seemed determined to keep pushing the scent at me.

"So, you gonna help me move?"

"Say what?" I blinked at him, and he grinned.

He laughed. "It was worth a shot." He looked from me to the darkened, empty house across the street. "I know you're not crazy about me moving in over there . . ."

Understatement of the century. Actually of all time. It was right up there with Noah saying, "I think it's going to rain." Or Custer muttering, "I think I saw an Indian."

"But," he went on, oblivious to my thoughts, "it's important to me. I want to be a part of Thea's life."

"I know."

"Of *your* life."

"Logan . . ."

"I'm back, Cassie." He stopped the swing, looked me square in the eye and said, "And I'm not going anywhere. We could start over, you and me. Maybe we'd be good together."

"And maybe it'd be a disaster."

His mouth quirked. "Disasters can be fun, too."

He always had been able to make me smile. I pulled a piece of cinnamon roll free, nibbled at it and said softly, "Things are different now, Logan. You don't even know me anymore."

He shifted on the swing to look deeper into my eyes. "Yeah, I do. You're still Cassie. You're still the only woman who haunts me."

Hmm. Good? Bad? "I'm not that sixteen-year-old girl you remember."

"I'm not a kid either," he said, and nipped the piece of

cinnamon roll from my fingers to feed it to me. "But we could find something together, Cassie."

Tempting. Too, too tempting. Which was pretty darn scary from my point of view.

Oh, boy. "Jeez, Logan." I took a deep breath, shook my head and said, "Why don't you concentrate on Thea for now? You want to be a dad? Great. But you just moved back. Your divorce papers from Binky are still wet—"

"Misty."

"Whatever. My point is, what's the big hurry?"

He leaned back on the swing and set it rocking again. "I feel like I've wasted a lot of years, Cassie. Years with you and Thea. I was a dick when I was a kid. When we were together. No question." He squeezed my shoulder. "But that was then. This is now, Cassie. And I don't want to waste any more time."

I felt a ping in my heart, and a rush of emotion charged through me. Logan was still the only man who could make me feel this much, this deeply. He scared the crap out of me. What if I softened up? Let myself get close to him again? And what if I screwed up not only my life, but Thea's too?

"I already have a life, Logan," I said, taking another bite of the cinnamon roll. "And you're not in it."

He winced. "Fair enough. But that could change."

I watched him watch me, and the sizzle in his eyes was pretty powerful. Logan had always had that certain something designed to drive me insane. When I was sixteen I'd fallen head over heels for him. I gave him my virginity; he gave me Thea and then life had rolled on.

Could you really back up and start over again?

And *should* you? I mean, I had just ended a fling with a demon. Did I really have the energy to try to get something going with my ex?

When did *I* become Miss Popularity?

While I was chewing and trying to unravel the secrets

of the universe, he frowned and lifted his head. "What's that chanting?"

I waved one hand. "Thea and Brady are working on her cheerleader routine."

He frowned harder. "You really think it's okay to have that guy living here? Spending time with Thea?"

So much for me trying to find a way to fit Logan into my life. He's been an official dad for, like, a month, and every time he offers his opinion, I want to shout, *I've been doing this on my own for nearly sixteen years and I've done a damn good job of it, so butt out!* Oh, yeah. We had a real shot at a future together.

But all I said was, "Yes, and let me think about this . . . Yes."

He dropped the rest of his cinnamon roll back in the bag, wiped his fingers on his jeans and looked at me. "What's going on around here, Cassie? Who is this Brady character, and why're you pissed off at Cole?"

"Brady is a Faery," I said, just because it was fun and I wanted to watch Logan's jaw do the twitch thing. I wasn't disappointed. "And why I'm mad at Devlin is none of your business."

"Okay, but just so we're clear, you're not seeing Cole anymore?"

I wished I could *stop* seeing him. But when I closed my eyes, I got the whole picture back in living color again. Probably not what Logan meant, though. "No, I'm not seeing him anymore."

"Good."

If I could have lifted an eyebrow, I would have. "Thanks for your support."

"Hey, never pretended to be anything but interested in you, Cassie." He slid one arm along the back of the swing and stroked my shoulder. Even through the fabric of my gray sweatshirt I felt the imprint of his touch. Logan's good like that.

I stopped chewing and looked at him. In the wash of moonlight he looked pretty spectacular. His black hair was a little too long, hitting the collar of the dark red flannel shirt he wore jacket-style over a black T-shirt. His jeans were worn in all the right places, and the boots he wore were scuffed. He was the anti-Devlin.

Devlin Cole was great suits and was polished perfection. Logan was down and dirty and way too touchable.

God!

I'm a *horrible* person!

I did a mental Hail Mary and got stuck only once on the second stanza. It had been a while. But I was thinking maybe I should go back to church. Light a candle or a bonfire. I needed an intervention here.

My hoo-hah got a little happy and all of a sudden I was hey-big-boy-want-to-play? This was sooooo not me.

I'm a mom.

A businessperson.

A Demon Duster.

For God's sake, could I find a little self-control? Was that really too much to ask?

I slapped one hand to his chest and held him off when he would have leaned in closer. I felt his heartbeat, and it was thudding hard and fast. Just like mine. "Look, Logan," I said. "Just because I'm not seeing Devlin doesn't mean I'm ready to see *you*."

"Would it really be so bad, Cassie?"

That was the problem. I was pretty sure getting together with Logan wouldn't be bad at all. It would probably be great.

Then my life would just get even more confusing. And who needed *that*?

My brain was racing like a mouse in a maze, going down one avenue after another, trying to find the cheese and only managing to stumble into one wall after another. Not a pretty image. I had to find a way to get us onto safer ground. Steer Logan off the subject of *us* and onto another one. So I blurted out the one thing sure to get his attention.

"Thea's in love."

"What? WHAT?" He looked panic-stricken—a good look on a man. His eyes were wide, and when he brought the swing to a sudden stop I almost tumbled off the damn thing. "Who is he? That thug's not back in town, is he? The one with all the armor stuck through his face?"

Ah. The unlamented Jett. Half-demon, Jett had had so many piercings I once watched him down a bottle of water just to see if he leaked. He didn't.

"Nope, it's not Jett. Somebody new."

"Somebody normal?" he asked, and it sort of sounded like a prayer.

"Depends on your idea of normal," I said. "He's a football player."

"Football?"

"Yep. Which explains why Thea's trying out for cheerleader."

Logan dropped the bakery bag onto the seat beside him, braced his elbows on his knees and cupped his face in his palms. Shaking his head, he kept talking, but his voice was muffled. "Football player. Jesus, Cassie. Why can't she fall for some chess geek?"

I sort of felt sorry for Logan. After all, he'd come into this whole parenting thing late. He'd hit the ground running, and he was still trying to play catch-up. And it actually felt good to be sharing the worry. Hey, if I suffer, everybody around me suffers. "She says he's cute."

"God." He lifted his head and glared at me. "Who is he?"

I ate the last of my cinnamon roll, thought about polishing off what was left of Logan's, then decided not to be greedy. "His name's Ryan Butler. He's a junior."

"He's *older* than her?"

Logan said this like I'd just told him the boy in question was thirty-five. "By a year, Logan."

"A year is a lot to a guy in high school." He sprang up off the swing and sent me into a wild arc. The chains were screaming, and I grabbed hold of the arm of the swing and set one foot on the porch to stop the swaying. "Jeez."

He wasn't paying attention to me, though; he was pulling a small memo tablet out of his jeans pocket and fishing for a pen in the pocket of his flannel shirt. "Butler, right? Ryan Butler, you said."

I watched him and shook my head. "What're you gonna do? Arrest him?"

He paused thoughtfully. "Hmm."

"Logan! He's a kid."

"He's a boy. A teenage boy. A football player," Logan added on a groan. "He's probably the king of the high school. Got girls falling all over him. Thinks he can get away with anything." He nodded to himself, as if approving of this weird-ass train of thought. "Well, he's not going to squash Thea like a bug. I'll run him."

"*Run* him?" I repeated. "You mean, like, hit-and-run? Run him down? Over? Roadkill? Come on, Logan; isn't this a little over the top?"

"What am I, crazy?" he asked. "I'm not talking about running him down in my car. I'm going to run a check on him. Look into his record."

"He has a *record* now?"

"See what he's hiding," he muttered, his eyes narrowing and a grim smile curving his mouth. "He won't be able to get away with anything around *me*."

"Overreact much?" I said, and stood up. As much as I was enjoying seeing Logan go bananas, I had to try to dial him down a little. If he went nuts, Thea would go over the edge, and she'd make *my* life a living hell. And I so didn't want that. "Logan, Thea says this guy doesn't even know she's alive. Relax."

"*Relax?* How the hell can I relax? You don't know what this means, Cassie. I know guys like him," Logan said, his voice rising. "I *was* him when I was in high school."

"Ahhh . . ." Suddenly it was all so very clear. *Well, hell.* No wonder Logan was panicking. He was imagining his little girl dating a guy just like him. Enough to make any man pause, I guess. As for me, I started thinking that maybe he was onto something.

After all, I remembered falling hard for Logan. If Thea was anything like me . . . I grabbed Logan's shirtfront and yanked him down to my eye level. "Run him."

✐

Whether I was speaking to Devlin or not, my company, Clean Sweep, still had the contract to clean his club. I couldn't exactly send Carmen in there alone to clean twelve rooms built for sin. Sure, I could have suggested she take one of her cousins, Rosario or Olympia, with her, but the truth was, I wanted to go. I wanted to see Devlin and walk right past him. I wanted to snub him so badly he bled.

Good plan, in theory.

"Damn it, Cassidy, you have to listen to me."

Hard not to when he had hold of my shoulders and was pinning me to the wall of the harem room. He'd ambushed me as soon as I entered the room.

Lots of silk scarves hung from the ceiling. Oriental rugs covered the floors, and dozens of pillows littered the surfaces of the rugs. The bed was a king-sized mattress on the floor, covered with silk sheets and yet more pillows. And just in case the sheikh you were with got a little testy, there were chains and whips on hooks by the door.

I tried not to look at the whips. I mean, come on. I like sex, but pain? *Ew.* No, thank you.

Devlin was big, and he was pissed. His eyes were locked on mine, and I swore I could see red flashing in there again. It was a weird demon thing, I guess. No matter what color their eyes appeared to be, when they were pissed the red came out. Not that I was worried about handling Devlin. Just in case, I'd squirted myself with eau de Demon Duster before coming on this job. If he got too close, the demon spray on my skin would make him sizzle like bacon in a pan!

He sniffed the air and made a face. "You sprayed yourself, didn't you?"

"You bet."

He dropped his forehead to mine. "Cassidy . . ."

His chest was pressed to mine, his long legs aligned with mine, and I have to admit he felt good. Too good, actually.

So just to make sure I didn't change my mind, I gathered up my strength, gave him a push and sent him back a few paces. (Apparently the little battery charge I kept getting from a certain Faery was really topping off my new Demon Duster powers!) With space between us I could think clearly and had no trouble at all remembering exactly why I was so furious with him.

While he glared at me, I flipped my hair out of my face and said, "Back off."

"If you'd listen to me for a damned minute—"

"What could you possibly say that you haven't said every time you phoned my house?"

"How can you know what I'm saying when you hang up on me every time I call?"

Had me there.

He shoved one hand though his thick black hair and looked like he wanted to kick something. *Join the club.*

"I didn't expect to see you that day," he started.

"Oh! Well, then, that explains everything." I pushed off the wall, stomped right past him and kicked a pillow into the far wall. It knocked a couple of scarves loose, and they fluttered to the floor. "You're right. I feel so much better now. Thank God you trapped me here in Sheikhland to clear that all up. Don't know what I was so pissed about. Wow. This is good. Thanks. Now, if you don't mind, I'll just finish cleaning and get the hell out of here."

"Damn it!" His voice thundered out around me, and I was pretty sure I heard the glass in the windows rattle. "You make me insane!"

To be fair, I get that a lot.

"What do you want from me, Devlin?"

"I want you to give me another chance."

I was speechless—for about two seconds. "HAH! Why would I do that?"

"Because we had something."

Had we? Or was it more that Devlin had been there when the Duster thing first started? That I'd been grateful to have someone who knew what I was and wanted me anyway?

I folded my arms across my chest, hitched one hip higher than the other and tapped the toe of my tennis shoe against the rug. "And how does Three Boob feel about this?"

He rolled his eyes. "She's got nothing to do with this."

"Not the way it looked to me."

He threw both hands in the air. "Fine. I fucked up. I made a mistake." He came toward me, but I narrowed my eyes, and he was smart enough to take that for a sign that he should keep his distance. He stopped and nodded. "Okay. Just listen. I'm . . . not used to monogamy. It's not the way we live. In the demon world that's a rare thing."

"News flash. I don't live in the demon world," I said, and points for me. I must have been growing as a person.

"I know." He shoved his hands into his pockets and looked about as uncomfortable as a man-demon could look. *Good.*

"Finished?" I asked.

He blew out a breath. "Would it help to keep talking?"

"Probably not."

"Okay, then, I'm finished. For now," he said.

"You give up easily, don't you?"

"What?"

"I tell you to stop so you stop?" Yes, I know I wasn't making much sense. So what? Who said a rant had to be logical? "What kind of demon are you, anyway?"

"I'm trying to be patient. . . ."

"Wow, thanks again. That's just so special." I bent down to my cleaning caddy and grabbed a pair of rubber gloves. I snapped them on. (This was a *sex club*, remember? I wasn't touching anything in that room without a layer of latex between it and my body.) Then I turned and looked at Devlin, who was still standing there looking like he was torn between leaving and strangling me. I get that a lot, too.

"Are you gonna let me get to work now?"

"Are you going to think about that second chance?"

If I could ever get the picture of him and his freakishly endowed demon slut out of my mind, then maybe. But until then it wasn't going to happen.

"I don't know."

He scowled a little and finally said, "It's all right. I understand. I can wait. You're worth the wait."

Was it wrong to think that was really nice? Yes, it was wrong. And stupid.

Yet he was looking at me, and my hormones were doing a skip and jump, and my hoo-hah was warming up, just in case I decided to forgive him. My heartbeat sped up a little, too. Jeeezz. All he'd had to do was say something sweet and endearing and I was a puddle of goo.

Yes. I'm an idiot, all right? What's your point?

The important thing here is, I didn't give in. I told my hoo-hah to go back to sleep, moved around Devlin and went for the vacuum. *Keep busy, Cass. That's the way.* "I'd better get busy."

"All right. I'll let you get to it," he said, and started for the door. He stopped on the threshold, though, and said, "One more thing. The demon queen? She's losing patience with you. Something about wanting her Faery back and you dead."

Good to be me.

Chapter Ten

The next few days were pretty busy.

Demons, demons everywhere.

The only bright spot was that Jasmine hadn't been around to torture me with training. She was off doing whatever ancient, crabby demons did in their downtime. But, hello? Demon queen after me. You'd think my trainer would be concerned enough to stick around. But whatever.

I had Devlin calling me all the damn time, and I was getting tired of hanging up on him. (Points for him on persistence, though.) Logan had stopped by once or twice, but every time he looked at Brady his head exploded, so he never stayed long.

Thea and Brady were practicing cheerleader routines every afternoon in the backyard, and I had the stupid jingle stuck in my head.

How funky is your chicken? How loose is your goose?

What does that have to do with football?

Anyway, Thea's as physical as I am, which is not saying much, so she was doing a lot of complaining. But she wasn't quitting. Apparently Ryan Butler was plenty motivating.

Me, I was just trying to keep my head down. I was busy with the denial thing, the reward for my tortured, mutilated body was up to twenty-five thousand and I still had to deal with Carmen and her cousins.

"My cousin Teresa is willing to do the Chambers house

now that the ghost is gone." Carmen's voice sounded clipped and businesslike over the phone.

"Good. Mrs. Chambers makes me nuts." Ella Chambers is about a hundred and ten, and when you're there cleaning her house she follows you with a white glove and a Q-tip. She checks every crevice, every nook, and God help you if she finds a speck of dust. Fortunately she had us in to clean only once a month. And she was so old she'd probably die soon.

You're wondering why I didn't even mention the whole ghost thing that Carmen was talking about. Well, turns out the demon spray I'm perpetually squirting people with is not only great for identifying demons and cleaning windows so well they shine like diamonds, it also cleans ghosts out of haunted houses. Apparently ghosts are no fonder of the scent of oregano than demons are. Who knew?

Amazing that I'd gone my whole life not knowing about any of this otherworld stuff. And now my whole life revolves around it.

Maybe *amazing*'s not the right word, here.

Maybe *screwed* is.

While Carmen was talking, scheduling my working life, I walked around the kitchen nibbling on a cinnamon-and-brown-sugar Pop Tart and dodging Sugar every other step. They're my dog's favorite, too.

"Olympia says she will not use the spray anymore because she is half-demon and it will give her demon cancer."

"What?" I stopped at the window overlooking the backyard and stared blindly at Brady and Thea, working on their cheerleader routine. Brady could really kick high. "Demon cancer?"

"This is what she says."

Ouch. Watching Thea kick was painful. "Is that even possible? Is there such a thing?"

"Pfft."

This was Carmen's favorite expression. I have no idea what it actually means, but she uses it all the time.

"So what do we do about Olympia?"

"I will tell her that if she does not use the spray, you will fire her."

"God, I'm a beast." I rolled my eyes, then realized Carmen couldn't see me, so what was the point? Besides, we both knew I didn't hire or fire anyone in my own business. Carmen did that. Technically she worked for me. The reality was, Carmen was in charge and occasionally let me think I was. The situation worked for both of us.

I used to have trouble keeping workers. I mean, come on, cleaning houses can be disgusting. But since Carmen started hiring her cousins, no more employee troubles. They're all too afraid of Carmen to quit. Still, maybe I should look into liability insurance against demon cancer. *Oh, God.*

"Hmm. Be fired or get demon cancer. Wonder which one she'll pick?"

"There is no demon cancer," Carmen pronounced. "Olympia only wants more money, which she cannot have. I've already told her that you will not give her a raise."

"Well," I said, nodding and wincing a little as I watched Thea try to do a split. "I am a tough boss."

"Yes. So Olympia will work or I will send her back to her mother in Mexico." Carmen huffed a little in disgust. "Trust me when I say that she will choose working for you over such a possibility."

How this tiny person got to be in charge of everybody was beyond me. But she'd survived a bad marriage and three teenage sons, and now had a ten-year-old boy who made the older ones look like saints, so I figured God had made her tough just for self-defense.

Then He sent her to me to keep life interesting.

"After all, you know that many hands make light work," Carmen intoned, and I groaned and thunked my forehead into a kitchen cabinet.

Sugar whimpered in sympathy, but I think mainly to remind me she was still there and still hungry.

I sighed a little and said, "But if Olympia's worried about the spray . . ."

"She will take one for the team," Carmen muttered.

The clichés were coming fast and furious now. But I was feeling bad for Olympia. I didn't know if there was such a thing as demon cancer. After all, the demons I squirted with the spray either got dusted by yours truly or they ran for the hills and I never saw 'em again.

If oregano gave 'em demon cancer, what would be their equivalent of chemo? Basil?

"If Olympia doesn't want to use the spray anymore, then don't make her," I said, using my firm voice that occasionally got a response from Thea. "Send her out with one of your nondemon cousins and—"

"Most of the mountains we have in life are ones we build ourselves," Carmen said, sounding sort of like a short, Mexican Buddha. Clearly my firm voice had no effect at all on her. Of course, I'd known that before I tried it. "Olympia will work and she will stop complaining."

I took another bite of my Pop Tart. "So why did you tell me about this at all?"

"Because it is your business, Cassidy. I only work for you, so I must bring you the problems."

"And the solutions."

"What does not kill Olympia will make her stronger."

"Okay, then. Thanks for calling."

"I will see you tomorrow at the clinic?" Carmen asked.

"Oh, you need me, do you?" I grinned, set the Pop Tart

down on the kitchen table and reached for the coffeepot. I poured a cup, turned around to pick up my Pop Tart and was in time to see Sugar swallow. Perfect.

"And bring more spray with you," Carmen said. "I'm running low."

"Yes, ma'am."

Sarcasm was lost on Carmen. She hung up, and I stood there for a second, debating whether I should have another Pop Tart. Talking about work made me hungry.

"MOM!"

Thea's scream lifted every hair on my body and seemed to slice right through my heart. I didn't think. Didn't bother to look out the window. I just threw the door open and started moving.

I grabbed a bottle of spray off the washing machine and hit the back door running.

Sugar ran outside with me, made it a few short steps, then skidded to a halt and slid three feet on her butt. I tripped over her hundred pounds of quivering terror, sprawled on the grass and looked over to see my watchdog cringing back and trying to hide under a dead chrysanthemum.

Let me just say, elephant behind a fire hydrant. But I totally understood why she was going for it.

Brady was standing in front of Thea like a big, brave Faery. Thea was peeking out from around him, eyes as big as Moon Pies, staring at the demon that had just jumped our fence. (*Mental note: Do something about the fence situation.* Clearly it wasn't enough to dissuade every demon in the county from jumping into my yard whenever they felt like it. Maybe razor wire? Broken glass? Electricity?)

This demon was pretty damn impressive. It was yellow, for one, with pale green spots like overgrown freckles dotting its face. It didn't have hair, but it did have white, rubbery dreadlock-looking spirals shooting back from its skull. It also had the requisite red eyes and a full set of teeth displayed through a gleaming pool of drool.

Ew.

"You," it said, nodding at Brady. "I take you or the Duster. Then I'll have the whelp."

"Hey!" I pushed off the lawn and went charging into the fray. "Nobody's taking anybody! Thea, get inside."

But she wasn't moving. I think she was just too stunned to do what I wanted her to do. I mean, she'd seen a few demons, but this one was a prize. It had to be seven feet tall, with long, scaly ape arms jutting out of its Dodger-blue T-shirt. Great. A baseball fan.

"Brady," I told him, never taking my eyes off the big guy, "get Thea inside."

"I won't leave you," he said, glaring at the demon with fire in his eyes. "It is my duty to help. To offer assistance—"

God knows how long he would have gone on in that vein if the demon hadn't interrupted him. It jabbed a bony finger toward me and said, "You harbor the Faery. All bets are off now, Duster. I will kill you and take the girl."

Just when I thought I couldn't get any madder. Jasmine had explained all of this to me a month ago, when I was having some serious doubts about Thea's safety. She had assured me that it was absolutely impossible for a demon to attack a Duster before she came into her powers. Which gave Thea, in theory, another sixteen years of relative safety.

Of course, this rule hadn't prevented the judge from kidnapping Thea and planning to sell her off into demon sex slavery. Apparently it only kept the bastards from actually *killing* her themselves. They could hire it done—as I'd discovered the judge had done to my own mother.

Now *this* guy was standing in *my* yard, threatening *my* kid? Oh, I so didn't think so.

I gave him a squirt right between the eyes and smiled when

his howl roared out around us. "Listen up, buddy. You can just keep your scaly-ass tentacles away from my daughter. I *know* the rules. You can't touch a duster until she's come into her power. That means Thea's off-limits to you."

"It is a rule!" Brady shouted.

"Mom . . ."

"Get inside, Thea." I still wasn't looking at her, but I could feel her fear pulsing in thick waves that joined with mine.

The demon hissed and swiveled its head, sort of like a lizard does, in a slow, smooth move. It looked at me and ran its tongue across its fangs in anticipation, sort of like Sugar when she first sees a bowl of popcorn.

"Once you're dead," it said, "she's mine. You can't save her, and no one is here to stop me."

See, the demons just can't seem to get this one thing: *Nobody* threatens my baby. I thought I'd made that point to the whole demon community the month before, when I'd ripped out Judge Jenks's heart. But apparently they were slow learners. I don't care what you do to me—I'll take the bumps and bruises and the occasional broken heart, but mess with my baby girl and you're gonna be a pile of lint so fast the wind won't be able to catch you.

I gave it another squirt just for the hell of it, then lunged. It was still screaming when I hit it square in the middle with my shoulder. Jasmine has tried to pound all these sophisticated moves into my head, but the only judo shit I'm ever going to know is what I picked up from watching the DVDs of *Buffy* and *Angel*.

But when it came right down to it, I just jumped in and started beating the crap out of that damn demon. I was beyond mad. I was so far over the edge I slammed everything I had into this guy and never took a breath.

The demon put up a hell of a fight, determined to get its hands on Brady and Thea. I took a shot to the side of my head that had bells clanging around inside. I bit my cheek and my mouth filled with blood, which was just so disgusting I fought even harder.

Sugar was barking like a maniac, Brady was running in a wild circle around us, trying to help and not sure when to jump in, and Thea was making like a cheerleader already.

"In the head, Mom!" she shouted. "Elbow. Right. That had to hurt. Okay, now his eyes. Fingers in the eyes!"

Even in the midst of the fighting I remember thinking, *Ew*. Where did she come up with that stuff?

The demon grabbed hold of me and lifted me high over its head, and for a moment, I thought I was going to fly. Then I grabbed hold of its dreadlocks—slick and slimy; I had to fist them around my hand to keep a grip on them—and when the demon flung me like a five-foot-seven Frisbee, it came along for the ride.

It landed hard, facedown in the dirt, and I was on it in a second. It was big and it was mean and it was determined, so I didn't have any time to waste. I sat on its butt, shoved my hand through its back and ripped its heart out, and the damn thing exploded right out from under me.

Adrenaline was still pumping inside me, but my breathing was coming along a little better. My heart rate was steadying out at about two hundred beats a minute, and if I didn't stroke out I might just live out the rest of the day.

"Duster," Brady said, giving me a bow.

"That was SO cool," Thea said, smiling despite the fear still shining in her eyes.

WOOF. Sugar had a comment too. And then she peed on the pile of dust. I thought that about said it all.

"A Terrasco demon." A very familiar, crabby voice spoke up, and I swiveled my head to watch Jasmine stroll into the back-yard. The wind was brisk, kicking at the hem of her ugly gray dress, but her steel gray hair didn't budge. Her sharp blue eyes were fixed on me, and her already grim mouth took a turn for the worse. "The queen sent one of her best killers after you."

"WHERE THE HELL HAVE YOU BEEN?" I shouted, and scrambled to my feet. "This guy was going to kill Thea."

She snorted.

"I would not have allowed that," Brady said, straightening up and squaring his shoulders.

"Faeries," Jasmine muttered.

"He was seriously huge," Thea pointed out, and walked a wide berth around the puddle of pee-stained dust.

Jasmine looked at Thea. "He could not have harmed you. There are rules and—"

"Yeah, he looked like a real law-abiding citizen," I said.

"Attacking Thea would have killed him."

"Damn straight," I said. "And it *did*."

"No," Jasmine countered, walking to Thea and dropping one bony, amazingly strong arm around her shoulders. "Whether or not your mother had succeeded at destroying the demon, he would not have been able to harm you."

Thea didn't look convinced, and, hey, neither was I. "Why not?"

"To harm a duster before her time is forbidden. The gods would have killed him."

Hmm. Gods? "Small G or big G?"

"Small," Jasmine said with one of her rare smiles. "There are otherworld gods who maintain the balance between the worlds. This demon would have been destroyed by them had he directly attacked Thea."

Yeah, well, she could believe it if she wanted. But I figured that gods, small or big Gs, were too busy to handle the day-to-day crapola. And who was to say they'd be paying attention when Thea needed help? But then, protecting Thea was *my* job, and I trusted nobody else with it. Heck, I didn't even trust Logan with it completely, and he was her father.

"Cassie?"

"Crap!" Speak of the devil.

"Out here," Thea shouted before I could scream, *Nobody's home!*

Logan came through the house, stopped on the back porch and looked at all of us. "What's going on?"

"Nothing," I said.

"A demon attacked," Brady said.

"Mom killed it," Thea told him.

"A Terrasco," Jasmine said, always a stickler for details.

"Oh, for . . ." Logan's blue eyes narrowed on me. "You've got everybody playing the demon game now?"

"Yes, Logan," I said, brushing off what was left of Dread-lock Boy from my jeans. "This is all a big conspiracy to make you crazy. Is it working? Will you go away now?"

"No and no," he said, and shook his head. "I don't know what you're really up to, Cassie, but I'm not falling for it. Thea's my kid too, and I'm not going to stop coming around just because you want to act like a loon."

"*Very* nice," I said.

"MOM IS NOT A LOON," Thea said, and I saw Logan wince at the tone and the capital letters. When Thea's crabby she can make a point pretty fast.

"I meant *loon* in a nice way," he said, backtracking right away.

Sure, I thought. Loon in the party sense, not in the Hotel-Funny-Farm kind of way. I frowned at him, but Logan forced a smile. True, he didn't want to piss off his daughter, but the whole truth was, that smile was for me, too.

"Anyway," he said, "I didn't come to get into this. I came by to see if Thea wanted to go with me to pick out some paint for my new house."

Ah, yes. The one he was moving into. Across the street from *me*. Could this day slide any farther down the drain?

"Can I?" Thea asked.

"Go ahead," I said, taking small comfort in the fact that Logan was sure to be sorry for stopping by. Thea's taste in paint colors went really wide of the beige I was sure Logan would want. It would serve him right to have a purple living room and an orange bathroom.

As for me, I wanted a beer and a bottle of aspirin. Not to mention a chance to lather, rinse and repeat to get what was left of Dreadlock Boy out of my hair.

Brady made spaghetti—always a hit at my house, although pretty much everything is, so there was no way for him to lose. But while we were eating at the kitchen table, Jasmine was talking. And talking. And talking.

About the queen, of all things. Almost enough to make me lose my appetite.

Almost.

"She's losing patience," Jasmine said.

"She's not the only one," I told her, and reached for the last slice of garlic bread. Thea beat me by an inch and shouted "Ha!" in victory. Fine, fine. Didn't need a third slice anyway. Instead I concentrated on more spaghetti and another meatball.

Sugar moved under the table and sat on my foot, reminding me that *she* was hungry too. Kibble doesn't count as food in my dog's world.

"Logan's living room is gonna be green," Thea said, taking a big bite of *my* would-be garlic bread. "It's a great green. Sort of a cross between iguana green and the color of a Nile crocodile."

"Fabulous." Lizard wall color.

"Green is a good color," Brady said solemnly. "Faeries like the colors of nature. Green, blue . . ."

Jasmine snorted and started talking right over Brady's list of nature colors. "The queen is furious, and so she's not thinking clearly. Sending the Terrasco demon is only one sign that now is the time you should make a move on her."

"Yellow, orange . . ."

"Oh," I said, also talking over Brady, mainly because I so didn't care what color Logan's house was or what colors Faeries preferred. "So the idea is for me to face down a furious, out-of-patience queen? Good call."

"If you wait much longer she'll have the time to gather her forces for an all-out attack on both you *and* the city of La Sombra."

"Red, purple . . ."

I glanced at Brady, shook my head and looked back to Jasmine. "I thought you told me I wasn't ready to face the Queen."

"Saffron, brown . . ."

Jasmine bristled, and I wasn't sure, but I thought I actually saw her hair move with the action. She shot a beady-eyed glare at Brady, then shifted that same glare to me. "You are more ready to face her now than you will be should she gather her strength."

"Wow, that makes me feel all warm and cozy," I said, and took another bite of spaghetti. *Just keep chewing, Cassidy.*

"Mom . . ."

"Ivory, red . . ."

"The queen is right now in a house by the beach. . . ."

"Figures. Only a queen could afford beachfront property." And I tried not to be bitter about that.

"Heliotrope—"

"Heliotrope?" I looked at Brady.

"Cassidy, are you listening to me?" Jasmine shouted.

My grandmother insists that when Jasmine was *her* trainer, the old demon was calm, cool and collected at all times. Never raised her voice. Never lost patience.

Apparently I can push anyone over the edge.

"Yes, I'm listening. Fight the queen. Got it."

"You cannot." Brady set his fork down and folded his arms over his pretty impressive chest. "The queen is most formidable."

"And will only get more so the longer you wait," Jasmine said.

"Mom, if you fight the queen, can I come and watch?"

"No," I said, still eating. I was secretly hoping that if I just kept my head down and kept chewing they'd all disappear. Along with this pesky little problem of a demon queen who wanted me dead.

Then I lifted my head and met three sets of eyes—four, counting Sugar.

No such luck.

Chapter Eleven

*A*n hour later, as I got ready to head out, the spaghetti wasn't sitting so well.

It takes a lot to put me off my food. Apparently the thought of bitch-slapping a demon queen was enough to do it, though. And I was busy asking myself how I'd gotten myself into this situation. An hour ago we were *talking* about me taking on the queen. Now I was getting ready to go face her.

How had *that* happened so fast?

"You cannot," Brady insisted, staring at me from his seat at the foot of my bed. "You are Sanctuary. You are the only one who can save me. You must not risk yourself with the queen."

"Hmph!" Another Jasmine snort. She was leaning against my bedroom wall, keeping a sharp eye on all of us. "Your concern for Cassidy's welfare," she said, "would be more touching were it not for the fact that you're mainly worried for your own well-being."

A polite—who knew Jasmine could be polite?—way of telling him he was trying to save his own ass. And he was. But could I blame him for that? Besides, he was still the only one trying to talk me out of this!

"You can beat her, right, Mom?" This from Thea, stretched out on my bed, clutching one of my pillows to her chest like it was Einstein the Beloved.

"Sure!" I am the Duster. Superhero. Able to punch out

demon queens and get back home for dessert. Did we have anything for dessert? *Oh, God.* For the first time in my life the thought of dessert was turning my stomach! This was not a good sign. What was I doing? I couldn't face a demon queen in a fight! She'd clean my clock. And I couldn't even find a cookie to take the edge off, because I was seriously feeling like I was about to yak (something I usually avoided at all costs).

At the moment my stomach was sort of twisting and squirming and feeling like all of those spaghetti noodles had come alive and were writhing like snakes.

"If you remember your training," Jasmine said, "you'll be fine."

Fine.

Well, there was a stellar vote of confidence. Although, coming from Jasmine, that was a pretty strong statement, right? Right. I could do this.

"Training. Okay. Training is good." I did a couple deep knee bends and winced when my right knee popped. Should've trained harder.

"Vanessa is dangerous," Brady warned, his features tight, his voice a low note of dread. "You should not attempt this, Cassidy. You should stay here. With us. I will make you a cake. A chocolate cake," he added, sounding a little like the snake in the garden must have. "With whipped cream. *Extra* whipped cream. You will be safe, and so will we all."

"The Faery is trying to dissuade you from your duty," Jasmine said tightly. "Don't listen to him."

At least he's on my side, I almost said, but let it go, because, hey, I was already looking forward to one fight. Did I really want another one?

I slapped one hand to my stomach and swallowed hard. With all this talk about Vanessa the Villain, I was really wishing I hadn't eaten so much. Maybe I should have waited to go fight her until the next day. Or next week.

Or, hey, next *year*.

But as soon as I considered it, I let it go. No point in putting it off. Jasmine was right: The bitch queen was only going to get stronger and madder, and I might as well try to face her down before she got her shit together.

"Maybe we should go with you," Thea said softly, and I turned around to look at her. Her blue eyes were filled with concern, and she was chewing on her bottom lip.

"No way." I didn't want Thea anywhere near this business. What if Jasmine was wrong about the whole "forbidden" thing? Until I could look into that theory myself, I wasn't going to take any chances. "You stay here, with Jasmine and Brady. Stay in the house. Doors locked. Got it?"

"Got it."

Wow. Cooperation. This was a big day for me.

"You should not go, Cassidy," Brady said, standing up to walk to me. He laid one hand on my shoulder in a warm, insistent kind of grip. "This is not wise."

Nope. Probably not. But then, I wasn't generally known for my wise decisions. Sugar whined from the bathroom. I knew how she felt. I wanted to lock myself in there and hide in a bubble bath.

Later, I promised myself.

"Cassidy . . ." Brady was holding my shoulders, looking down into my eyes, and I knew he was reading my mind again when he smiled and whispered so only I could hear, "I will help you with the bath if only you will stay."

Tempting.

But I had to do this. Brady's life was at stake. But it wasn't only him. Thea had been threatened only a couple hours ago. I had to stop the queen before this got even more out of hand.

"Hey!" I looked up at Brady as a wild thought popped into my brain. "I just thought of this. You're a Faery. Can you fly?

You never said, and if you can, then maybe you could sprinkle a little Faery dust on me and—"

"No," he said with a slow, sad shake of his head, and shattered my little dream. "I cannot. Male Faeries don't fly."

"Well, that sucks." I heard how disappointed I sounded but couldn't seem to help it. Flying would have been very cool and would have given me a nice way to exit the fight if it wasn't going well. Excuse me for looking for a safety valve. And yes, I was stalling. Sue me. I was in no hurry to go fight a demon queen.

"Female Faeries fly, though," Brady said solemnly. "And they never let us forget it." The look of disgust on his face led me to believe there was an interesting story about female Faeries I'd have to get out of him another time. "And Pixies, of course," he added.

"Pixies?" I asked.

"Pixies?" Thea echoed. "They're real, too?"

"Pixies are even worse than Faeries," Jasmine said, pushing away from the wall. "Nasty, troll-like little things. Completely untrustworthy."

I looked at her. "So not just a little untrustworthy."

"They are evil," Brady said, looking like he hated to agree with Jasmine about anything. "But they can fly."

"So what do male Faeries do?"

"We guard the power."

"Power?"

What power? Before I could ask, he gave me a slow smile and added, "We also do *other* things."

I headed Jasmine off at the pass. "Snorting is really unattractive."

She scowled at me. "Are you ready?"

I hooked a bottle of demon spray to my belt loop. "As I'll ever be."

I sure wished I had a female Faery handy. I could have really used one. Or an Uzi. Or a new job.

I looked from Brady to Jasmine to Thea. Every light in my house was on, and the air still smelled like spaghetti. It was cozy. Safe. And I soooo didn't want to leave. I was still new to this dusting business, and the longer I thought about facing off with the queen, the harder those spaghetti worms in my stomach did their little tangos.

"Guess I'd better go," I said, hoping someone in the room would convince me not to.

"Good," Jasmine said, and I sneered at her. She was supposed to be on *my* side. Why was she in such a big damn hurry to send me off into battle? If she lost me, she'd have to wait another sixteen years before she got to order Thea around.

"Fine," I said. "I'm going." Because I had to. Because Brady needed help. Because if I didn't kill this bitch, she might wait around for Thea to come into her power, and it was better for me to face the queen than to worry about my baby girl doing it.

I hitched my jeans up, shoved the sleeves of my gray sweatshirt back over my forearms and headed for the door. I didn't look back.

Because I knew if I did, I wouldn't leave.

&

Queens lived well.

At least, this one did.

I parked my VW on the street, in front of a mansion that looked a lot like Tara from the old movie *Gone with the Wind*: lots of columns and second-story balconies and lights glowing in practically every window.

It sat alone on a bluff overlooking the ocean, and its nearest neighbor looked to be at least half a block away. Apparently demon queens preferred privacy.

I swallowed hard, hoping the spaghetti would stay put, and told myself I could do this. Hereditary Demon Dusters were *born* to do this. *Go, Cass! Kill the queen! Yay, team!* Okay, too much time spent listening to Thea and Brady in the backyard.

When my cell phone rang I shrieked, jumped straight up, then yanked the damn phone out of my jeans pocket before the tinny version of "Every Breath You Take" could alert the queen that her doom had arrived.

I didn't even glance at the caller ID, just flipped it open and said, "What?"

"Tell me you're not at the queen's house," Devlin said.

I looked around, half expecting him to pop out from behind one of the wind-twisted cypress trees. How the hell did he know where I was? Good question, so I asked it. "How the hell did you know where I was?"

"Doesn't matter how I know. Damn it, Cassidy, I was afraid you'd do something like this," he muttered. "Go home. You're not ready to face Vanessa."

He was right, of course, but that so wasn't the point. And *Vanessa?* He was on first-name terms with the queen? Well, why not? He'd been working for Judge Jenks when I took him out. Seemed like Devlin was pretty high up in the demon food chain in La Sombra. Back when I thought we were a couple, that might have actually been comforting. The way things stood now, though, I had no idea what—if anything—it meant for me.

So when I answered him, I went for my standard. When in doubt, attack. "Excuse me? Who're you to tell me what I'm ready for?"

"I'm the guy who . . ."

Long pause.

Interesting.

I realized I was holding my breath. Did I actually *care* what he might be about to say? *Hmm.* Okay, yes, focusing issues. I was about to fight a demon queen and I was wondering what my demon ex-lover might be thinking. But, come on. So would you. "Yes?"

"The guy who cares whether you live or die," he finished.

Not what I might have hoped for usually, but nice nonetheless. Even if it was coming from the demon who had cheated on me. And *that* thought was enough to bring me back to focus. "I'm hanging up now, Devlin. I've got places to go, queens to kill."

"Damn it, Cass. Don't do it. Or at least wait for me to get there. I can help."

"Why would you help me kill your own queen?"

"She's not my queen," he said, then blew out an exasperated breath. (He did that a lot around me.) "And before you ask me, it's a long story."

Wasn't everything?

"Some other time, then." The longer I stood there, the harder it was going to be to make my feet move. I *had* to go face her down. After all, I was already there. Might as well be now. Right?

"Cassidy . . ." Devlin's voice was low, thick and warm. "Please don't go in there alone."

"Bye, Devlin." I hung up. See? I can be brave. Or stupid, depending on how you looked at it. Yes, it might have been nice to have Devlin's help. He'd helped me out with the judge, after all. But things had changed. We'd been a couple back then, and now we weren't, and maybe he was holding a little grudge for me squirting him and his demon babe with all that acid.

Now was definitely not the time to test that theory.

The phone rang again almost instantly. Mental note: Turn the damn thing off. I snapped it open. "Devlin, I don't need your help to kill the queen."

"Good to know, but I'm not Devlin, and why would you want to kill the queen? I mean, sure, she never treated Diana very well, and she has hideous taste in purses, but Cassidy— some restraint, huh?"

"Rachel." My shoulders slumped and my chin hit my chest. Who else but me would be fielding phone calls while planning an assault on a demon queen? "God. I can't talk right now, okay?"

"Yeah," she said. "Sounds like you're busy, all right. What with queen killing and everything."

"Rach." I cut her off because Rachel could talk even more than I could, and that's saying a lot.

"What's going on, Cass?"

"Um . . ." I turned my back on the queen's house, as if she could look out a window and read lips or something. Hearing Rachel's voice had made me realize there was something I had to take care of before I started this little rumble. "Look, I'll explain all the queen stuff later. But just in case . . . if I run into trouble here, you'll take care of Thea, right?"

Cut me a little slack, okay? I mean, I knew Jasmine would watch out for Thea—the next little Duster, after all. But I hadn't had time to actually realize that there was a really good chance I might not make it out of this fight alive. If I didn't, I wanted Thea to be with someone who loved her nearly as much as I did. Sure, Logan was her dad, but he was new. And yes, he'd be right there to step into Thea's life. But Rachel was as close as Thea could get to having *me* around.

Terrifying.

I really wanted to not die.

"Take care of Thea . . . Cass, what're you doing?"

"I'll tell you tomorrow." There. I had made plans to meet Rachel, so I couldn't possibly die now. If you had plans to meet someone, you had to be there. So now I was sure I'd survive this. Almost sure. "So will you?"

"Of course I'll take care of Thea, but what're you—"

"Thanks." I blinked away a sudden sting of tears, hung up,

turned the phone off and forced my feet to move. They didn't want to, and I have to say I agreed with my feet. This was *such* a bad idea. Every step that took me closer to the queen's mansion only made me realize that more completely.

She was a *queen*, for chrissakes.

I stepped up onto the manicured grass and slipped down the wide, graveled drive to the back of the house. The moon was playing peekaboo with the clouds, so light filtered down in an unsteady wash of silver. The lights in the house weren't able to reach into the dark surrounding the huge place, and I was squinting while I crept along, hoping like hell I didn't trip on a sprinkler or a car or, God help me, a demon hound from Hell.

GULP.

Great. I scared myself.

Shadows were thick and the night was quiet. On this exclusive street there were no basketballs, no howling dogs, no Van Halen pumping out of a garage. Here there was just quiet and the steady slap of the ocean against the rocks below the house.

Well, and the pounding of my own heartbeat.

Fear slid through the pit of my stomach, mixing with the spaghetti in an ugly way. My mouth was dry and the palms of my hands were damp. I wiped them off on my jeans, then slipped my demon spray out of the belt loop. Wrapping my hand around the neck of the bottle, I rested my finger on the trigger and told myself Vanessa was just another demon.

No big deal. I'd been doing this for a month now, and I almost never screamed and ran away anymore.

Who's afraid of the big, bad queen? Yes, I hummed to myself. It was too dark. Too quiet. Too scary. And I don't do scared real well. Let me tell you, the Fates or the gods or whoever had picked the wrong Burke woman for this duty. I was a weenie. And a very happy weenie. The only reason I was really here at all was that I'd been backed into a corner. There was no way out but straight ahead—or maybe digging through the wall at my back, but I couldn't think of a way to do that.

So here I was, singing to myself and trying to get the drop on a demon queen.

"Duster."

CRAP!

She came out of nowhere, sliding out of the shadows as if she were a part of them. She moved like smoke, wispy and insubstantial. She was tall, probably six feet. She was also gorgeous, damn it. I had been hoping for a troll.

Her pale gray dress hugged what looked like a great figure and fell all the way to the tops of her bare feet. Her skin was milk white, and her eyes glowed yellow as she smiled at me. (At least they weren't red.) Her long, dark brown hair lifted in the wind and swirled about her head like writhing snakes, and when her smile widened she flashed a set of teeth that looked razor-sharp.

Oh, boy.

"I've been hoping you'd come. But you certainly took your time about it," she said, and kept floating in a wide circle around me. It was really pretty eerie.

She was moving without *moving*, if you know what I mean, and it was seriously creeping me out. So I kept moving too, wanting to keep an eye on her so I could pretend to be ready when the time came.

"I've been busy," I said. "You know, dusting takes a lot of my time these days."

She frowned, and those yellow eyes narrowed. Not a good look. "You've taken many of my kind."

YIKES.

"Yeah, well . . ." *Good one, Cass!*

She paused, lifted one elegant hand to her chin and tapped a long finger against it. "You have my Faery."

"I sure do."

"I want him back."

"Why's that?" *Stall, Cass. Stall.*

"The Faery's mine, Duster. Hand him over and I'll allow you to live."

"Wow. Generous." I have to admit, even if it's only here, that just for a second I actually considered handing Brady over. You would have, too. I'm not brave or very good at this fighting thing. And if Brady went back to her, I'd get to live! Big bonus.

But I couldn't turn him over, and I knew it. In a flashing instant, thoughts of Brady spilled through my head. Him at the stove. Him in the backyard, working with Thea. Him sneaking Sugar food. Him on the couch, watching *Buffy* DVDs with Thea and me. Him in my bed in the morning, making my hormones sing the "Hallelujah" chorus.

Besides, in the next second I had to wonder just how long the queen's generosity would last. Once she had Brady back, what was to stop her from deciding to get rid of me anyway?

"I think it's very generous," the queen said. "After all, I've invested some time and money into ridding myself of you."

"So I heard. Dollars to kill the Duster?" I shook my head, swallowed hard and tried to keep talking without choking on the heart currently lodged in my throat. "Don't you think that's a little tacky? Going online to get demons to kill me?"

She shrugged and kept floating. "I use what's available."

"Afraid to do it yourself?" Even *I* couldn't believe I'd said that! What was *wrong* with me? I was practically *daring* her to kill me!

I took a step to one side, just to see if she'd keep pace with me. She did. That was when I noticed something else: That slow circle she was moving in was also *shrinking*. She was getting closer and closer to me.

Not a happy thought.

"You don't frighten me, Duster," she said, and her voice was almost lost in a sudden gust of wind. "You're a bug. A nuisance. A fly to be swatted."

I glanced around me, hardly daring to take my eyes off of her, but, let's face it, wanting to know if she had help stashed close by. I thought I saw a pair of red eyes staring at me from under a bush, but I might have been hallucinating. It was a pretty weird situation.

"You're becoming more of an irritant than I'm willing to put up with, though," she said, so reasonable. So relaxed. Just another day at the office.

Then she smiled. Were her teeth growing?

YIKES.

She wanted me out of her way. For what? Global domination? "So why do you want Brady so badly?" I asked, and I wasn't sure why I was stalling. Okay, I knew why: Terror's a real good motivator. "Brady's a great guy, but—"

"I have my reasons, and they're none of your business."

She was even closer now, and breathing was getting harder—for me, not her. She looked calm and cool. Totally relaxed. Just a couple of girls having a chat.

Me? I was hanging on by a thread. Every nerve in my body was humming. My blood was pumping thick and fast, and my heart—still in my throat—felt like it was swelling, cutting off my air.

Fabulous.

How did I get into this? My brain started racing and my feet were wishing they were, too. All I wanted to do was turn around, bolt for my car and speed back to my house. This demon was *way* out of my league. I could feel it.

Jasmine had said the queen was weaker now than she would be, and there was no way I wanted to see her at full strength. In fact, now that I was there facing her and it was way too late to run, I knew I couldn't win this.

So . . . what did that tell me?

When in doubt . . . attack.

Without warning I did one of those snappy Duster jumps—straight up. It almost felt like I was flying. Must have cleared seven feet, because when I looked down I was staring into her wide, startled yellow eyes. Her mouth dropped open, and when I dropped from the sky like a rock I planted my fist in her face and felt the punch of it sing up my arm.

Brady, bless him, had been giving me that little extra battery charge for days. If male Faeries were really in charge of guarding the power, I could only be glad he'd been sharing it with me. When I hit Vanessa she crashed to the ground as if she'd been hit by a truck. I didn't give her much time to regroup, either.

As soon as I landed I shot her dead in the eye with a stream of demon spray. It splattered across her pale skin and had her making like popcorn.

She SHRIEKED so loud I felt as if my ears were bleeding. The hair on the back of my neck lifted, and I sucked in air like it was one of Tully's margaritas.

"You're ruining everything," she shouted, furious as she wiped desperately at the demon spray still blinding her. "I *must* have my Faery! Everything depends on it, and no Duster is going to stop me!"

"Oh, yeah?" (Not the best comeback, but I was under some pressure!)

While she was screaming I slammed my hand at her chest, going for her heart.

Except nothing happened.

No hand through chest.

No heart.

No pile of dust.

All I got for my trouble was what felt like a broken hand. Reaching into her chest was like trying to penetrate a solid steel wall.

Funny that nobody'd bothered to mention that.

"OH, SHIT."

She hissed at me and leaped to her feet. Her yellow eyes were glowing, and she peeled her lips back from teeth that glinted in the moonlight. Then she hit me, and I really knew what it felt like to fly.

Chapter Twelve

𐤟

The next few minutes are still, thankfully, a blur.

All I really remember is incredible pain. The queen was seriously pissed off and didn't have any trouble letting me know about it.

She beat me, kicked me and threw me all over the yard like I was a cheap plastic purse at a garage sale. Every time I landed I felt the jolt shoot through my bones. There was pain everywhere.

I remember feeling the dampness of the grass seeping into my clothes. I remember looking up at the night sky, seeing the stars and a slice of moon peeking out from behind a cloud. I remember trying to breathe despite the agony gripping my chest. I remember looking up into the queen's flashing yellow eyes and seeing my own death written there.

And I remember thinking that it was a damn shame I was going to die and never get the chance to tell Jasmine she was full of shit. No way had I been ready for this.

Mostly, though, I remember feeling something inside me tear as Vanessa picked me up and threw me against a rock wall surrounding her yard. When I landed I knew it was over. And I wanted to tell Thea I was sorry for leaving her the way my mom had left me. And I *knew* that my mom had felt just like this. There was so much left to do. So many things I'd miss.

Thea's first prom. Thea graduating from college with a

million degrees. Thea winning a Nobel prize. Thea getting married. Thea having her own babies.

I wanted to see it all.

And now I wasn't going to see any of it.

Tears filled my eyes, my heart, my soul. Tears for the waste of it. Tears for the ending that had come too soon. And tears for the pain roiling inside me.

"You're a fool," Vanessa said as she stood over me. Her gaze caught mine, and her yellow eyes spit disgust. "And worse, you're a useless fool. You're going to die, Duster, and I'll have my Faery back anyway. You should have given him to me."

"I'm here."

She whipped around, and I groaned. I knew that voice, and God help me, I was *really* glad to hear it.

"Brady!" Queen Vanessa cooed his name, and even dying I was grossed out by it. Desire and greed laced her voice, and I hated knowing that she was going to get exactly what she wanted.

"Let her go, Vanessa," he said, and I sensed, more than saw, him moving closer to me. "Let her go and I'll stay with you willingly."

From my perspective, on the ground I watched Vanessa's beautiful features shift into a thoughtful expression. Brady was even closer now. I could look up and catch his profile. Handsome. Worried. Resigned.

"Why should I let her go?" Vanessa said, again totally reasonable. Hell, she wasn't even winded from all of her kicking my ass. "You're here now. I can have you and rid myself of the Duster."

"Because if you kill her," Brady said, "you'll get nothing from me. Ever."

"I don't like being threatened," Vanessa told him, and I was really starting to feel superfluous.

I mean, I was lying at their feet, quietly dying, and neither one of them even glanced at me. The two of them were so locked into whatever it was they had going on, I was nothing more than a lump on the lawn.

Brady smiled, and even half-dead, the woman in me responded to the magic in that smile. So I knew Vanessa would be feeling the same thing.

"My queen," he asked, making his voice as tempting as his smile, "what interests you more—killing the Duster or having me back in your bed?"

There was a long pause, where I was forced to wonder if the queen really *did* want me dead more than she wanted Brady. And then the suspense was over.

"Very well," she said, reaching across my prostrate body to cup Brady's chin in the palm of her hand. "Come with me now and the Duster lives."

He inclined his head and caught my eye as he did. I wanted to tell him not to do it. Not to sacrifice himself for me. And maybe a better human being would have. But I was so grateful to be alive, I couldn't find the words to tell him to run. To save himself.

Vanessa turned and started floating back to the house, her tall, elegant body sweeping across the lawn, through the shadows and into the puddles of lamplight streaming through the long windows. She was clearly confident that Brady wouldn't be going anywhere, and just as confident that I was no kind of a threat. Hey, she was right.

Pain washed over me with such a rich, deep pull that I felt myself drowning in the misery gripping my body. I sucked in air carefully, and when Brady went down on one knee beside me, I released that breath and managed to say, "Thank you."

His gaze met mine, and I read sympathy and worry glittering in those beautiful eyes of his. I wished I could do something to help, but at that moment it was all I could do to keep breathing.

"It will be all right, Cassidy," he said, holding his hands out over me and rubbing his palms together with a brisk, frantic movement. I watched as Faery dust shimmered in the night, rising up from his hands and then falling over me in a glittering sprinkle.

Instantly the pain receded, and I began to breathe easier. My body felt as though it were healing itself while I lay there, and the more Faery dust that drifted over me, the better I felt.

A few moments later he finished and helped me to sit up. He threw a glance at the back of the house, but Vanessa had already disappeared inside. When he looked back he forced a smile and gave an eloquent shrug. "You'll be fine now, Cassidy. I will miss you and Thea. But you must leave. Go home before she changes her mind."

"Brady," I said, reaching for his hand and holding on, "I can't just leave you here with her." I seriously owed him. Not only had he saved my life; he'd *healed* me. Without that Faery dust I had no doubt at all that I'd have been weeks healing even with Duster strength.

"You must. But first I must do this." He leaned in and covered my mouth with his.

His lips moved on mine, and a zing of something incredible shot through me. Brady's Faery fingers were good, no doubt about that, but his kisses were even better. Despite the aches and pains still lingering in my body, my hoo-hah sat up and did a completely inappropriately timed rumba. Heat erupted between my thighs, and when his tongue pushed into my mouth and tangled with mine, I wanted him more than I'd ever wanted anything.

It was no wonder at all why Vanessa was willing to go to so much trouble to get him back.

Brady pulled away suddenly, ran his thumb over my bottom lip and smiled. Then he looked into my eyes and said, "Get to safety, Cassidy. Go now."

My sizzling, needy, pain-ridden, completely turned-on body just *sat* there on the damp grass while I watched him walk to the house and step inside.

And then he was gone.

⟨⟩

"Hmmm . . ."

"THAT'S IT?" I demanded while Jasmine stared at me. "THAT'S all you've got to say?" I sounded like Thea, the way I was shouting.

The TV was on, but for the first time in remembered history we weren't watching it. A rerun of *The Gilmore Girls* was on, and usually Thea and I watched it together and laughed at the mother and daughter. I mean, please. Nobody talks like Lorelai and Rory do to each other. Besides, we were *not* happy about what the writers had done to Luke and Lorelai. Hello? Pay attention to the characters you created much?

And Thea had issues with Rory, of course, but not that night. That night I wanted answers. Poor Jasmine—Thea wasn't looking any happier with her than I was feeling.

Thea was on the couch, Jasmine was perched on the edge of a chair, Sugar had her face in the popcorn bowl and I was pacing like a crazy person. Arms flying, feet stomping, I marched around the living room, circling Jasmine just like Vanessa had circled me—with a lot less floating.

"You told me I could beat her."

"Yes."

"You were wrong."

"Yes."

As fascinating as it was to hear Jasmine admit to being wrong about anything, it didn't change anything.

"My MOTHER could have been KILLED," Thea said, then added, "and now Brady's missing and maybe dead, and what are we going to do about it?"

Jasmine looked completely uncomfortable—not something I was used to seeing, and it didn't make me feel any better. I mean, this crabby old demon was my mentor. My link to what had happened to my life. My road map to the world of killing demons. If *she* looked uncomfortable, how do you think it made *me* feel?

She took a breath, smoothed her impossibly stiff hair with one gnarled up hand and said, "It's true. You were not prepared. I take full responsibility for that."

"Boy howdy," I said, still pissed off and a little sore. The Faery dust was really spectacular stuff, evidenced by the fact that my bruises were nearly gone, but walking didn't help anything. So I took a seat next to Thea and waited.

Jasmine looked from one to the other of us. "I was told the queen was weakened."

"Well, if that's *weak* I don't want to see strong," I said.

"Clearly," Jasmine agreed.

"Is she going to kill Brady?" Thea asked, and I patted her hand. I wished there were somebody to pat mine.

"No," Jasmine said.

"No?" I asked. "And this you're sure of?"

"I am."

"Like you were sure I could beat the queen, or a better kind of sure?"

Again with the tight-lipped smile. I think I irritate Jasmine on a cosmic scale. But just then I didn't really give a shit.

"She won't kill him. She needs him."

"For what?" Then I winced. Of course. The queen needed Brady for sex. Hello? Sex slave? And was that something I wanted to talk about in front of Thea? "Never mind."

Jasmine knew what I was thinking. One of her eyes twinkled. Briefly. "While you were fighting Vanessa, I was speaking to one of my sources—"

"You have sources now?"

She gave me that smile that looked as if it were the edge of a rusty knife blade. "Yes. Unfortunately this source wasn't available before you went to meet the queen."

"Fabulous." I flopped back onto the couch.

"Yes, well . . ." Jasmine stood up, and Sugar lifted her head for a pat. Jasmine obliged. My dog isn't very persnickety about whom she gets her petting from. "The queen needs Brady to accomplish her plan to take over the human world."

I was stunned. Vanessa really *did* want global domination? "Isn't that more of a Lex Luthor kind of plan?"

"Who is—"

"Superman's nemesis."

Jasmine's eyes rolled so far back in her head, she was probably trying to see through her hair. "Of course. But if we could put aside comic-book heroes and television shows for one moment and deal with reality . . . if it's not too much trouble."

I stood up too. I'm only five-foot-five, and there aren't many people I'm taller than. Thea is one. Jasmine's another. So I took the opportunity to loom a little while I said, "You don't get to be snippy tonight, Jasmine. I almost DIED."

"Yes," she said, backing off a bit, though she didn't look happy about it. "I know. But to the point . . ."

I thought my near-death experience *was* the point, but what did I know?

"Male Faeries are . . ." She glanced at Thea, and I thought about having my girl leave the room, then remembered that she had to deal with all this stuff too. So no point in keeping secrets. Besides, knowing Thea she'd only slip back in and eavesdrop, so why pretend?

"Go on," I told Jasmine.

She met my eyes for a second, almost seemed to approve, then said, "Very well. Male Faeries bestow on their lovers a battery charge, for want of a better term."

"Huh?" Thea looked confused. Good. I was just as happy she didn't immediately get it.

"I know that much," I said. I'd felt lots of little power bursts every time I woke up to find Brady in my bed, playing a surprise concerto on my naked body.

"Yes, but there's more," Jasmine said. "A male Faery not only enhances his lover's innate strengths; he can also bestow a supercharge, giving his chosen one an incomparable amount of strength and force. Male Faeries are the guardians of Faery power. They have it within them to bestow that power on someone else."

"Oh, boy." Too much information. I dropped back down to the couch and thought about Vanessa. Weak, she'd wiped her yard with my battered body. If she got a supercharge out of Brady there'd be no stopping her. She'd mow through La Sombra like I went through cinnamon rolls, and then she'd move on to the rest of the world.

But then again, maybe not. Maybe Vanessa wasn't as upwardly mobile as I was giving her credit for. Maybe Brady wouldn't surrender that supercharge of strength to Vanessa. He'd held out for more than a hundred years already. But sooner or later I knew he'd have to crack. No one could be held as a slave forever. When the day came that Vanessa got all of Brady's power . . .

"Hmm . . ."

"Exactly," Jasmine said. "You see"—her voice took on that oh-so-loathed master-to-dummy tone—"centuries ago the female Faeries, tired of their males' egos and selfishness, cursed them."

So, I thought, females everywhere were pretty much the same. Good to know.

"Now the Faery realm is a matriarchal society. Males are used in two ways—one, to guard the magic, and two, for sex, at which apparently they are very talented. . . ."

"Is this experience talking?"

Jasmine looked appalled. "I beg your pardon?"

"So that's a no," I said. I felt Thea's curious gaze on me and forced myself not to look at her.

"If we could stay on topic . . ."

I nodded.

"There is a danger," Jasmine said in her pay-attention-because-this-is-serious voice. "If a female isn't careful during sex, the male Faery can steal a female's power for himself."

"WHAT?" I jumped up again—easier to be outraged on my feet. Funny how Brady had never mentioned *that* little nugget of information all the time he was trying to get me to have sex with him. My brain was tired, but it managed a few more wild thoughts. Brady hadn't come to me for safety; he'd come to try to steal my dusting powers so he could save his own scummy ass. I was more grateful by the moment for my supreme self-control in never having had actual sex with Brady. If I had, he might've taken my Duster strength, and I'd be one dead Duster pretty damn fast.

Rat Faery bastard.

"There's more," Jasmine said.

"What's left?" I demanded.

"The males alone decide whether to gift a lover with their power center. It is not involuntary. The power must be given freely."

"Fine," I said, waving one hand as though I could wipe away the whole damn night. "But why does Vanessa think she can get Brady to hand over his power? He's held out a long time already."

"True," Jasmine said. "But if the queen can seduce Brady into feeling loved, he might allow himself to be melded with the demon queen. Even if the transfer of power isn't complete, this would give Vanessa a temporary supercharge of powers that will allow her to conquer the human world."

"CRAP." So Jasmine was thinking what I'd been thinking

Vanessa was thinking. Well, that sounded confusing, but you know what I mean. This was serious trouble. Potentially.

"Precisely."

"Mom, we have to get him away from the queen."

Out of the mouths of babes, right? "Yeah, we do," I agreed. Not just because we soooo didn't need Vanessa getting a supercharge of whatever, but because Brady'd sacrificed himself for me.

He hadn't had to. He was free and clear. He could have disappeared. Okay, yes, he hadn't mentioned that he might be trying to steal my powers through sex, but that hadn't actually happened, either. Could I really blame him for trying to save his own ass when that was what *I* was doing every damn day? Besides, damn it, Thea and I *liked* him. A lot.

The house felt lonely without him trailing Faery dust everywhere he walked. There were no good smells coming from the kitchen. He wasn't here to make Logan nuts (always a good time). And he couldn't help Thea with cheerleading.

"We'll get him back," I promised my daughter. I just didn't know how yet. All I did know for sure was, I wasn't going to be able to free him alone. I wasn't looking for another smackdown from Demon Babe.

I needed the cavalry.

E

"You're alive."

"Barely," I said into my cell phone the next morning as I drove down PCH to Magic Nights.

"Well," Rachel said, in her hissed, I'm-really-mad-at-you-but-can't-scream-'cause-I'm-at-work voice, "you could have *told* me. I was up all night worrying about you until I saw your Bug back in your driveway."

I rolled my eyes. Vanessa wasn't the only drama queen in my life. "I was home by ten, Rach."

"It *felt* like forever," Rachel pointed out. Then she half covered the receiver with her hand, and I heard a muffled, "Yes, Mrs. Harris, the doctor knows you're here. I swear it on the head of my child." Then back to me. "I swear, these people are driving me insane."

Rachel was the receptionist in her husband's dental office, which probably wasn't the right job for her. Rach really isn't a people person.

"I was worried, damn it," she said. "Asking me to look after Thea . . ."

"You're right," I said, knowing I had to take my mea culpas on this one. I should have called her. But the night before I was too pissed off, and this morning I'd been too busy coming up with a plan to get Brady back.

I swerved around an idiot trying to parallel park on the busiest street in La Sombra, but because I had one hand on the wheel and the other on my phone, I couldn't spare a hand to flip him the bird. "It was crazed; that's all."

"What happened?"

"Demon fight."

"You won, then."

"I sooo didn't. Lost. Big-time. Brady's been captured, my whole body hurts, Thea's crying, Jasmine's all huffy and this morning when Logan picked Thea up for school, he told me he's moving in early. As in *this* weekend early."

"Brady was *captured*?" Rachel honed in on the most important point to her. "By who? When?"

"Demon queen. Last night."

"They have queens?"

"Really strong queens, too. She must eat her Wheaties, because she seriously kicked my ass." I wheeled the VW into the parking lot of Magic Nights and cut the engine.

"What're you going to do?"

"I have a plan."

"Why doesn't that make me feel better?"

"It's not doing anything for me; why should it for you?" I asked—pretty reasonably, if you ask me. "Gotta go," I told her, and snapped the phone shut before she could ask for details. Yes, I'd hear about it later, but at the moment there were bigger problems to face.

$\mathscr{E}$

"You want me to help get the Faery away from Vanessa?"

"His *name* is Brady, and yes, that about sums it up."

Devlin stood up from behind his desk and walked toward me, and God help me, every nerve in my body did that I'm-on-fire, let's-get-busy dance. Yes, apparently I'm a slut. But I've made peace with it. So should you.

His office at Magic Nights was sleek and elegant—just like him. I hadn't had any trouble getting up to see him. Serena hadn't tried to stop me. She'd just hissed at me and let me go. Apparently she was still a little pissy about the demon spray and the ass kicking.

"Why should I?"

"Well, Logan's already agreed to help." (He hadn't yet, but I was willing to use whatever bargaining chip I had.) "How would it look if you turned me down?"

His gaze narrowed and his mouth tightened. Funny, the mention of Devlin's name did the same thing to Logan.

"If I do help what do I get?"

"Me thinking you're a nice guy?"

He smiled, and the man packed some serious power in a smile, let me tell you. Six feet five inches of gorgeous demon looming over you will definitely give a woman a charge she can travel on all day. "What else?" he asked.

"Um . . ." I hadn't really thought this part through completely. Give me a break. I'd been up all night trying to come up with ways to save Brady.

He leaned in, planted his hands on the arms of my chair and lowered his face until he was so close I could see my reflection in his dark eyes. "If I help you get the Faery away from Vanessa, I want another chance with you."

Was it hot in there?

I wanted to fan myself, but he would have enjoyed it. There was definitely a sizzle in my bloodstream and a fog settling over my brain. Yes, Devlin had cheated on me, but, okay, maybe he *didn't* think about relationships in the same way humans did. To be fair, maybe we should have straightened out the whole cultural-differences thing before we started anything.

"Okay," I said, not really sure if I meant it or not, but what the hell—a little lie to get me the help I needed wasn't really that bad, was it? "You help me out and we'll talk about second chances."

"Deal."

E

"You want me to fight who for the sake of a what?" Logan leaned back in his chair at Starbucks. His black hair needed a trim, and he was wearing worn blue jeans, black boots and a dark green flannel shirt over a black T-shirt. And yes, the anti-Devlin got me just as hot as Devlin did.

These slut issues were really getting out of hand.

I glanced around and noted the usual crowd gathered. The geeks hovering over their laptops like they were impressing everyone in the room. The terminally trendy with their mocha frappé whatsis, and the housewives looking for five minutes to themselves. The baristas kept the line moving, the hiss of the espresso machine sounded like a disapproving crowd and I was going to need more than one stinking doughnut to get through this conversation with Logan.

I took a bite, let the chocolate slide around on my tongue for a second or two, then leaned in toward him and whispered, "The demon queen took Brady."

"The Faery."

"Yes."

He shook his head, grabbed his latte and took a long drink. "You're a nut."

My chin hit my chest. Naturally Logan would be the hardest of the two men in my life to convince. But then, the other man in my life was a demon. He didn't need convincing.

Logan sat up and leaned across the table. He locked his sharp blue gaze with mine and said, "If you want my help for something, just ask. You don't have to make up all this shit to get it."

"I'm not—" Then I stopped myself. What was the point, anyway? Logan wasn't going to believe me, and did it really matter? "Okay, I need your help."

"See? How hard was that?"

Irritating, I thought, counting to ten, then twenty. It wasn't helping. "Look, whatever you want to believe, I can't help Brady alone. Devlin's already agreed to help me. What do you say?"

This piece of news had exactly the reaction I'd been hoping for.

"Cole? Devlin Cole?" His features went stiff and tight. "I thought you were finished with him."

I shrugged. "I need help; he's helping. The question is, are you?"

"Hell, yes," Logan said. "You think I'm leaving you alone with that guy?"

Chapter Thirteen

By the time Carmen and I finished cleaning our houses for the day, I'd about had it. Starting the day off talking to Devlin and Logan had just put the wrong kind of spin on an already crappy day.

Now I was tired of men, cleaning, Faeries and demon queens. I didn't want to train, didn't want to squirt potential demons, and I sure as hell didn't want to rip out any hearts.

What I wanted was a little normalcy. Something simple. Fun. As if reading my mind, my VW Bug headed straight for the mall. While my trusty car took off, practically on autopilot, I made a quick call on my cell phone and then sat back to enjoy the ride.

La Sombra's not a big town, but we've got the necessities. A few Starbucks, Taco Bell, In-N-Out Burger and a mall with a Nordstrom. With these slices of civilization, you could live and be happy.

I parked closest to Nordie's, because that's where I do my purse shopping and my purse daydreaming. I wanted to wander through the narrow aisles and inhale the scent of fine leather. I wanted to stroke silver clasps and examine suede linings. I wanted to choose which handbag would be my next goal. I wanted to slip straps over my shoulder and admire the hang of the bag in the mirror. I wanted to relax.

That's not too much to ask, is it?

Of course, walking into Nordie's wearing frayed jeans and a

T-shirt that had CLEAN SWEEP emblazoned across the boobs was not the way to snag a personal shopper. But who needed help? I had my black Fossil bag hung on my shoulder and an atomizer of demon spray hooked to my belt loop as if it were Mace.

Hey, I said I didn't *want* to kill any demons. Didn't say I wouldn't if pushed.

I figured that life kept getting more complicated, so to combat all of that, I was reclaiming the life I'd had up until a month ago. Back then I didn't know a thing about demons. I lived in blissful ignorance. There wasn't a lot of bliss to be found here lately.

I passed the makeup counter and tried not to look into the mirrors as I went. Cleaning houses doesn't require me to do the glam thing. I was lucky most days to swipe some mascara on and hit my cheeks with a little blush if I looked especially pale. And I hadn't bothered to clean up a little more for Logan's and Devlin's sakes. I mean, I wasn't looking to *seduce* them into helping me.

Then I caught a glimpse of myself in a hand mirror on the nearest counter and figured it was a good thing seduction hadn't been on the morning's menu, after all. I *still* hadn't gotten to the highlight portion of my hair color.

So, I was going to put everything out of my mind. At the mall this happens easily. The scents from the food court alone are enough to smooth all my rough edges.

And I had plenty of rough edges right about then.

"I got here as fast as I could."

I looked over and smiled when Rachel hustled up.

"I knew I'd find you in purses," she said. "Anything interesting?"

"Plenty," I said wistfully, staring at a Dooney & Bourke clutch. "But my purse account's empty after my Marc Jacobs."

She nodded. "But it was worth it."

"Yeah." If, I thought, I could get the demon-caused scrape

rubbed out of the leather. Whoops. The tension was back. Clearly purse drooling was over for the day. What I needed was some fries and some sugar.

Not necessarily in that order.

"Anything new on Brady?" she asked, opening up a Fossil wallet to check out the compartments inside.

"Not yet, but I've got a plan."

She put the wallet back down and watched me warily. "Is this a better plan than asking me to raise Thea?"

"Here's hopin'."

"Glad to hear it." She leaned on the glass counter housing the DB purse collection and looked at me. "So, have you told Logan this plan?"

"Actually," I said, remembering our little meeting at Starbucks that morning, "yeah. I have."

"Points for you. Did he believe the demon thing this time?"

"Nope."

"But he's helping anyway?"

"Yeah, but mostly because he knew Devlin was going to help me."

Her eyes bugged out. "You went to see Devlin and he's not a pile of dust?"

"He lives to annoy me another day."

"Impressive restraint. Now you've got *both* of them helping you save the Faery you're sleeping with?"

"I'm not sleeping with Brady!"

She lifted both hands. "Not yet anyway."

"Maybe not ever." Sad, but true. I felt a lot of things for Brady: tenderness, affection and sure, irritation. Yes, he'd tried to sucker me into handing over my powers during sex, but who could blame him for trying to stay alive? He'd done nothing to hurt me. He'd helped my kid and saved my life. How could I not care about him?

But sleeping with him? Did I really need to make my life even more complicated?

"You know," Rachel said, straightening up, "your life is way better than most fiction."

And less believable. Sad, but true. "You hungry?"

"Am I breathing?" Rachel said, and fell into step beside me.

We left Nordie's, walked out into the mall and swerved in and out of the strolling shoppers. I don't care if you want to take your time in the mall, but do you have to walk at a snail's pace with your entire family and stop dead in the middle of the aisle? Hello? Share, people.

There were kiosks of diet aids, silver jewelry and the decorate-your-own-coffee-mug spot. There were photo booths, cell phone booths and the big black massage chairs. (Put in a dollar and have a chair poke and prod at you like it's done to every other person in the county. Can you spell "cooties"?)

But all I noticed were the Halloween decorations.

"DAMN IT."

"What?" Rachel skidded to a stop, lifted both hands as though she were a B-movie karate expert, and looked around wildly.

"What're you doing?" I asked.

"Getting ready for the attack." Then she noticed I wasn't. She let her hands fall, glared at me and asked, "What the hell was the yelling about?"

"Halloween. It's two weeks away, and I haven't done anything about it yet."

Rachel slumped, rolled her eyes and said, "Oh, for God's sake. Did you have to give me a heart attack? And aren't there enough demons in your life at the moment?"

I knew she didn't really mean that. Rachel loves Halloween as much as I do and I'm crazy about Halloween. Christmas is nice, sure. Who doesn't like presents? But come on. An entire holiday devoted to *candy*? This is the kind of celebration I can really get behind.

Usually, in a world where Thea and I are not being visited by Faeries and demons and other miserable members of the otherworld, we have the house decorated for Halloween by the first weekend in October. Every year we add a few more goodies, like cutout witches on the front door, the hanging guy from the tree, fake cobwebs dotted with plastic spiders (the only kind of spider we approve of, by the way).

On the actual night we dress up, hand out candy to the kids, and buy way too much so we can eat the rest of it ourselves. I know people who only buy the kind of candy they *hate* so they won't be tempted to eat their own stash. What's the point of *that*? If I'm going to buy candy, it had better be Hershey's. Or Milky Ways. Or Three Musketeers. Or Baby Ruths.

God, I love Baby Ruths. And those little snack-sized ones? Hell, there were hardly any calories in them, they were so small. It was like you weren't really eating them at all.

"You're thinking about Baby Ruths, aren't you?"

I looked at her. Best friends since we were kids. Nobody knew me better than Rachel. "Yeah."

"Do you really think you've got time for the Halloween thing this year, Cass?" she asked as we started walking again. "I mean, what with queens out to kill you and kidnapped Faeries and all?"

I glanced in the window of a costume shop as we passed and I saw the mannequin wearing a Wonder Woman costume. *Hmmm.*

Rachel saw it too, and laughed. "Until they make a Sugar Woman costume, you should just go as you are."

Then she grabbed my arm and tugged until I was walking again. *Fine, fine.* But on the way home I was stopping at the market to get some candy. This weekend, come Hell or high water, (which in my life meant *actual* Hell), Halloween was coming to the Burke house.

A woman pushing a stroller and dragging a screaming toddler by the hand briefly got my sympathies, but the kid trying to force flyers on us for a free makeover at Merle Norman got a snarl. Was he saying we *needed* makeovers? True or not, how rude was that?

Then I caught the scent of garlic, pepperoni and cinnamon and concentrated on following my nose to nirvana. Rachel, though, could find food *and* talk. Multitasking.

The hallmark of a woman.

"Thank God you called and rescued me from another day of dental misery. Simon was working on a Pacheko demon when I left," she said, a twinge of disgust in her voice.

I winced, stopped, looked around, then hissed, "Maybe you could say 'demon' a little louder?"

"What?" Rachel asked, her voice rising. "You think anyone's listening to us? Watch." She looked around at the wandering shoppers, put both hands on her hips and called out, "Beware, people! There are demons in La Sombra."

Most people kept walking. A fat guy with a bald, sweating head jolted like he'd been shot and scuttled off down the escalator. I was guessing, *Demon*. Then an old woman handed Rachel a dollar bill, said, "Get some help, dear," and kept walking.

Rachel shrugged, tucked the money into her purse and laughed. "See? Nobody cares."

The little fat guy had cared, I thought, but didn't bother saying. After all, she was right about everyone else. No one was stampeding the exits or tying to call a cab from Nutcake Hotel to come pick Rachel up and give her a private suite. They were just going on about their lives as if demons didn't matter.

Lucky bastards.

"Fine. You win. It just makes me a little nervous talking about it, that's all."

"You'd have been more nervous if you'd seen the Pacheko demon," Rachel said, walking again now that she'd made her point. "They've only got four teeth in their pointy heads, but they've each got to be three inches long, at least. He couldn't even close his mouth over them. Which explains the drool."

She shuddered, hitched her bag higher on her shoulder and followed me to the front of the line at Dairy Queen.

Hmm.

In hindsight, maybe I should have steered clear of anything with *queen* in the title, but I needed a sundae. Then some fries. Maybe a slice of pizza. Cut me some slack. Brady hadn't been around to cook, and Thea and I were making do with cereal, bagged salad and the last of my Pop Tarts.

Pitiful was what it was.

And my life was too iffy to risk leaving dessert till last.

"Can I help you?" A woman with blond hair teased into a lacquered tower, bottle green eyes and bright red lips looked at me from behind the counter.

"We need sugar, honey," Rachel said for me. "Ice cream smothered in hot fudge. Don't forget the whipped cream." She paused thoughtfully. "Actually, make that *extra* whipped cream. It's been a tough day."

"Right." The blonde kept one eye on me while she went about filling two cups with the soft swirl ice cream, then spooning hot fudge over it.

She was creeping me out a little with the steady staring, but I was willing to let it go. I didn't even care at the moment if she was a demon. As long as she handed over the hot fudge, live and let live.

I was having a Zen moment.

"No nuts," I warned her. I don't like polluting my ice cream with salt. Salt had its place, and it wasn't in my sundaes. Nuts in a Baby Ruth? Completely different situation.

The blonde nodded, slid the finished sundaes across the counter, and when I reached for mine, she locked her long fingers around my wrist and squeezed till I wanted to yelp. "Duster."

Crap.

So much for Zen.

"Can't I get away from this for a minute?" I demanded, trying to wriggle free of her grip. *Damn*. She had fingers like steel bands or something. "Can't I have ice cream in peace?"

Rachel jumped in and started hitting the blond bitch's hand with her purse, trying to spring me. The blonde didn't even glance at her, just picked up one of the sundaes and smashed it into Rachel's face.

Rachel was sputtering and wiping thick hot fudge off her face, and I was getting madder by the moment.

"Is there, like, a rule or something where you guys have to jump out at me from everywhere?" I asked, really pissed because my hot fudge was cooling, and the ice cream was going to be melted before I could get to it. And I really needed that ice cream. Not to mention Rachel was wearing her sundae. "Because you know, if there is a rule, I want it changed."

Rachel gave up with the wiping of chocolate and ice cream and swung her purse in a wide arc, aiming for the tower of bleached hair. But the blonde ducked, used her free hand to give Rachel a shove that sent her staggering back and managed to tighten her grip on my wrist until I thought she was going to twist my hand off.

"*What* is wrong with the world?" I asked nobody in particular. "I can't go to the *mall* anymore? Is no place sacred?"

"That's it. You stupid demon bitch, if I had you at the office I'd use one of Simon's drills on you!" Rachel was back and grabbed me from behind, her high heels sliding on the marble floor and slipping on the ice cream. I appreciated the effort, but this wasn't going to work.

"The queen's going to pay me well for this," the blonde said, and she ran her tongue across her chapped lips and sort of reminded me of Sugar when she was anticipating a snack. Which just grossed me out.

Enough was enough. She'd pushed my friend, shoved ice cream in her face, ruined my appetite and was cutting off the circulation in my arm.

I drew my free hand back, bunched it into a fist and slammed it into the blonde's face. I felt her nose crunch and watched a shower of green blood spray across the counter. What was left of my sundae looked almost festive.

If disgusting.

"Oh, gross," Rachel said, letting go of me to skip back out of range of the green flow.

"You ruined my ice cream, you bitch," I said, too mad at the moment to think about who might be watching. Besides, Rachel was right. Who noticed?

The blonde's fingernails were biting into my skin, and her grip was really starting to annoy me. She was shrieking, which I couldn't blame her for; I'd have been shrieking too if somebody just broke my nose. But she seemed determined to hold on to me, so what was I supposed to do?

I planted my feet at the bottom of the counter for balance, gave a hard tug, and my Duster strength sent the blond demon flying across the counter and smacking into me like a bag of cement.

We both careened back with lots of momentum, knocking Rachel over. On her way down to the floor Rachel yelped and slammed into the ATM machine. The poor old outdated thing toppled with a crash, and a couple of teenagers ran over, eagerly stepping across Rachel's prone body to get to the ATM, thinking maybe they'd hit the jackpot.

The demon was all over me, snarling and spitting, and when I looked up into her narrowed (now red) eyes, all I could think was, How did this *happen* to me? Why the hell was I the damn Duster?

Blondie grabbed a handful of my hair and yanked, and that really pissed me off. A demon doing the girlie-fight thing? I bucked her off me, planted my foot in her flat belly and lifted her back and over my head. This was finally enough to break her grip on my wrist (without actually breaking my bone, and yay for me). She hit the floor hard and slid across the shining marble like she was a ball in one of those skeet machines at a game arcade.

She slammed into the wall of Macy's, smacking her head against the faux stone. It had to ring her bell, because the impact had knocked her tower of ugly-ass hair to one side, and now she looked like she had the Leaning Tower of Pisa on her head. She was still trying to focus her spinning eyes when I went up to her.

"You should've just given me the damn ice cream," I said, and reached into her chest.

Her eyes went wide, and she had just enough time to say, "Oh, shit."

A second later I had her heart in my hand, and a moment after that she was the janitor's problem.

I just sat there for a minute, too tired to complain. So you know how tired I really was.

Rachel staggered up to me, using a napkin to wipe the rest of the mess off her face. She grabbed my arm and pulled me to my feet, then looked down at the pile of dust, gave it a kick to scatter it and said, "You know, maybe ice cream isn't the best thing right now. We should get a burger instead."

"Good call."

Then we leaned into each other and walked like drunks to McDonald's, at the back of the food court.

Nobody paid any attention at all.

La Sombra.

Home of the selectively blind.

⸙

I needed music. *Terminator* music. Or maybe the *Rocky* theme. Something to get me pumped without worrying about the pesky details of death and dismemberment.

Unfortunately, all I had was a houseful of demons.

Yep. You heard me. *Demons.*

Devlin had called in some favors. Now I was hip deep in demons loyal to Devlin. He'd made them promise not to try to kill me and got them to fight on our side during the Assault on the Queen.

This little maneuver had taken on capital letters in my mind. Who could blame me? I had demons helping me fight demons and an ex-boyfriend looking at all of them like Halloween had come early.

Thea was sitting on the couch with a one-hundred-pound chicken/dog in her lap. Sugar's whimpering was almost enough to carry over the sounds of shuffling demon feet and the whisper of demon murmurs. Jasmine was wandering through the crowd giving everybody looks designed to turn their souls to salt.

And let me say . . . demons? Not the prettiest branch on the evolutionary tree.

Logan pulled me aside, got me up against a wall and leaned in close. "Who did you say these people are?"

I glanced to one side and caught a glimpse of a two-nosed guy with a single horn in the middle of his forehead. *Yeesh.* Then I looked back at Logan. "They're friends of Devlin's. He got them to help us get Brady back."

"Friends." Logan swiveled his head around to look over the bizarre collection of demons in my living room. "Figures he'd have freakish friends wearing masks. I keep telling you there's something off about that guy."

"I know. He's a demon."

Logan's eyes did the roll-back-into-his-head thing. "Let it go already."

I was on edge anyway. I hadn't had my ice cream, and my hamburger, fries and chocolate shake were nothing but a fond memory. So I grabbed Logan's black sweater with both hands, curled my fists into the cashmere and said, "Take a look around, Logan. These guys didn't show up in costume for a fight. They're demons. Actual demons."

His mouth worked as if he wanted to say something but he was forbearing (a word? who knows? and who cares?), since he knew it would only piss me off. Good call.

"I'm just saying," he finally said through gritted teeth, "I'm keeping an eye on Devlin Cole."

"You do that." I let go of his sweater and smoothed down the lumps my fingers had made in the fabric. Really nice fabric, cashmere. "While you're doing that, though, don't forget you're here to help me."

"I know why I'm here," Logan said, and leaned in closer. Now I could feel his chest against my nipples, and my heart started slamming against my ribs.

"I'm watching out for you, Cassie," Logan said, dipping his head until his mouth was so close I could have licked it. "I don't trust Cole, and I'm going to make sure he doesn't drag you into anything stupid."

Ha! I was the one dragging the two of them into something stupid. But apparently Logan still had his illusions about me. Like I was still the naive sixteen-year-old girl he'd gotten pregnant one fine summer. Which was exactly why I couldn't give in to whatever I was feeling for him. He didn't see the real me. He didn't get what my life was like now.

"As for the rest of these guys . . ." Logan shook his head. "I didn't know there were so many freaks in La Sombra. It's like an early Halloween party."

Yeah, only with real demons. Okay, fine. Logan likes living in the land of denial. Not much I can do about that. I was just grateful he was here to help.

Devlin came up beside me, completely ignored Logan and said, "You ready?"

No.

Absolutely not.

Does terrified count?

"Sure," I said, and my voice cracked only twice on that one-syllable word. "Let's do it."

Devlin grinned like he knew I was faking the whole Dirty Harry attitude and approved.

Logan dropped one arm around my shoulders, pulled me in close and said, "Stay where I can see you, Cole."

"Detective," Devlin said with a barely perceptible nod in Logan's direction, "I didn't realize you were in charge of this little operation. Not exactly police-sanctioned, is it?"

Hell, no, it wasn't.

"I'm not here as a cop," Logan said, giving me a squeeze just to prove a point to Devlin. "I'm here to watch out for Cassie."

"Funny," Devlin said, not looking as though he found any of this amusing, "that's exactly why I'm here."

The testosterone was rising to a dangerous level. The air was practically bristling. Just what I needed before a big fight— a big fight.

"Logan, get a grip," I said. "Devlin, get your demons."

I squirmed out of Logan's grasp, even though a part of me really appreciated that big, strong arm around me. Then I walked out in front of both of the men in my life to lead the way to the Faery in my life.

Chapter Fourteen

Things started happening pretty fast after that. And you know me—I'm all for top speed. But there was a part of me that wondered if we weren't rushing into trouble. Which, of course, we were.

I felt the stares of dozens of demon eyes boring into my back as we walked to the cars and knew that some, if not most of Devlin's little handpicked army would like nothing better than to kill me and forget this whole thing. Apparently, though, they were more scared of going against Devlin than they were of facing the queen.

Worked for me.

Logan drove his SUV. I was in the front passenger seat, and Devlin was in the back, with Jasmine right beside him. The other demons were behind us in a parade of cars that I tried not to pay attention to. I was twisting my hands in my lap and trying to ignore the flutter of dragon wings in my stomach. My mouth was dry, my palms were damp and I was suddenly wishing I were anywhere but there.

"Nothing to be nervous about," Logan said, and I heard Jasmine snort from the backseat. One day she was going to blow her nose right off her face.

"Right," I said.

The headlights of passing cars flickered across his features, and I took a second to admire the view. Even when he irritated me—which, yes, was often—Logan could still make me think of hot summer nights and long, slow kisses. (I already explained how I have inappropriately timed fantasies.)

He glanced at me. "I'll talk to this chick, get her to let Brady go."

Now Devlin snorted.

"Logan . . ."

He threw a dirty look into the rearview mirror and said, "If Brady's there against his will, it's a police matter. I'll explain it and we'll go home."

"You make a mistake if you underestimate the queen," Jasmine said, her voice soft, but heavy with dire portents. (She was excellent at that.)

Logan steered the car along PCH until he came to the right drive, and I told him to park on the highway. No point in letting ol' Vanessa get a heads-up that we were coming.

Let's not forget my ass had been kicked by this queen already, and I was in no way ready for *that* to happen again. Although I have to say that I really wanted another shot at the bitch. Yes, yes, Cassidy Burke, allergic to exercise of all kinds and known to need a nap after just watching someone *else* being athletic, was ready for a smack-down.

Logan parked the car, turned the engine off, then shifted in his seat to look at me. "So what's your plan?"

I don't really like being in charge, but it was up to me. I unhooked my seat belt, squared my shoulders and gave myself a mental pep talk. I could do this. I had Duster strength. I had a bunch of demons with me. And Devlin, Logan and Jasmine. How hard could it be? I wasn't alone this time, and Brady was counting on me. Go, team! Kill the queen!

"You okay?" Logan asked, grabbing my shoulder to give me a shake. "You sort of look like you're having a conversation with invisible people."

"I was talking to myself."

"Do any good?"

"Not really." I swiveled around and looked into the back-seat, and then beyond, through the window at the demons piling out of their cars like clowns in the circus. *Ooh*. Not a good analogy. Never liked clowns. "Okay, half of us in the front, half of us in the back. We find Brady and we get the hell out."

Devlin reached out to touch my shoulder briefly, and I could feel Logan bristling beside me. "Good. Don't stick around trying to take Vanessa on, Cass. Complete the mission and leave."

The mission. Aren't we just covert operatives?

"I will go in the front with Logan," Jasmine said, and opened her car door. "It's better if you stay with Devlin, in case his 'supporters' forget that *you* are not the target."

Hmm. Good point.

"The queen," Jasmine said, "is probably holding Brady in her bedroom. My sources say it's the corner room on the second floor."

"Right." I got out too, and the cold ocean wind pushed at me, like somebody somewhere was trying to tell me to get back into the car and forget this whole thing. While I appreciated the sentiment, there was no way out. We had to do this. Now.

Devlin looked down at me, and in the pale wash of moonlight his familiar features looked hard and sharp. "My men won't turn on you," he said.

"I'll hold you to that," Logan told him as he came around the front of the car to stand right behind me.

"I wasn't talking to you," Devlin said.

"Okay, enough!" I slapped one hand on each man's chest and pushed them back a little. "We're on the clock here, okay? A little less with the growling and snarling and more with the queen kicking—what do you say?"

The men were still doing the big-dog glare. Each of them

willing to go for the throat of the other. Oh, this should work well.

"Another time then," Devlin said.

"Anytime," Logan told him.

Aaarrrggghhh . . .

All around us demons were gathering. My Spidey sense was tingling like you wouldn't believe. This was just wrong in so many ways. Trusting my hereditary enemies to watch my back? Oh, yeah. Good plan. I hadn't seen so many demons in one place in, well . . . ever.

Not something I'd really like to see again, either.

I didn't have a clue how Logan was explaining all of this to himself. I mean, you could only carry the Halloween thing so far. These guys defied description, and there wasn't a costume maker alive who could come up with these looks. Not even the monster makers on *Buffy* came close.

There were red demons, green demons, horned and winged demons. There were scaly demons and some dripping with some kind of icky fluid that made me want to take a bath just from standing this close to them. There were demons with cloven hooves, and one with a tail like you'd expect to see on the devil.

Hmm.

I worried about that for a second, then let it go. Hey, if it really was the devil, then the queen would have her hands full. And if it wasn't . . . whatever.

While the United Brotherhood of Demons were all meandering around, I looked at Logan and said, "Just be careful."

He pulled me in tight and laid a hard, brief kiss on my mouth that made my toes curl. My head was spinning, and other parts of me were doing a wahoo dance. When he finally let me go he said, "You too."

Not to be outdone, Devlin spun me around before I even had time to recover, bent me back over his arm and kissed me like he was dying of thirst and I was a cold jug of Kool-Aid. When he set me upright again my head was spinning even faster, and I was pretty sure I heard Jasmine mutter, "Oh, for chrissakes, somebody dust me."

I snapped the old crab a look that said, *Don't tempt me.* She lifted one eyebrow and made her point.

Right, I thought. *Priorities. Demon fight.*

Bitch queen of the universe.

Brady in danger.

"Okay," I said, tamping down the sparks in my body, "let's just do this and get it over with."

Then I forgot about everything else but the mission, because let's face it—if I didn't have my mind on what was about to happen, I wouldn't survive long enough to experience any more hoo-hah parties.

The demons were quiet; I'll give 'em that. They melted into the shadows as we moved up the long drive toward the house. The night was quiet too. Foreboding? Oh, yeah. All I heard beyond the slamming of my own heart was the relentless pounding of the ocean waves on the rocks at the bottom of the cliff.

As we slipped through the darkness, though, I looked up and realized something. Hello? *Four* corners on the damn house. Why hadn't Jasmine been just a touch more specific? *Crap.* This meant that we were going to waste some extra time searching the upper floors for the room where Brady was probably stashed. Where the hell else would the queen keep her sex slave?

Devlin was right beside me, and I glanced to my left to watch Logan, Jasmine and a handful of demons break off from the main group and slink up to the front door.

There hadn't been any outcries. So, good—Vanessa didn't have lookouts or security posted. But then, who needed security when you could mow down any intruders by your damn self?

The outside of the house was dark. No cheery little lantern lights lining the wide walk to the front porch. No motion-sensor lights on the driveway. In fact, the place looked pretty much exactly the way it had the night before, when the queen had used my battered body to rake up her leaves.

The scent of sulfur rose up around me, and I gagged. Demons? Not exactly smelling pine fresh.

I tightened my grip on the demon spray bottle in my left hand and bent over double to hurry past the windows overlooking the drive. We came around the edge of the house and I looked ahead at the wooden deck spilling out from the back of the mansion.

A few details I'd missed the other night. Pretty lawn furniture gathered in conversation spots, lamplight spilling through the French doors onto a deck that spread all the way out to the edge of the cliff. The wind was sharper here. Colder. I shivered a little and felt Devlin's arm come around me.

He leaned in close to whisper, "Vanessa's bedroom's at the back of the house, overlooking the ocean."

I turned my head and just looked at him. *Big* surprise. Three Boob–lovin' Devlin knew which bedroom was hers. *Hmm.*

"I know what you're thinking," he said, but I didn't think so. If he'd known what I was thinking at that moment, he'd have moved farther away from me. "But I've got a guy on the inside. He told me where her room is."

Uh-huh. If you'll buy that, I've got some oceanfront property in Phoenix I'd like to sell you.

He blew out a breath. "Do we really have time to do this right now?"

I scowled at him. No, we didn't have time. But, boy, I wanted to. Fighting with Devlin sounded like a lot more fun than fighting with the queen again.

"Fine," I said, but I didn't sound happy, and I think he

picked up on that, because he dropped his arm from around my shoulders.

"We don't know how many demons are in there," he said, "so we go in fast and hard."

I nodded. I couldn't talk. Weird sensation for me. But my throat was closed up tight. I wasn't even sure I was breathing. *Come on, Cassidy. Get in. Get Brady. Get out.* "How hard could it be?" I whispered in my best cheer-myself-up voice.

"Very," Devlin said.

"I wasn't talking to you," I told him.

A demon came up too close behind me, and my instinct was to turn around and rip out his heart. I remembered in time that for tonight, anyway, these demons were on my side.

Swallowing hard, I started forward, Devlin practically glued to my side. And right about then I was glad to have him. He was big and strong and probably didn't want to kill me most of the time.

I took the four narrow steps at a quick run, crossed the wooden deck, and my sneakered feet squeaked so loud it sounded like a scream. Well, the element of surprise was most likely gone, so I grabbed the handle on the French door and threw it open.

I don't know what I was expecting, but this wasn't it. Somehow I figured queen equaled elegant. Nope. This was more like demon queen had collectible addiction.

She had more knickknacks, doilies, china dogs, porcelain dolls, afghans, pillows, end tables, chairs, coffee tables and candy dishes than I'd ever seen in one place before. It was like an auction house had exploded inside.

And it smelled funny.

But, then, *demons.*

Speaking of which, a greenish demon with red spots on its cheeks leaped up off one of the couches when I stepped into the room. It tried to rush me, but it tripped on an umbrella stand. It sort of fell into me then, but I just swung out one arm and threw it behind me. Devlin and his boys took care of that one, and I kept going. I raced though the family room, ripped out the heart of a demon that jumped out at me from a corner (scared me big-time) and headed down a long hall toward the stairs that would take me to the second floor.

There were grunts and groans and shouts all around me. Someone shouted out what I guessed was a warning but sounded more to me like, "Alley boatem floss ares." Demon languages are pretty ugly, really. All guttural. Sort of like German but without the poetry.

The front door flew open when I rounded the corner and grabbed the banister. Logan and Jasmine were right there, side by side, with a handful of demons backing them up in their fight. Logan took a punch to the face and came up swinging. The demon he hit went down and stayed down, and I caught a glimpse of Jasmine leaping up to plant her orthopedic shoe in another demon's face.

They were holding their own.

Good. One less thing to worry about.

"Go, Cass, go!" Devlin's voice from right behind me. He gave me a shove to start me running up the stairs, but it didn't take much. Get in. Get Brady. Get out. My plan. Brilliant in its simplicity.

I hit the head of the stairs and turned left. The landing was wide and carpeted with a bloodred rug. Appropriate? God, I hoped not.

Devlin kept pace with me, and from down below the sounds of the fighting just rose up and up, like cheers at a football game.

My squad of hit demons was getting it done, and I hadn't run into the queen yet, so I called that a win.

The last door on the left was locked when I tried it. Was Vanessa inside? *Please let her be gone*, I thought, wildly making deals with whatever God might be listening. *I'll say the rosary. Go to Mass.* I thought about that for a second and figured it probably wasn't wise to lie to God. Especially in an emergency situation. *Okay, I probably won't go to Mass. But I'll feel worse about missing it.*

"I just suck at making deals," I muttered, and kicked the door just above the brass knob. Duster strength smashed though the lock as though it weren't there, and the door crashed open, slamming into the wall behind it.

"Brady?" I shouted for him, because who knew how much time I had left? For all I knew Vanessa was hiding behind the big-ass bed, waiting to spring at me and finish what she'd started the other night.

Devlin waited in the doorway and called out, "Hurry up, Cass. We gotta go. . . ."

Well, duh. I bolted into the room, tying not to notice that, at least in her bedroom, Vanessa had some style. Silk duvet, a million pillows piled against a gleaming carved wood headboard. There was even a fireplace with a couple of cozy chairs pulled up to it. *Bitch.*

She had the bedroom I'd always wanted.

And she had Brady.

I looked in the closet—big-ass walk-in, bigger than Thea's bedroom. Then checked the bathroom. Can we say day-at-the-spa? She had a damn Jacuzzi tub. What the hell did she need a sex slave for?

"Damn it, Brady," I shouted, frustrated now and getting more scared by the minute. Plus I wasn't breathing real steady, either. I'd done a lot of running in the last few minutes, and my body wasn't used to that. "If you're here say something!"

"Duster?"

I knew that voice. It was muffled, but familiar. I sprinted across the room, threw open the only door I hadn't opened yet and stumbled into a connecting bedroom. Not quite as plush as Vanessa's, but pretty damn impressive. There was a fire in the hearth, an acre of gleaming wood floor unsoftened by rugs, and a four-poster bed that looked big enough to sleep a family of ten.

And on that bed was Brady.

Six feet, five inches of toned, tanned *naked* flesh. Brady's dark blond hair hung over his shoulders. His arms were splayed wide, his wrists tied to the twin posts of the gigantic bed's headboard. The silk sheets beneath him were a twisted-up mess, and he looked exhausted.

Even his Mr. Happy was in a coma—still damn impressive, if you know what I mean, but lying there limply, as though it had had quite the workout over the last twenty-four hours.

Apparently Vanessa hadn't wasted any time.

I couldn't stop staring at him.

(And here in these oh-so-private pages, I'll admit that I got a real rush just looking at him. Sure, yes, I know. Big trouble. Big danger. Poor Brady, captive and bound to a bed. But I don't think there's a woman alive who wouldn't have thought, at least initially, *Hoo, baby, lemme at him.* There was seriously something very intriguing about seeing a gorgeous naked guy tied up and waiting for you. Or maybe that was just me.)

Anyway . . .

His pale blue eyes—absolutely *stunned*—locked on me, and a tired smile curved his mouth. "You came for me."

Him speaking was enough to break whatever spell I was under and get me moving again.

"Why didn't you answer me?" I demanded, rushing to the head of the bed and going to work on the thick ropes holding him in place.

"I heard a voice. Thought it was Vanessa toying with me. I never believed you would come." His eyes shone with gratitude and worry as he looked up at me. "Cassidy, you shouldn't be here. It's too dangerous."

"I'm here now. No talking. Stealthy escape." Someone downstairs screamed. "Well, not stealthy. But escape, anyway."

The damn rope was as strong as it looked. I was never going to get it untied. "Devlin! A little help here!"

He burst into the room an instant later, took in the scene in a single glance, and went to the other side of the bed across from me. He grabbed hold of the top of the bedpost and said, "We don't have time to cut him loose. You're strong enough to snap that post. Grab hold and pull."

"Right." I hadn't even thought of it. You try keeping your thoughts focused with a naked Faery in front of you and demons out for blood just a floor below you. Devlin and I took hold of the posts, gave them mighty yanks, and they snapped like toothpicks. The ropes slid off, and as soon as they were loose Brady was able to shake off the ropes coiled on his wrist.

"Let's roll," I said, reaching for Brady's arm and dragging him to his feet.

His legs went rubbery, which told me he'd spent the last twenty-four hours or so flat on his back. But a second later he managed to straighten up. He grabbed the black silk top sheet, wrapped it around himself, and this time, when I got hold of him, he moved with me.

The three of us left Brady's little love-slave shack, bolted through Vanessa's room and headed into the hall. Brady was having a hard time keeping up with us, but Devlin just kept dragging him along.

"Cassie," Logan shouted from below, "gotta jet!"

"Right there with you." And I was. We hit the bottom of the stairs and ran for the front door. The demon assault on the queen was almost over. I looked at Logan on the way out.

He had a split lip and a cut on his forehead, but his blue eyes were clear and he was royally pissed. Jasmine, naturally, looked exactly as she had when we first got there: not a single hair out of place. She wasn't even *winded*, for chrissakes, and she had to be two hundred years old. I was so out of shape, I could hardly breathe at all, and I had a stitch in my side that stabbed at me every time I tried to breathe.

My troops and I were out of the house and racing across the darkened yard when lights blazed into the night, bright enough to blind us all.

Well, that couldn't be good news. We just kept running. I heard a very female scream of fury and knew the queen had shown up from wherever the hell she'd been and had just found her sex Faery missing.

Well, and a few of her pet demons dead. I was guessing her furniture was all knocked over too, though in a house that cluttered, I didn't know how she could tell.

Anyway, so not my problem.

None of us stopped running till we hit the cars. Then I pushed Brady into the backseat with Devlin and Jasmine and jumped into the front.

"Hurry, Logan," I urged, my foot tapping on the floor, my fingers drumming on the dashboard.

"I'm hurrying," he muttered fiercely, and fired up the engine. He slammed the gearshift into drive and peeled out just as some hideous Hell beast threw itself against the car.

"Fuck!" Logan didn't even look back. My kind of guy, he just kept driving

It felt like we'd been hit by a boulder, and frankly I'd just as soon not know what it was that hit us. It was enough for me that we'd all gotten out of there.

Even if I wasn't sure exactly how it had happened.

"Demons," Logan said, reaching across to grab my arm. "Those were *real* demons, weren't they? And the guys with us. Those weren't costumes, right? Actual demons. There are *demons.* They exist. And they hit pretty hard. Demons. *Demons.*"

"Yep. Real demons." I patted his hand. I sympathized, but I

didn't have time to walk him through his epiphany. I'd *tried* to tell him the truth the month before. But had he listened? Um, that's a big no.

I looked into the backseat. "Brady? You okay?"

"Yes," he said, shaking his head as if he weren't really sure. "Yes. I am fine. Thank you, Cassidy. You risked yourself for me. I am honored."

I smiled. "You're welcome."

"All of this for a Faery," Jasmine muttered.

I didn't even look at her. "Devlin? You okay?"

"Fine." He leaned forward in his seat. "We were lucky we got out when we did. Vanessa must have transported into the house just as we were leaving. We must go before she follows."

This information left me suddenly speechless. Needless to say, that didn't last long. "*Transported?* Like on *Star Trek?* 'Beam me up, Scotty'? Like the Asgard on *Stargate?*"

"Again, television," Jasmine muttered just under her breath.

"Give me a break," I shouted, and didn't care that my voice was hitting notes that usually only Sugar should have been able to hear. "Nobody mentioned transporting to me! This is the first I've heard of it. If she can just biddy-bop in and out of places, why didn't she just pop into my house and get Brady for herself?"

"Sanctuary," Brady said, laying his head on the seat back, clearly exhausted, either by the surprising escape or from his arduous hours with Vanessa. Clearly it was hard getting used to the fact that he was once again a free Faery.

"I claimed Sanctuary," he said, "and she cannot violate that. It is a rule. She cannot enter your house without an invitation."

"I thought that was just vampires."

"Oh, for . . ." This from Jasmine again.

"You know," I said, "you're being awfully snarky for somebody who's withholding a shitload of information! You're the big kahuna. The master to my grasshopper! The Obi-Wan to my Luke—though I prefer Han, and who the hell doesn't? The Giles to my Buffy! How come you didn't tell me all of this stuff?"

Jasmine's usually blue but now suspiciously black eyes narrowed at me. "You clutter your mind with more trash than anyone I've ever known."

"What's your point?"

"I've been your trainer for a month, Cassidy. That's hardly time to fill you in on all aspects of demon life."

"How about the pertinent ones?"

She opened her mouth to speak, but Logan beat her to it.

"Demons," he whispered, as if he were trying the word out to see how it tasted. Judging by the expression on his face, I was guessing it didn't taste very good.

"You'll be okay, Logan." I gave his shoulder a quick squeeze. "It'll get easier." Not really, but why give the guy any more grief tonight?

When we got back to the house Thea was so happy to see us, even *Jasmine* got a hug. Sugar barked and spun around so fast in a show of dog joy she made herself sick and barfed on the rug. (She couldn't have hit the wood floor?)

Logan had dropped us off in a sort of stupor I hope wore off on his drive home. Nights like this would be easier on him when he lived across the street. *Yeesh.* They wouldn't be any easier on *me*.

Devlin had hopped into his car, but not without giving me a look that said we had a talk coming in the near future. None of that mattered at the moment, though. We'd survived, Jasmine had gone off to wherever cranky old demons went in their off time, and it was just Thea, me, Brady and Sugar in the house.

Brady used Faery dust to make some clothes for himself—

and wouldn't that be a handy skill? No more fitting-room nightmares with bad lighting and funhouse mirrors! Then he made hot cocoa and cookies. (It seemed to relax him; what can I say?) By the time we all went to bed I was so tired I fell into unconsciousness.

And I woke up tingling.

Chapter Fifteen

*B*rady was back!

I didn't try to stop him either. Forget it. If you've been paying attention to the state of my life, then you have to agree I'd *earned* an orgasm. And damn it, I wanted one *now*. But it wasn't all about the trip to Orgasmland. I'd spent the last week or so being hurt by a demon I'd thought I could trust and being pursued by a man who claimed to love me, though I knew he would never be able to accept the world in which I lived.

I was feeling alone and put-upon and downright miserable. To have Brady act as though he wanted me was just too much temptation to resist.

My eyes slitted open, and I noticed it was still dark out. *Good God.* Yet I was tingly enough not to care that I was actually awake before the sun! That had never happened to me before.

"Cassidy," Brady's voice whispered to me in the darkness while his fingers were doing some whispering of their own.

Magic fingers, I tell you. While I was busy enjoying myself completely, my mind dredged up the image of how I'd found him the night before—tied up to a bed, stark, gorgeous naked—and everything inside me lit up like the Strip in Vegas.

And I was naked. How convenient.

Apparently Brady was as skillful as using Faery dust to take off clothes as he was in making them appear.

Whoa.

His mouth was on one of my nipples, and his tongue was doing some seriously fabulous things. The man had talent. Real talent.

I mumbled something like, "NeverstopbecauseifyoudoI'll-havetokillyou," or words to that effect.

In response he used his teeth on me, too—nibbling, tasting, sucking. He made love to that one nipple so long, my other breast was thinking about suing for alienation of affection.

While he nibbled, his fabulous fingers explored. He stroked my hoo-hah with the tips of his fingers, his touch so light it was almost just the impression of a touch. I opened my legs wider. (I dare you to say you wouldn't have done the same.)

His breath was hot on my breast, his fingers delving deeper and deeper with every stroke, and I was so twisted up, with every nerve jangling, I felt like I was going to boing right off the bed.

I arched my back, because it was impossible just to lie there and not move. I stroked my hand through Brady's hair and fixed my gaze on him while his mouth tugged gently at my nipple, and I wondered absently if I could just spend my days like this . . . you know, walking around with his mouth on my nipple.

My hips started rocking when he set a languid rhythm with his fingertips. We were in this together now, a team. Working it, building to something I knew was going to be amazing.

Suddenly I knew I wanted Brady like I'd never wanted anything else in my life. My breath was fast and hard and short. My heart was pounding, and my mouth was so dry I kept licking my lips just so they wouldn't stick to my teeth. I wanted that impressive Faery penis I'd seen the night before. I wanted it deep inside. I wanted Brady pumping his hips against mine.

At least I'm honest about what I want.

I've been with human males. And a demon.

Now I wanted to take that Faery ride.

"Come on, Brady," I said breathlessly, catching his face in the palm of my hand and turning him so I could look into his eyes. "Show me what a sex slave can do when he's a free Faery."

"Yes, Cassidy," he said, and gave me a smile that told me I was really going to like what was coming next. He leaned in and kissed me, his mouth moving over mine with lazy abandon. His tongue traced the outline of my lips, then dipped inside to tangle with mine. I was so primed, I was ready to explode by the time he finally meandered down my body.

Boy, do I mean *meandered*. He took his mouth out for a stroll around my personal block. He kissed and licked every inch of me. There wasn't a spot or crevice or curve he didn't pay attention to in detail.

But I was no closer to that Faery penis than I had been when we'd started.

He flipped me over onto my stomach and nibbled my spine before biting my butt. He kissed the backs of my legs and all the way down my calves. Then he flipped me back over and worked his way up again.

I was flummoxed. (I know that's a word; my dad used to use it, but not exactly in this kind of situation. Well, as far as I know, anyway.) Completely flummoxed and discombobulated, and didn't know whether to breathe in or out. My skin was humming, my brain was trying to keep up and my heart felt like a jackhammer in my chest.

Imagine what happened to me when Brady paused on his "stroll" up my body right at my hoo-hah!?!

Oh, yeah.

Brady lifted my legs and dropped them over his shoulders; then he scooped his hands under my ass and picked me up off the mattress. Moonlight swam in the room, sliding through the windows opened to the night. His pale eyes seemed to glow, his skin looked like polished bronze and his hands felt like they'd been sent from heaven.

I was just hanging there, hoo-hah exposed, mouth dry, watching him. Waiting. *Please, God, let me have this orgasm and . . .* What kind of deal was that to make? *Never mind,* I thought wildly, *leave God out of this.*

"Brady . . ."

"You saved me," he said, dipping his head to lick me once. Twice.

I went completely still and shook my head. Suddenly this didn't seem right at all. Yes, I still wanted him, and I still needed to be wanted myself. But gratitude shouldn't be the reason behind any of this.

"No, Brady. You don't owe me anything." If I just used him, what made me any better than the bitch queen? "You don't have to do this because you're grateful to me."

He smiled, and his eyes burned with desire. "I am not. I do this because we both wish it. Because to touch you gives me pleasure as well."

"Are you sure?" *Please be sure,* I thought.

"Will you allow me to touch you? Taste you? Pleasure your body until you weep with the joy of it?"

Wow.

How many women ever get to hear *that* from a guy?

What'm I, Saint Cassidy? I don't think so.

"Yes, Brady, it's okay by me, and—" *Wow.* Hard to talk to a man when he's got his tongue in your hoo-hah. Hard to keep your mind on anything but the amazing sensations flying around your insides.

So I shut up. I quit thinking.

If he wanted to give me a present, who was I to say no?

He played me like a virtuoso. Brady was amazing. He had a real gift for sex. Made me want to take him out for a spin even more than I had before. He knew when to lick, when to suckle, when to nibble. He knew when I was on the very edge of reason and stopped long enough to pull me back, to make it all last so long I thought I was going to die from the whole lack-of-breathing thing.

My hoo-hah trembled with an orgasm that seemed to shake me right down to my bones, shock waves rolling through me one after another, and I figured I was finished. But Brady had other ideas. Even after a second time he wouldn't let me go. I didn't think I could survive another climax, but I was willing to give it a try.

Brady the Faery was every woman's dream come true: a man who not only knew how to do the tongue thing, but really seemed to like doing it.

That was the last rational thought I remember having. After that it was me twisting in his grasp, rocking my hips and reaching down to hold his head in place for fear he might stop. Then the earth exploded.

Or maybe it was just my little corner of it.

All I know for sure was, I'd been orgasmed (trust me, it's a word) by the best damn Faery in the world.

When I finally stopped trembling he set me down and smiled at me. God, he was cute.

But now that the festivities were over, I had a couple of questions. Not that I didn't enjoy what was happening, and I was still hoping that it would happen again. But there were some things we had to talk about. *Might as well do it now*, I thought.

"That was really incredible," I said first off, because you don't insult a guy who'd just rung your bell *three* times.

"I am pleased you enjoyed it," he said, idly stroking the inside of my thigh. "Do you wish to have more pleasure?"

"Oh, yeah—I mean, no. I mean . . ." *Damn it.* "Not right now."

"Whatever you like, Cassidy."

"Uh-huh." I scooted back, reluctantly moving away from that oh-so-insistent touch. "Look, Brady, now that you're back and everything, I think we should talk."

He looked worried, and also as if he were going for confused innocence. "About what?"

"I know," I said, and scooted off the bed. (I've already admitted to slut-puppy issues. No point in testing my restraint.) I found my jammies tossed to the floor and grabbed them up. While I tugged them on I threw my hair out of my eyes and slanted a look at Brady, still on the bed, looking completely comfy. "I know about the whole male-Faeries-stealing-female-powers-during-sex thing."

"Oh."

Hmm. Not exactly the dropping-to-his-knees-and-begging-for-forgiveness that I'd expected. So I kept talking while I got dressed. Hard to be large and in charge when you were naked and the guy looking at you had just had his head between your legs.

"Jasmine told me. Everything you ever wanted to know about male Faeries but were afraid to ask."

A brief smile curved his mouth, then disappeared.

"I know about the curse on you guys. . . ."

He scowled. Apparently the males still weren't real happy with the female Faeries.

"I know about the whole being-able-to-give-someone-your-power thing. *And* I know that you were trying to seduce me into losing my powers to you."

"Ah . . ." He nodded solemnly.

"That's it?" I asked, pulling my T-shirt on over my head. "That's all you've got to say?" The floor was cold against my bare feet, but I hardly felt it. "You didn't come to me just for sanctuary. You came here to tempt me into sex"—not too difficult, but I wasn't saying *that*—"and steal my strength for yourself."

"Yes," he said, and stood up. His shirt gaped open over his

chest, and he scrubbed one hand across his face as if he were both irritated and uneasy. "I did plan to do that."

A cold ball of something ugly dropped into the pit of my stomach and settled in deep. Funny, but even though I'd known this since Jasmine had spilled the beans, hearing him admit to it hit me pretty hard. "Even knowing I have Thea to protect?" I demanded. "You were going to leave me defenseless against the demons who keep attacking me?"

His gaze shifted to mine, and the sweet, sexy Faery I thought I knew was gone. He'd become a strong, tough male, looking at me through defiant eyes. "I had no choice. It meant my survival, Cassidy. You don't know what it was like being held by the queen for more than a hundred years." He paced off a few steps, spun around and glared at me. "I enjoy sex. I *don't* enjoy being held as a slave. Being used as a battery charger. Or being threatened daily to either give her the power she wants or to remain a slave for eternity."

"And that makes what you were going to do to me okay?"

"I don't expect you to understand," he said tightly, and reached up to shove both hands through his thick, dark blond hair. "But I didn't know you when I came here. All I knew was that a powerful Duster had been called. You were a stranger to me. Thea was a stranger. Things are . . . different now."

The cold spot in my belly was dissipating. Because whether he realized it or not, I *did* understand. In his place, wouldn't I have done anything I had to, to survive? To protect Thea? Keep her safe?

I sighed and asked, "Different how?"

He smiled, and behind him I saw the first signs of dawn beginning to filter through the window. "I know you," he said. "I *like* you. And I care for Thea. I wouldn't harm you like that, Cassidy. I would never leave you unable to protect your child. I hope you can believe me."

I walked around the edge of the bed and stopped directly in

front of him. He was so damn tall that tipping my head back to look into those blue eyes of his was damned uncomfortable.

"I do believe you," I said, and it was the truth. But even knowing that, I'd be keeping my guard up if we ever did have sex.

"Thank you." He cupped my face in his palms, and tingles of anticipation rushed through me like the bubbles in a freshly poured beer. "You have given me a great gift, Cassidy. You have delivered me from the queen."

I covered his hands with mine. "It's not over. I'll have to face her again," I said. "I know that. Not sure yet how I'll beat her, but you're safe for now."

"Yes. Safe and with you."

Ooh. There were those bubbles again. I moved in closer to him. He dropped his hands to my waist and pulled me tightly to him. I felt his Mr. Happy—awake, alert and oh-so-ready— pressing into my abdomen. *Oh, boy.* I swallowed hard, moved into him and watched his eyes darken with the same kind of desire I was feeling.

Sex with Brady? Was I ready for that? Okay, yes. I was.

"There is something you should know, Cassidy."

"There's more?" I asked.

"Yes." He bent low, kissed my forehead, then straightened up. "I will not make love with you."

"Huh?"

He let me go and took a step back for good measure. "We cannot."

"Why the hell not?" (Yes, I was crabby. And probably a little greedy. I know—I'd had three orgasms already, but I wanted more. Brady wanted me, and I wanted him back. I wanted to forget about everything else in my life for a few crazed minutes and simply be Cassidy. I wanted . . . I wanted a Faery-driven, penis-enhanced ride to Happyland.)

"Because I like you."

Now I was really confused. "When you *didn't* like me, you would have had sex with me. But now that you *do* like me, you won't?"

He beamed at me. "Exactly!"

Could my life get more screwed up?

⌇

"You want the ghoul hanging from the roof or the tree?" Rachel shouted.

"Ghoul in the tree, ghosts on the house," I called back, and thought for just a second that this would sound like a very weird conversation to any strangers who happened to be listening. Fortunately, everyone *I* knew was cool with it.

Two days after escaping the demon queen's house, Faery in tow, I was finally getting our Halloween decorations up. I'd decided that we needed a little normalcy. Well, as much normalcy as we ever had, anyway. There was another fight coming, I knew. But at the moment the sun was shining, Thea was safe and I was getting tingled by a Faery every morning. (Still no actual sex, damn it, but the tingles were nothing to sneeze at! And Brady really did have a terrific mouth.)

Now I glanced around my yard with pride. Could I sucker my friends and family into helping out or what? Even Logan was there, stretching out fake spiderwebs from the driveway to the front porch. Zoe Cohen was right behind him, planting plastic spiders (the only kind I could accept) in the webbing.

Rachel had climbed the tree in the front yard and was currently wrestling the stuffed ghoul into position, and Thea was attaching blinking eyeball lights to the insides of the front window. Jasmine was muttering under her breath and setting up the coffin in the front flower bed. (All my dead flowers were suddenly looking pretty good as ambience. Good for me that I suck at gardening.)

Brady was wandering around looking like he was helping.

The real surprise, though, was Ryan Butler.

Apparently he'd finally noticed Thea. I wasn't real sure how I felt about that. But I'd taken the precaution of squirting him with the demon spray, just in case.

He'd blinked at me and wiped the green-flecked liquid from his eyes. No smoking going on, so at least I knew he wasn't a demon. He was cute, too, in a way that a fifteen-year-old girl would find dreamworthy. About six feet tall, he had brown hair, brown eyes and a letter jacket that made him the stuff fantasies are made of. (A big improvement from the last guy Thea'd had a crush on. At least Ryan Butler wore his pants higher than halfway down his butt—and as far as I could tell, there were no piercings.)

Still, he was a guy who was looking at Thea as if she were a tasty steak, so I had a little chat with him anyway.

"So, you and Thea, huh?" *Smooth, Cass. Real smooth.*

"Yes, ma'am," he said.

Oh, dear God. When did I become a ma'am?

"Thea's great."

"Yeah, she is," I said, agreeing with him as I glanced into the house to smile at Thea through the wide front window. She didn't smile back. In fact, she gave me the death look. You know the one. A teenager's way of silently saying, *Don't embarrass me, Mother, or I will never speak to you again.*

Not a real threat in Thea's case. Like me, she's incapable of going without talking. So I smiled again, gave her a finger wave and looked back to the guy who was currently making Thea's heart go pitter-pat.

"See that guy over there?" I said, pointing at Logan.

Ryan looked at him, saw Logan giving him the hairy eyeball, then shifted his gaze back to me. "Yeah . . ."

"That's Thea's dad."

"Yeah, I know."

"He's a cop. So he carries a *gun.*"

Ryan blinked. Good. I had his attention.

"Logan's very protective," I added.

Ryan swallowed. "Yes, ma'am."

Then I gave him a pat on the shoulder and smiled up at him. He really was cute, and for Thea's sake I was glad he'd noticed her, but not glad enough that I was willing to give him a clear path to my baby. "Just so you know, I'm really protective, too." I leaned in and gave him my Mad-dog Mother glare. "And I don't *need* a gun."

He looked nervous.

Well, my work here was done.

I grinned and said, "Thanks again for helping out with the decorating!"

"Yes, ma'am," he said, but he looked like he was having a hard time not running for his life.

But Mr. Football was apparently made of sterner stuff. He hadn't made a run for it, and at the moment he was on the roof, stringing pumpkin lights along the eaves.

I was pretty sure I'd have to listen to a speech from Thea all about how I'd mortified her and scarred her for life, but that was for later. Right then life was looking pretty good. I had bags of candy in the house, pizza had been ordered and there was cold beer in the fridge.

And in a life as filled with craziness as mine . . . you learn to appreciate the slow days.

Because tomorrow all hell might break loose.

Chapter Sixteen

My unbelievably long day was over, and my street was settling in for the night. Behind wide front windows, televisions flickered and lamps glowed. Dinners had been eaten, homework was done, and now it was time to close up the house and lock out the night.

Streetlights shone with a wavery yellow light, and the Sanchez's dog, Rosie, had started her nightly howl. Sugar flinched at the end of her leash and looked around as if expecting something to jump out at her from the shadows. It was all so normal. Comforting. In a world of weirdness I held on to the familiar like I would a cinnamon roll from Sun and Shadow bakery. I needed this. I needed to take the time to remember that not everything revolved around demons.

Sugar lumbered forward a few steps, then stopped, out of breath. That was embarrassing.

From my backyard came the sounds of Thea and Brady, chanting and working on her cheerleader routine. My next-door neighbor, Harlan Cates, had his TV on too loud again, and I could hear Alex Trebek offering somebody a shot at Double Jeopardy. His door was open, the security screen probably barred and his front porch light on, no doubt so Harlan could keep one wary eye on his precious lawn even while watching TV. The man was just a touch psychotic about his yard.

I swear, once I saw him using manicure scissors to even out the pruning on his oleander bush.

Sugar whined and tried to head back to the house.

"No way," I told her. "You're walking even if I have to drag you."

I wanted a little time alone. A little time to think about where my life was going (the toilet, currently circling the rim), about what I'd do next about the queen (hiding being the best first option) and the highlights my hair needed (give me a break. If I was going to die sometime soon, I wanted my hair to look good).

"What're you thinking about?"

I jolted. Some superhero I was. A voice in the dark and I was ready to jump out of my skin.

"Jesus, Logan." I slapped one hand to my chest. "Wouldn't it be easier just to shoot me as to give me a heart attack?"

"Sorry. Thought you saw me coming."

Actually, no, I hadn't noticed him. In fact, I was doing everything I could to pretend he hadn't really moved in today. He'd hauled what little furniture he possessed into the house that morning before coming over to help decorate, so he had to be tired. But did he stay at home and rest up? No. Instead he was standing next to me in the dark.

And all of a sudden it felt really crowded. "What's up?"

"I was going to ask you that," he said, waving one hand at me holding on to Sugar's leash. "You're really taking this dog on a walk?"

"Something wrong with that?"

"It's almost like exercise, isn't it?" He grinned, and Logan has a really good grin. It hadn't changed much since the summer the two of us had made Thea.

Probably not a good thing that I was noticing this.

Sugar walked over to him and leaned, which forced Logan to lean back. The only way to keep from falling over, remember? "This dog is *fat*."

"Hey, don't you be insulting my dog." Of course she was

fat. That was why I was forcing her to take a walk. But that didn't mean I let other people pick on her. "Come on, Sugar. Let's move."

Instantly Sugar sat down, whimpered pitifully and held up one paw. Like I was going to buy that excuse. If she'd had thumbs, she'd have been playing a violin.

Logan laughed. "Damn, Cassie. Your dog's just like you!"

What could I say? He was right. If I'd had an active dog, it would have run away from home years ago in disgust.

"She's had a long day," I said.

"Yeah, all that lying in the shade, snoring, must have really taken a toll."

I didn't even respond to that, just tugged on the leash, and Sugar was forced to come along.

We hadn't gone very far, our footsteps echoing in the silence, Sugar's heavy breathing playing counterpart, when Logan abruptly said, "That football player was watching Thea like she was dessert all damn day."

I'd noticed that, too.

"Bound to happen," I said, trying to be nonchalant about the whole thing. "She's gorgeous."

"Yeah," Logan said with a mixture of pride and fear (a combination I knew and identified with), "she is. What do we know about him?"

I shrugged. "He's not a demon."

Logan's steps faltered; he shoved his hands into his jeans pockets and said, "Demons. Jesus, I can't believe we're talking about demons and I'm not laughing my ass off at you."

"You mean like you did last month, when I tried to tell you all about it?"

He had the decency to look a little uncomfortable at the memory. "Okay, fine. I shouldn't have blown you off like that. *Or* laughed," he added before I could. "But in my defense, who the hell would have believed you? I *still* wouldn't believe it if I hadn't seen them for myself."

Judging by the expression on his face, I was guessing he wasn't real happy about having this new reality foisted on him. *Well, hell. Get in line.*

We stopped so Sugar could rest up and spend her break sniffing at the base of Harlan's tree. Dogs are easy to please. Give 'em the scent of old dog urine and they're happy. To make *me* happy right about then, I would have required a giant margarita and a plate of nachos. Or pizza sticks from Tully's. Or some KFC Original Recipe—extra-crispy only got you more batter, nearly burned. Or a sundae. Hot fudge.

"Earth to Cassie."

I blinked.

Logan looked down at me. "I talked to a couple of the guys at the station, and they said there've been rumors about demons for years. Most of the guys aren't buying it, and I didn't work real hard to convince them. I didn't want an appointment with the police shrink. But one guy, Mahaffey, he's convinced. Said he saw a guy with shark teeth once."

Rachel's husband, Simon, dentist to demons, had a client with shark teeth. I wondered if that was the same demon or if, God help us, there were more of the *Jaws* guys running around town.

"Weird to think about, I know."

"Think about?" Logan blew out a breath and shook his head. "I'm trying not to. Regular bad guys—dopers, armed robbers, hell, *murderers*—I can live with. Demons? Not so sure."

"You think *I* like it?" I tugged at the leash, but Sugar wouldn't budge. This particular tree must have been the neighborhood watercooler. Every dog in town must pop by to leave messages. Bet Harlan loved *that*.

Disgusted but resigned, I said, "I know how you feel. I didn't know about them myself till last month. Didn't believe it until I squirted my first demon and his head started smoking." Poor Leo, my washing-machine-delivery demon. Short, fat and bald, he'd hit the ground running after I squirted him and nobody had seen him since.

"So then," Logan mused, "that night we went to the beach caves to save Thea . . . Judge Jenks really was a demon and you . . . *dusted* him?"

"Yeah." I smiled to myself at the memory.

"And this guy Brady?" Logan asked. "He's really a Faery?"

"Yep."

"And Jasmine?"

"Demon."

"Cole?"

"Him, too."

His features went hard and tight. "I can't believe you were dating a demon!" Logan shouted, and Sugar's head snapped up as if she'd been shot.

"Hey, did I give you grief for marrying somebody named Busty?" I countered.

"Misty."

"Whatever."

I started walking again, and Sugar practically crawled behind me like a dog taking its last long walk through the pound. At this rate it'd take us an hour to get past Harlan Cates's house.

But I wasn't really mad at Sugar. It was Logan bugging me. *This* was why I hadn't wanted Logan moving in across the street. It was hard enough trying to figure out where the two of us stood without him living so close by. Now here he was, tagging along on my forced march, making me mad again.

He grabbed my arm, dragged me to a stop and said, "You're through with Cole though, right?"

Was I? I didn't know. The only thing I was sure of was, "So none of your business."

He didn't let go of my right arm, and Sugar was straining against the leash I held in my left hand, trying to go home, so it was sort of like being drawn and quartered. Good to be me.

"I *want* it to be my business," he said, and his blue eyes, so much like Thea's, stared down into mine.

Oh, boy.

It was damp and getting colder by the second. I was wearing my winter coat (red sweatshirt), and I was suddenly so hot I needed to fan myself. But I couldn't do that. Logan would enjoy it too much.

This just wasn't fair. Wasn't my life already full enough? Hadn't I reached the top of my cup and now it was runnething (yes, I know it's not a word) over? Wasn't there a karmic limit to some things?

Logan's hands moved up and down my arms, and even through my sweatshirt I could feel the heat from his body pumping into mine. His eyes warmed up, too, and shone with something that looked way too interesting.

This was one of the reasons I'd wanted those stolen moments with Brady. Because what I felt for Logan was too confusing.

Heck, *everything* was confusing. I was still mad at Devlin (helping me notwithstanding, I still had the image of Three Boob stuck in my brain). I had a lot of affection for Brady, and Logan? Well, Logan still made me *really* nervous. He'd always been able to slip past my guard. Make me want him even when I knew it was a mistake. He was gorgeous and funny and knew me really well, even though he seemed to like me anyway. Logan, I guess, was my Kryptonite. One touch of his hand and weakness set in.

He was my past and somehow had wormed himself into

my present and he kept hinting about my future. All very discombobulating. (One of my grandmother Harry's favorite words.) So was I baffled by my life? Oh, yeah. Was I worried? Damn straight. Was I going to let him kiss me?

You betcha.

Mist rolled down the street in tendrils of gray, thickening the shadows as the fog drifted in from the ocean. Wind sighed past me, and the night was so quiet it was as though the world had taken a breath and held it.

Logan leaned in close, tucked my hair back from my face and smoothed the pad of his thumb across my cheekbone. I was trembling. My body was humming, my brain was screaming and my hoo-hah just didn't know what to do with itself. It hadn't seen this much action in years.

Then Logan kissed me, and I'm sorry to say I can't even describe it to you. My brain shut down. Hell, I was lucky I could still stand up. Logan's got some great lips, and he's not afraid to use 'em. There was some tongue action, too, and his hand was sliding up underneath my T-shirt, reaching for my boob, and I was leaning in, trying to help him with directions. Well, let's just say he had my complete attention.

Which was why I didn't hear anything right away and didn't know what the hell Sugar was up to until it was too late. Sugar doesn't react well to strange situations. When she's scared (which is pretty much all the time), all she wants is to climb inside my body for safety's sake.

Well, since Logan was trying to get there first, all Sugar could do was run in circles around us. She managed to wrap her leash around us once, then nearly strangled herself. Barking and backing up, she hit the backs of Logan's knees, and he bit my lip as we started toppling over.

My eyes popped open and stared up into his, and I winced and sort of braced myself, waiting for my head to crack open on the sidewalk.

Fortunately, Logan's reflexes are better than mine. He broke our fall with his hands and only let out a manly groan when his wrists bent back.

Instead of sidewalk, my head bounced off Harlan Cates's precious grass. Then, once we were on the ground, Sugar covered us with her body, but I wasn't fooled. She wasn't being brave, throwing herself on a live grenade to save her loved ones. She was trying to get lost in a crowd.

"Damn it, Sugar, you're killing me," I said.

"Your dog's a menace, Cassie," Logan said.

"Ahoooooooooooooo," Sugar said.

"Great," Logan shouted, trying to lift his head away from Sugar's gaping jaws. "Now I'm deaf!"

"Who's out there?" Harlan Cates threw his screen door wide and stepped out onto the porch. "Hey, you two, get off my grass! I just fertilized! What do you two think this is, Motel 6? I'm calling the cops on you kids, swear to God."

"Perfect," I said, hoping that at least it wasn't cow-poop fertilizer. Though God only knew what the chemical kind was doing to my hair!

"I *am* the cops, Mr. Cates," Logan shouted, then whooshed all the air out of his lungs when Sugar's foot came down on his nuts. "Logan Miller." How he managed to talk on a groan, I don't know. "I just moved in across the street!"

"And it's me, too, Mr. Cates," I called out, untangling the leash while Logan whimpered—in a manly way, of course. "Cassidy Burke!"

"Should've known it was you!" the mean old coot yelled. "You think you can TP my lawn again? I'm ready for you this time!"

Jesus. Let it go, already. Rach and I toilet-papered the old goat's yard when we were in high school. Clearly Harlan wasn't the forgive-and-forget kind of guy. Guess we were still public enemies numbers one and two.

"Everything's fine," Logan assured him in a voice a notch or two higher than normal.

"Everything's not fine, you idiot!" Harlan yelled again. "Get off my grass!"

"Ahoooooooooooooo," Sugar howled, and Rosie down the street picked up the echo and sent it on. From a distance I heard another dog and then another. *Great.* It was *101 Dalmatians and the Twilight Bark.*

"Sugar, get off me," I said, and fought with the leash and the dog and—whoops—Logan's hand. "Cut it out!"

"Hey, I deserve some kind of reward here."

"On Harlan's front yard?"

"Wherever I can get it."

"He's *watching*!"

"He's old. He can't see anything."

"Get a room somewhere!" Harlan shouted.

Logan muttered something but tried to slide his hand back up the inside of my thigh anyway. Then Sugar decided this was all too much for her and tried to run back home. Too bad the leash was still around Logan's leg.

He was grappling with the dog, and the dog was howling, and Harlan Cates was still shouting from his doorstep, and Brady and Thea were chanting in my backyard, so ask me how I heard the kid crying?

I don't know. Duster ears? Did the little charge I got from Brady give me Superman hearing? Would my ears grow? God, I hoped not. I stood up and looked around, and it took me a minute to follow the sound of the soft sobbing. But finally I spotted the little girl.

Across the street she was sitting on the curb. The yellow fog lamp shone down on her, spotlighting her in the mist. She had her arms crossed on her knees and her forehead on her arms and she was crying, her long blond hair hanging down on either side of her head.

Oh, man . . .

I left Logan with Sugar and ran toward the girl, trying to figure out who she was and how she'd gotten there. I mean, I knew everyone on my street and she didn't live here. So what was she doing out all by herself with the fog coming in?

"Cassie, damn it, wait for me!" Logan called out, but I didn't pay any attention. I was working in pure mother mode. It's involuntary. Once your uterus has produced a child, you're forever stuck in the land of answering the call of a kid in need. I don't know how it happens; I just go with it.

"Hey, honey," I cooed, slowing down so I wouldn't startle the kid by running at her full-bore. "Are you okay? Where's your mom?"

She sniffled a little louder, and my uterus twisted in response.

"It's okay," I assured her, getting closer. "Everything'll be okay."

"It will be," the little girl answered in a voice that was way too deep for her size, "as soon as I'm finished with you."

Yikes.

Goose bumps raced along my spine, and my throat snapped shut.

The little girl lifted her head, and I backpedaled as fast as I could. Her eyes were slanted upward at the edges and glowing a deep, violent red. Her fangs dripped out of her mouth and brushed the bottom of her pointy chin.

She leaped up and stood about three feet tall in her tiny Winnie the Pooh sneakers. She lifted both hands, and the tips of her fingers grew. I am not shitting you—her fingers *grew*! They curved out and down until they looked like a picture I saw once of this ancient Chinese guy whose fingernails were, like, a mile and a half long.

Ew.

"Cassie!" Logan shouted.

"Ahooooooooo," Sugar howled.

"I called the cops!" Harlan shrieked.

It'd be nice if he had, but Harlan was all talk, no show. Besides, even if he had called the cops, they wouldn't come. They didn't like him any more than I did.

"The money's all mine now, Duster," the weird-ass little girl promised.

That damned Web site again. Even when Vanessa wasn't around, she was trying to have me killed!

"Have to get me first," I taunted, and points for me. I was shaking in my tennies. My tremors had tremors, and a cold sweat was breaking out down my spine. Now we all know how I feel about sweating, so this was not a good experience!

I got in my (ha!) fighting stance and looked like a poor imitation of Buffy. Perception is everything, though, and I figured that if this midget demon thought I wasn't scared, maybe she'd back off.

Nope.

She *flew* at me.

And by flew, I don't mean she ran really fast. I mean she freaking *flew*. That's right. Flying midget demon, looking like a second grader from Hell. Somewhere in the back of my mind I put it all together, which was pretty impressive, considering I was terrified!

Yikes!

Pixie!

I have to say, Jasmine was right about them. They *were* nasty little troll-like creatures!

I ducked as she sailed over my head, and then I turned to watch her bank like a helicopter to come at me again. Man, even scared, I remember thinking, *What a cool power to have.* I'd fly everywhere. No more traffic jams. No more worrying about keeping my Bug in working order. I could fly Thea and me to Europe, though I'd probably need a rest halfway there.

The Pixie from Hell flew right for me again, all fangy and long fingers, and I braced myself for what I hoped would be a really lucky dusting.

She screamed bloody murder, her mouth hanging open, drool sliding off her fangs. Her hands were outstretched, her tiny feet kicking in the air as if she were swimming or something, and as she swooped in low I ducked a little, jolted my right hand up and grabbed that nasty Pixie heart right out of her chest.

The freaking thing exploded into dust overhead, and I was instantly covered in Pixie dust.

Not in a happy way.

"What the *hell* was that?" Logan said as he ran up, gun drawn, hobbling from the groin smash Sugar'd delivered.

"I think a Pixie," I said, and brushed at the dust covering my sweatshirt. I was going to have to boil it. Or burn it. Or buy a new one. The dust in my hair was already itching and really creeping me out. God, I needed a shower.

And cookies.

Can't even take a walk on a nice fall night, I thought, and felt the sting of tears in my eyes. *Damn it*. I hated crying. I never looked good crying. I got all red and splotchy, and my eyes swelled up like I'd been punched in the face.

I blinked the tears back and told myself to call off the pity party. Better to be pissed off than weepy. I look *good* when I'm pissed.

"That's it," I said to nobody in particular, heading toward Sugar, who was trying to curl up into a ball small enough to actually make herself disappear. "Tonight's little walk is over."

"That was a *Pixie*?" Logan said from behind me. "Pixies are real too? I thought Pixies were supposed to be cute! That thing wasn't cute. That thing was . . . Pixies are demons?"

"Isn't everything?" I muttered, and grabbed up Sugar's leash. "Come on, baby; no more nasty exercise tonight."

My dog was almost as relieved as I was. Quivering and panting, Sugar trotted at my side. Harlan had given up once we got off his precious grass, and now his front door was closed. He was probably hiding behind his drapes, watching me, but damned if I could find it in me to care.

I could hear Brady and Thea still chanting in the back-yard. Apparently hearing me scream and fighting for my life wasn't distracting enough to tear them away from cheerleader practice.

"This is nuts, Cassie," Logan said from right behind me. "These damn things are all over, everywhere."

"Welcome to my world," I said, and stopped dead when I spotted a shadow standing alongside the back fence, looking into my yard. At my kid.

Crap.

I'd had enough. There was disintegrating Pixie in my hair, grass stains on my back, a traumatized dog drooling on me and a pissed-off cop yammering in my ear. I did *not* have the patience for any more demons that night. It was one thing for them to come after me, but no way was I going to let some drooly, hairy, ugly-ass critter peek in at Thea while she was learning her cheerleader routine, trying to be normal!

I shoved Sugar's leash into Logan's hand and stomped up the driveway like Frankenstein's mama. "Who the hell are you, and what are you doing?"

The shadow jumped, leaped backward and landed in a splash of light. Not a demon—as far as I could tell without my spray. But her eyes didn't glow and she didn't drool or spit on me, so I was going with not a demon.

A teenage girl (which, okay, could give a demon a run for its money at times) looked up at me through too-long brown bangs hanging over her eyes.

"Hi, Ms. Burke!" (Perky, perky, perky!) "I'm, uh, Elle, uh, you know, a friend of Thea's from school and, uh, I was, uh,

like, walking and stuff, you know, and, uh, heard her working out and, uh, thought I'd wish her, you know, good luck
at tryouts and, you know, uh, then I figured I shouldn't, you
know, uh, interrupt and stuff, uh, so I, you know, was, uh,
quiet and stuff, so I, uh, wouldn't bother her, you know, and
stuff."

My eyeballs were spinning by the time she got to the end
of her oh-so-eloquent speech. Plus, I was, uh, you know, out
of patience and stuff.

"Right," I said, holding up one hand to prevent her from
ever trying to speak again. "I'll tell Thea you stopped by."

Her eyes got big and round (what I could see of 'em behind the bangs, anyway). "Uh, okay, you know, if you think,
you know, you should and stuff . . ."

"Go," I said, pointing to the end of the driveway. "Fly free,
little Elle."

Saying her name made me think of Elves. Now I knew
there were Pixies and Faeries. Were there Elves, too? Did they
look like Orlando Bloom? Were they nicer than Pixies? Would
I care as long as they looked like Orlando Bloom?

"Okay, uh, you know, bye," she said, and bolted down the
driveway.

"And stuff," I added, gratefully watching her go. Man, all it
really took to appreciate your own teenager was having to talk
to another one for a minute or two.

"Was she speaking English?" Logan wanted to know.

"A derivative," I said. "Teenglish." (It is a word. I just made
it up.)

"Cassie . . ." His voice dropped, and I knew he was through
talking about demons and weird teenagers. He was ready to get
back to that interrupted kiss. Apparently his groin smash had
healed and his Mr. Happy was feeling hopeful again.

I looked at him, and even though something inside me was
wanting the same thing, I was just too tired to think about it

at the moment. Who would have guessed it was possible? Too tired to think about orgasms?

"Logan, no more tonight." I sighed and leaned against the fence. "Just go home, okay?"

He smiled, and that something inside me bubbled and frothed. "I could change your mind, you know."

Boy howdy, he could.

"Yeah, I know," I said, and had to admit that Logan had come through. He was new to the whole demon thing, but he'd taken it really well and *still* wanted me. So maybe he was seeing the person I was now and not just the sixteen-year-old girl who'd adored him. But either way, I was so tired all I wanted to do was sit down in the dark.

So I told my hoo-hah to go to sleep and stop with the tingling. It wasn't going to be seeing any action that night. "I'm just too wiped, Logan."

He nodded, rocked back on his heels and said, "Okay, if that's what you want I'll go. For now."

The "for now" told me he wasn't going anywhere.

And the tingle in my hoo-hah, not to mention my heart, told me that at least *parts* of me were happy to hear it.

Chapter Seventeen

There's a lot to be said for routine. Sure, it can start to look like a rut if you're in the damn thing too long, but after a couple of weeks of demon fighting and Faery rescuing, a routine looked pretty good to me.

For a few days that was just what I had. It was like we were in the eye of a hurricane. Everything was still. Quiet. Uneventful. Thea did the school thing, Brady did the cooking thing, Jasmine did the rolling-her-eyes-at-my-pitiful-attempts-at-training thing and I did the have-a-life thing. Everyone was happy.

Well, Logan wasn't happy, and I don't think Devlin was in a whoopee state of mind. But I couldn't worry about the two of them. Let them find their own routines.

Of course, eyes in the hurricane never stick around forever. Eventually the winds pick up, rain slaps you in the face and before you know it you're like the Wicked Witch of the East, with only your feet sticking out from under a house.

(Hey, hurricane/tornado . . . same diff.)

I stumbled into the house after cleaning old Mrs. Gomez's house (she has four cats, and you sooo don't want to know the rest of that story). Once a month I went into that house a normal (seminormal) human being and came back out again a changed woman. If I ever own that many cats, somebody shoot me.

At any rate, I was tired, crabby and spitting cat hair like you wouldn't believe—I swear, all four of those animals wait until I arrive to shed enough hair to build three more cats. It was in my lungs, up my nose, in my hair and all over my clothes. I smelled like demon spray and litter box, and all I wanted was a *huge* glass of white wine, a big dinner and a good dream.

Was that too much to ask?

Must have been. Because what I got was Jasmine.

"The news isn't good, Cassidy," she said, like I'd expected her to tell me I'd just won Publishers Clearing House or something. The woman never had good news. What? I should be surprised?

"Shock, gasp," I said, rummaging in the fridge for the wine. With wine all things were survivable. Since Brady'd been there, we actually had *stuff* in the refrigerator. Edible stuff. Which was great, but made the wine hunt that much more complicated.

"This is serious," Jasmine said in her stern, will-you-please-pay-attention voice.

"Aha!" Triumphant, I stood up and held the chilled bottle aloft. When I noticed my gray-haired nemesis wasn't sharing the joy, I sighed. "When isn't it serious, Jasmine?"

"I will get you a glass," Brady said, snagging the bottle from my hand.

Jasmine's beady blue eyes followed Brady for a sec, then shifted back to me. "I need to speak to you, *alone*, about something terribly important."

Brady stopped and looked at her. "Vanessa?"

Jasmine didn't want to answer, but did anyway. She loved having the stage. "Yes."

"Well, then," I said, slumping down into a kitchen chair. "No point in keeping it a secret from Brady."

This clearly frosted Jasmine's cookies. "In case you've forgotten, he tried to seduce you into giving up your powers."

I glanced at him and he smiled. "Yeah," I said, "but he didn't actually do it."

Jasmine sucked in air through gritted teeth, and I thought I heard her say, "Give me strength."

Who did demons pray to, anyway? A question for the ages. But not one for now. I accepted the glass of wine from Brady and took a long, grateful sip. Then I fished a cat hair out of the wine. *Yeesh.*

Thea and Sugar came in the back door, and I watched Jasmine's frown deepen.

"Hi, Mom," Thea said, then looked at Brady. "You ready to practice?"

Sugar came running over to greet me; then, with a look of horror on her hair-covered face, she changed her mind, dropped and skidded on her butt, and slammed into the wall to avoid touching me in any way. This happened every time I cleaned Mrs. Gomez's house. Sugar did *not* like the smell of cat. And she always managed to look at me as if I'd cheated on her or something.

"Relax," I assured her. "The smell will go away." *Please, God.*

"Your mother and Jasmine and I must speak first, Thea," Brady said solemnly.

"Is this about the queen?" Thea asked.

"Yep," I said, taking another sip and letting the cold, tart liquid slide down my throat. I pulled a cat hair from my mouth and flicked it onto the floor. Sugar shivered.

"Perhaps this would be best done somewhere else," Jasmine repeated, giving me the hairy eyeball.

"Give it up, Jasmine," I said, and slumped low in my seat, stretching my feet out in front of me. "Brady and Thea are in this too. They might as well know what's going on."

"Of course we're in this," Thea said, and dropped into a chair beside Jasmine. "The demons are, like, everywhere all of a sudden, and on the queen's Web site the reward for Mom is up to forty-five thousand dollars." She pushed her hair back from her face. "Besides, I'm almost an adult. Didn't I help Mom fight off that demon just yesterday?"

True. Okay, my routine had had a couple of bumps in the road. Like the demon that had been hiding in my hydrangea bush when I got home from work the day before. I'd taken to wearing my demon spray hooked on a belt loop on my jeans, and felt pretty much like a gunslinger in an old Western movie. I was minding my own business when this tall, skinny demon unfolded himself from under the dead and or dying hydrangea and hissed at me.

Now, I get that they're demons, but is all the hissing really necessary? I mean think about it. Demon equals bad guy. We already know this. (Okay, not all of 'em are bad, but 99.999999999 percent are bad, so a little profiling really isn't out of line.) So my point is, if we know you're evil and everything, do you really need to hiss and snarl every time you show up? If you're going to try to kill me, just do it already and spare me the theatrics! Jeez.

So Tall and Skinny reached out one arm that had to be five feet long, and before I could even think about it, he plucked my demon spray bottle off and tossed it over his shoulder as if it were salt and he were making a wish.

I just stood there like a big dummy. Well, until he ran at me waving those bony arms as though he were thinking about actually touching me. And I've got to draw the line somewhere. My first Demon Duster instinct was to scream. Loudly. And jump back out of the demon's reach. Then I wanted my spray. And a hammer.

"This was too easy, Duster," he muttered, and I told myself, *You know, it really was.* I *had* to start paying more attention to my surroundings.

When one of his long-fingered, black-nailed hands grabbed at me, though, I erupted out of my fugue state. I started swinging, throwing feet and fists at whatever I could reach.

It was hissing and spitting, and I was shrieking like a big girl and trying to stay one step ahead of it.

All my screaming turned out to be a good thing. Thea had raced out of the house carrying an iron skillet (the new one Brady bought online). She'd clonked old Reptile Boy in the head, and while he was distracted, I ripped his heart out.

Tag-team dusting.

Makes a mom so proud.

"She's right," I told Jasmine, with a smile for my daughter. No, I didn't really want her involved in this dusting thing; it was hard enough to imagine that one day she'd be stuck with the gig on her own. But I had to give her credit: She had a hell of a backhand. "Thea did great yesterday, and since she's going to have to deal with all this demon crapola at some point in her life, she might as well be in on it from the ground floor."

Thea looked too pleased, so I added, "As long as she stays out of the actual fights."

Now *she* scowled at me. Spreading sunshine and joy, that's me.

Brady stood beside me like a brave little soldier, hands behind his back, chin lifted, as if waiting for one of us to order him to his death.

Men are such drama queens.

"Fine, fine." Jasmine huffed out a disgusted breath and caved to the inevitable. She folded her hands on top of her ugly-ass vinyl purse and looked at me. "Vanessa is marshaling her forces. Amassing an army."

I waited, but she didn't say anything else. This was the big announcement? "Well, *duh*. That's not exactly a news flash, Jasmine. We all knew she was going to be pissed off about us rescuing Brady. She was bound to get her little demons together."

I sounded really brave, despite the fact that my stomach was twisting itself into knots. Hey, I was in no hurry to meet the queen one-on-one again. I still had vivid memories of the beating she had given me.

"She's using the beach caves Judge Jenks once used."

"Of course she is," I said. "Get one demon out and another one moves in. What is it with those guys and the beach?" I wondered.

"What's she going to do?" Thea asked, and her voice sounded so small, I thought for a minute that Jasmine might have been right. Maybe it hadn't been such a good idea to include Thea in this little chat.

Then Jasmine started talking again, and it was too late to change the game plan.

"She's planning an assault on the town."

"Mooooooommmmmmm . . ." Thea's eyes went wide.

"This is not good," Brady said.

"Crap," I said. An assault on the town. With only me to stand in her way? *Great.* Let's count the ways *this* was going to suck.

Jasmine nodded, and her eyes were more worried than I'd ever seen them before. It didn't exactly thrill me or fill me with confidence to know that my trainer was concerned. "My source tells me she plans to attack on Halloween night."

Even the air in the kitchen seemed to go still. Everyone was so quiet, I heard Sugar's heavy breathing and the ticking of the clock on the wall. Late-afternoon sunshine streamed in through the shining windows and lay across the table, highlighting the familiar faces all turned toward me as if expecting me to come up with something brilliant.

Me?

I licked my lips, picked a cat hair off and said, "That's just not right." I took a quick gulp of wine to ease the sudden tightness in my throat. Stupid, I know. I hear that a crazy, killer demon is planning to take over the world and I'm pissed off because she's planning to do it on Halloween. But come on . . . "Kids, costumes, candy. She can't ruin Halloween."

"More than your holiday will be ruined, Cassidy." Jasmine's voice sounded like she was at a funeral. *Oooh.*

Not a good image.

The crisp, cold wine wasn't going to do it for me tonight. I needed margaritas. A truckload of 'em. And nachos. With sour cream. Maybe guacamole. I settled for my wine.

Shaking my head, I said exactly what I was thinking and tried not to acknowledge the fear in Thea's eyes. If I did, I'd have to acknowledge the fear in *me*, and I so didn't want to do that. Cassidy Burke, queen of the mental block.

"She's already beaten me once. I don't know how you think I'm going to be able to stop her this time."

"We will think of something," Jasmine said, though she didn't exactly sound like she believed it. "We have time."

"Yeah. A week." I nodded. "Sure. We can do a lot in a week." Like move to Brazil. Change our names. Hide under a rug in Brazil. I'd have to take Carmen with us, though. I didn't speak Spanish. Or was it Portuguese?

I felt Brady's hand come down on my shoulder in quiet solidarity. I appreciated it; I just didn't want to have to think about that not only was the town, happy in its ignorance of all things Vanessa, counting on me, but so was Brady. He'd come to me for sanctuary—or to steal my powers, whatever—and if I didn't win, his future wasn't looking any brighter than La Sombra's.

Waiter? More wine!

I looked across the table at Thea and forced a smile I didn't feel. "It's okay, baby. We'll figure something out."

"How?" she demanded. Closing in on sixteen years old, Thea didn't buy my easy answers anymore. Damn shame, too.

"I don't know yet," I admitted, and sat up straight, plucking at a stray cat hair on my boob. "But I'll think of something." I looked at Jasmine. "We'll think of something. Right?"

"Of course," she said, but I thought I heard her mutter something about a snowball in Hell.

Feel the love.

I stood up and walked to the wine bottle on the counter. Pouring myself another glass, I looked at Brady and said, "You and Thea had better get with the practicing. Tryouts are in a couple days, right?"

My darling daughter looked at me as if I were crazy. But I wanted her to put this out of her head. Go concentrate on good stuff. Be a kid. No reason why she should have to obsess on this situation when she wasn't even old enough to have some wine to take the edge off.

"Mom . . ."

"Go on, Thea. There's nothing to do about this queen thing at the moment, so just forget about it for now. Go practice. Be a cheerleader. Make Sister Mercy crazy." I grinned. "Do it for me."

E

If Vanessa was planning on killing me, I needed highlights. Damned if I was going to die with roots showing.

The next day I called Castle Hair and begged, whined and pleaded until Cindy Fergus finally surrendered and promised to squeeze me in that afternoon.

Castle Hair had been in La Sombra for more than fifty years. Cindy's grandma started the shop, working out of the basement in her house. When her daughter took over she'd rented a store on Hill Street with an option to buy. By the time Cindy took over from her mom, they owned the shop free and clear.

Castle Hair had made its reputation in town with three generations of women. When I was a kid I'd had my bangs cut there, and one summer a disastrous pixie cut (didn't even want to *think* about Pixies anymore) had scarred me for life. But I got over it.

I had gone to school with Cindy. At St. Paul she'd been the

"good" girl. The one who never talked in Mass, got all As, had Father Dowd telling her mother that Cindy should be a nun and protected her virginity as if she were Saint Maria Goretti.

I, on the other hand, was the bad girl. The one who got detention for rolling her uniform skirt until it was practically a mini, smoked cigarettes in the bathroom (only the one time, because I accidentally set fire to the trash can when I threw the damn thing away, and the fire department was not amused), and I sneered when Father Dowd told me I was going to hell for suggesting that maybe Jesus had had a real life that probably included dating. Not to mention the whole getting-pregnant-at-sixteen thing.

So Cindy and I didn't really cross paths all that often in school. Still, she was the best hair person I'd ever seen, and she wasn't nearly as churchy as she used to be. Life had taught her a few things since then. She married Mike Fergus, the hero of St. Paul's basketball team, right out of high school, had two kids, and then Mike left her for a lounge singer named Darrin.

Guess Cindy realized not everything could be solved with an extra rosary.

Anyway, we sort of bonded over the single-mother thing and had become friends over the years. So while Cindy was working on a client, I took a seat at the shampoo bowl and looked around. Every time I moved my head I heard the rustle of the aluminum foil that was stacked all over my hair like shiny shingles. I'd had a glass of wine and a couple of fudge drop cookies. I'd been pampered and treated like a girl (nice for a change), and now I was ready to be finished.

It felt good to have a little normal in my life, though, you know? The scents of hair dye, perfume and burned coffee filled the air. Female conversation drifted through the room, with a couple of older women shouting at each other from under the hair dryers.

Cindy had redecorated since taking over from her mom,

and now the shop looked like it belonged in Tuscany: ocher walls, huge, dark wood–framed mirrors at every station, and soft enough lighting that everybody looked good. She had a great stereo system set up, too, and you could pretty much judge her mood by which CD she had playing. Right then Madonna was singing, and I knew Cindy was feeling all Woman Power.

When Gina, the shampoo girl, came around the corner with a dark brown towel, I smiled at her. Gina had short, dark brown hair, eyes so thick with eyeliner and mascara she looked as if she were wearing a Lone Ranger mask, and manicured nails at least three inches long.

"Hi, Cass," she said, and wrapped the towel around my neck, tightening it hard enough to make me gag. "Oopsie," she said, and loosened it just enough to let air through my windpipe. Then she lowered my chair, laid my neck on the rim of the black shampoo bowl and turned on the water.

I stared up at her while she slid the foils from my hair.

"So," she asked, "anything new with you?"

New. Hmmm. Demon hunting. Queen avoiding. Faery almost-sex.

"Nope," I said. "You?"

"Actually," Gina said, hitting my scalp with scalding hot water, "yeah."

"Hey! That's hot!" I jolted in my seat, but nobody else heard me over the blow-dryers, standing hair dryers, shouting old women and Madonna hitting a high note.

"Oopsie," Gina said, and blew a purple bubble with her gum. "So, like I was saying, I've got a chance to move to Paris and study hair for six months."

My head was still simmering, so I winced when she hit me with the water again, but it was just right this time, so I closed my eyes and relaxed into it. "That's great. When do you go?"

"Well," she said, massaging my head until I wanted to purr, "first I need to come up with some quick cash."

"Ah." I folded my hands over my belly. "Got any ideas on how to do that?"

"One," she said, and grabbed my chin, dragging my head further into the bowl.

Yikes! Shampoo girl goes psycho!

While I was struggling, she shifted the spray hose to shoot it right up my nose, and suddenly I was sitting in a chair, fully clothed, and about to drown!

My eyes flew open, and I had to squint to see past the splashing water, but I looked into Gina's brown eyes and watched them turn a glowy red. *Not* good. I was choking and gagging and fighting every instinct I had that was telling me to take a breath before I died.

Gina had her upper body pressing over me, holding me into the chair, and I was flailing my arms around, looking for something to hit. I was practically standing on my head in the sink, and the water was gushing into me, clogging my throat, cutting off all air.

Gina had a hell of a grip, too. Must come from the years of shampooing everybody in La Sombra. Funny, all the people around town I'd squirted with demon spray in the last month and I'd never stopped into Cindy's.

Why? Because it was so damn hard to get an appointment!

The roar of the water filled my ears, so I only barely heard Gina saying, "I really like you, Cass. Honest. It's just . . . well, it's nothing personal."

Well, it felt damn personal to *me*!

"I mean, you're really great." She lowered the hose closer to my face, pushing water higher up my nose, filling my mouth and throat. Little black dots sparkled at the edges of my vision. "You always tip me, not like *some* people, but the queen's offering big money for you, and I really *need* it."

So *my* dead body was gonna sponsor *her* trip to Paris? Oh, I didn't think so! My mind was fogging over, my chest was tight and hot water was pouring up my throat in a flood. Finally, though, I came out of my damsel-in-distress mode and found Duster power.

Gargling, groaning, spitting, coughing, I thrashed around like a crazy person, then managed to land a blow to Gina, slamming her off balance enough to make her stumble back a step or two. Before she found her balance again, I pushed out of the chair, dripping wet, my hair hanging down in my eyes. I spit out a mouthful of water and slapped my right hand into her chest. Her eyes went wide and horrified when I ripped out her heart and let her explode.

What was left of Gina mixed with the water on the floor and made a nasty little mud puddle at my feet.

That was when I noticed the quiet in the shop. I swung my wet hair out of my face and shot an arc of water droplets across the room. A couple of them caught Cindy dead in the face as she stared at me.

"Do you know how hard it is to find a good head massager?" she asked.

"Hey, she tried to drown me."

"Damn demons." One of the old women under the dryer sniffed. "Can't trust 'em."

"*You're* a demon, you dumb bunny," her friend snapped.

The first old woman sniffed again. "The young ones. Just can't trust 'em. They get uppity."

Uppity demons.

"Damn it, Cass," Cindy said, coming closer. "Look at that mess."

I glanced down at Gina's mud and couldn't feel bad. Better her dead than me dead. But still, I did make a mess. "I can clean it up. . . ."

"Never mind." Cindy waved a hand, then stepped in closer and peered at my hair. "The highlights look good. But you'll have to shampoo yourself now. My other shampoo girl's off today."

I shrugged. "I can do that."

&

Two days later I was back at school.

The gym at St. Paul High School smelled like sweat socks and raspberry lip gloss. Weird combination, let me tell you.

Brady and I took a seat on the bottom row of bleachers, with Zoe Cohen right behind us, watching the girls trying out for cheerleader. The first part of tryouts was simple enough. They lined up all the wannabes and had them do cartwheels and jumps (too bad Thea wouldn't get her Duster jumping abilities until way too late to help out in this department) and splits. Each of the girls dropped into a neat split, and the insides of my thighs screamed in sympathy.

But I smiled anyway, because Thea was looking good. Yes, her jumps weren't very high, but she didn't knock anybody over with her cartwheel (unlike a little brunette who was now dissolved in tears).

The kids and parents on the bleachers broke into applause as the girls came off the gym floor to wait for their names to be called. The group portion of the tryouts was over. Now came the hard part: Every girl had to perform, alone, in the middle of the gym with God and everyone watching.

"Am I late?" Logan rushed in and pushed his way into a seat beside me. He smiled at Thea as she came over to join us.

"You came," she said, giving him a big grin.

"Wouldn't miss it," Logan said, leaning across me to give Thea's hand a squeeze.

"Almost, though," I muttered.

He looked at me and shrugged. "I skipped out on a case. I've only got about a half hour; then I'm gonna have to bolt."

Staring at him, I had to give Logan points. He'd been an official father for only a month, and he was trying his best. He knew how important all this was to Thea, and he'd made a point to be here. *Damn it.*

How was I supposed to keep my guard up when he went behind my back and made my kid happy?

Thea sat between Brady and me, hands fisted in her lap, concentration furrowing her brow as she watched the first girl performing the original routine they all had had to create for tryouts.

"Dani's pretty good," Thea whispered when she leaned into me.

"You are better," Brady assured her.

Not to be outdone, Logan said, "You can beat her, Thea. I've seen you practicing."

Who hadn't? I thought.

"He's right," Zoe said. "You're way better than Dani. Look at that; she can't even smile and jump at the same time."

I sort of empathized with Dani. I couldn't jump and smile at the same time, either.

"Don't worry about it," I said, patting Thea's knee. "You're gonna knock 'em dead, baby girl."

"I hope so." Thea's gaze drifted to the other side of the bleachers, where Mr. Football, Ryan Butler, was sitting. He gave her the thumbs-up, and her eyes glittered with happiness.

Oh, boy.

Logan caught their little exchange and growled, but I ignored him.

Thea wanted this so badly, I was cringing inside. It's much easier to take disappointment for yourself than to watch someone you love go through it. And frankly, Thea had always succeeded at everything she'd ever done, so she had no experience with failure. I, on the other hand, had all kinds of experience with failure.

Then I caught the eye of Sister Mercy (Merciless the Evil), who glared at me—letting me know that Thea's ruining her brain and future by trying out for cheerleader was all my fault. One of these days I was going to spray that woman. Even if she wasn't a demon, it would feel good.

I pushed crabby nuns and nasty demons out of my mind and concentrated on Thea. I thought about praying, then realized that if I did, the chances were good that I'd bring the walls of this Catholic school gym crumbling down around us. Catholic-lites who actually *pray* run terrible risks.

"Elle Franklin," one of the judges called out.

I recognized the name and watched as the Peeping Thomasina I'd caught in my driveway the other night headed out into the middle of the floor. When she flew into her routine I started getting a little prickle of unease.

That prickle grew fast. I recognized that routine. Hell, I could probably perform it myself, I knew it so well.

"Damn," Logan muttered. "This is not good."

"Uh-oh," Zoe said from behind me.

"Pixie spittle," Brady whispered.

"Mom," Thea said, her voice shaking, "Elle stole my routine."

Crap.

Chapter Eighteen

Thea scuttled out of the gym, and the rest of us were right behind her. Logan looked like he needed somebody to punch. Zoe was muttering words I was pretty sure Rachel didn't even know her daughter *knew*, and I was right there with the kid.

That miserable little cheating cheer-creep had *stolen* Thea's original routine.

Who knew how many nights she'd been standing at our backyard fence watching Brady and Thea practice? Who knew how long she'd been planning this?

God, I hoped she was a rotten little demon so I could dust her ass.

"I can't believe this," Thea said, walking in circles. "I totally can't believe this. It was PERFECT. My routine was GREAT, and now Elle's using it and I'm going to look like the one who stole it from HER."

"Are there not *rules*?" Brady demanded.

"Yes, there are rules," I said, talking to him, but going to Thea. "Some people just cheat; that's all."

Watery sunshine shone down from a cloud-filled sky. The muffled roar of traffic out on the main street filtered to us from a distance, and from inside the gym came the sound of applause as Elle displayed Thea's routine. Looking into my baby girl's eyes, I felt her disappointment and hurt for her more than she could ever possibly hurt for herself.

There was nothing I wanted more than to march into that

gym, grab Elle by her hair and thunk her head against the gleaming wood floor a few hundred times.

Thea turned wide, blue, tear-filled eyes up to me. "Mom, what'm I supposed to do now?" She shook her head and her long black hair swung out behind her like a battle flag at half staff. "I can't go out there and do my routine now. Maybe I shouldn't be a cheerleader. I was happy before. I'm the captain of the math team. I don't need to be doing this. Maybe Sister Mercy was right. . . ."

I actually saw red.

Then in memory I saw Sister's sneering face telling me that Thea shouldn't splinter her focus. Suddenly I wanted Thea to be a damn cheerleader more than she'd ever wanted it. Nobody was going to put my girl in a niche and keep her there. She could do whatever she wanted. *Be* whoever she wanted. If anybody tried to stop her, they'd have to deal with me.

"Bull," I told her.

"Huh?"

I frowned. "Are you going to let that girl do this to you?"

"Really, Thea. That beyotch soo does not deserve to win," Zoe piped up.

I let that go. (Hey, Elle *was* a beyotch.) I dropped both hands to Thea's shoulders and looked her in the eye. "You can beat her, baby girl. You just have to believe you can do it."

"Your mom's right, Thea," Logan said, and put one arm around her shoulders to give her a quick hug.

"But she's using MY ROUTINE." A single tear rolled down her cheek and seared my heart. Seconds later, though, she swiped the tear away with one impatient hand, and I knew she was starting to get mad. Good. She'd need that to pull this off.

"We can change the routine," Brady said, moving up beside me. "Just enough to make it different."

"How?" Thea looked up at him, hope and resignation at war in her eyes.

From inside the gym more applause rolled out and slapped at us. Apparently the routine was a big hit. Thea grimaced and seemed to slump into herself.

"Is there time?" Logan asked.

Good question.

"When will it be your turn?" Brady asked.

"I'm last," Thea said, her voice a whisper. "We drew names before we started, so there are still five girls ahead of me."

"Good." Brady took Thea's arm, looked at me and said, "We will be back in time."

"Where are you . . ." But they were already gone, Brady whizzing Thea off to the track surrounding the football field.

I looked at Logan, then Zoe, who shrugged. *Right.* "Okay, then. While they're gone, Logan, Zoe . . . let's keep an eye on the competition."

We waited at the back of the gym, just inside the doors. Kids in the bleachers were clapping time and shouting encouragement to their favorites as girl after girl did her best to impress.

Was this payback for all the times I'd made fun of cheerleaders in high school? Was karma giving me a kick in the ass? Did it matter?

Logan checked his watch and his pager, then focused on the gym floor.

"Do you have to leave?" I asked, expecting him to make his excuses and get to work.

"Supposed to," he admitted. "But no way am I leaving until after Thea's tryout."

If he kept doing things like this, touching my heart with the way he loved our daughter, I was in danger of becoming a real marshmallow. I couldn't help smiling at him, and while I was feeling the warmth sliding through me, I told him, "You're a good dad, Logan."

His eyes went soft in pleased surprise. "Thanks, Cassie," he said, but when he might have said more, I patted his arm and turned my attention back to the gym floor.

I was busy cracking mental knuckles and chewing on mental fingernails. Zoe kept up a running commentary on each girl.

"That's Doanna Fredericks. She's such a cow. Totally mean, and forever talking about her uncle who knows Justin Timberlake. As if." I nodded but Zoe kept going. "And Carrie Hastings is completely uncoordinated."

Carrie tripped on her own shoelace and did a face-first sprawl in front of the judges—I was guessing Thea didn't have to worry about *her*.

Girl after girl performed and left the floor, and time kept ticking past. I was wound so tight I felt like I was going to *sproing* loose and ricochet off the walls of the gym if this didn't end soon.

There was only one girl left to perform when Thea and Brady finally raced into the gym and stopped alongside us.

"Well?" I demanded, looking from my girl to Brady and back again.

Thea's eyes were bright, and she was practically vibrating with excitement. Whatever she and Brady had come up with, it looked like it was working for her.

"I'm soooo ready, Mom," she said, flashing a smile toward Brady.

"Excellent," Zoe said.

"Go get 'em, Thea," Logan said.

"Thea Burke." The announcement was loud on the crackly microphone system and instantly caught all of our attention.

"OH, GOD." This from Thea, who went suddenly wide-eyed, fight-or-flight panic-stricken.

"Go, baby; you can do it," I said, and hoped I sounded way more sure than I felt. I've mentioned before that Thea's athletic abilities weren't much better than mine. Yes, she'd worked like a dog for a couple of weeks trying to make this squad. But were her splits and jumps going to be enough? Or would I be stopping on the way home at Sun and Shadow bakery for doughnuts to take the sting out of defeat?

God, I hate tension.

"You will be wonderful, Thea," Brady said. "You will show these other girls that you are the perfect cheerleader."

"Totally," Zoe crowed.

Thea nodded, pulled in a deep breath and plastered the phoniest smile I'd ever seen on her face. Nodding frantically she said, "Okay. I'm okay. I'm good. I'm . . ."

"Ready," Brady finished for her, and clapped his hands together. He rubbed his palms hard, then held his hands, palms down, over Thea's head. I saw Faery dust sparkle brightly, then settle over Thea.

"What the hell is that?" Logan demanded.

"Tell you later," I whispered.

Meanwhile, Thea took a deep breath and then smiled, relaxed.

Faery dust? Good stuff.

"Thea Burke?" The voice over the microphone sounded confused. And impatient.

She jolted a little, whispered, "Good luck to me," then turned around and walked into the middle of the gym all by herself. God, she looked so young and so alone. The crowd was quiet, just the usual stirrings of feet on bleachers and a low-pitched murmur as kids talked to each other.

I wanted to rush out after Thea, grab her and carry her out of there. Take her back home, where she'd never have to perform up to someone else's expectations ever again. My kid was *great*. She had nothing to prove to anybody. Why had I thought this was a good idea? Letting her put herself in the position of being judged by *other* kids?

Oh, good God.

"Christ," Logan admitted in a softly pitched whisper. "I'm actually nervous."

Funny, but hearing him—and knowing he meant it—made me feel better. About Thea. About Logan. I smiled up at him and enjoyed the little flash of solidarity we had going.

I'd been a single mom since the beginning. Of course, when Thea was little my dad was there, and he had been amazing. Once he'd gotten over the disappointment of finding his sixteen-year-old daughter pregnant he'd been an absolute rock. And he'd been totally nuts over Thea, so I guess I hadn't really been completely on my own. But it had felt like that a lot of the time.

I'd watched Rachel and Simon together with Zoe and envied them that sharing: the two of them together raising their daughter. When I wasn't pissed off about Logan being married to somebody named Sparky, I'd wonder what it would have been like to have him around. To have him watch Thea grow up with me.

Like on the nights when Thea was sick and I slept on the floor next to her bed, just in case she needed me. Or the day she rode her bike for the first time and she'd turned around to flash me a triumphant smile—just before crashing. Or the time she got her first A on a math test.

Through all of those milestones, it had been just me and Thea. We hadn't really missed having Logan as part of our lives because we'd never experienced it in the first place. But now that he was here, standing next to me, and we were together at last for one of Thea's big moments . . . it made me think about how different things might have been.

Not that I'd change anything, you understand. But a woman can't help wondering.

I looked up at Logan and found him smiling at me, and something inside me turned over. I didn't want to look at it too closely, though, because I still wasn't sure that starting up with Logan again would be a good idea.

Then Brady leaned in on my other side and said, "She will win," and my misty-watercolored-memory moment was shattered.

I glanced at Brady and noted the satisfaction in his eyes. Then I shot a look at Thea, standing there in front of the whole school—not to mention the table where the cheer squad sat making notes on the tryouts—waiting for her moment, and a niggling sense of suspicion rose up inside me. I turned my back on Logan, grabbed a fistful of Brady's shirt and dragged him away a step or two. Leaning in, I narrowed my eyes on him and demanded, "Did you put a spell or something on Thea?"

He blinked those big baby blues at me. "I do not understand."

I wasn't buying it. "Ha! You understand plenty." My eyes went even squintier, and he looked a little worried. "Helping Thea is one thing," I said, poking him in the chest with the tip of my index finger, "but she wouldn't like winning if you helped her cheat to do it."

Brady looked absolutely as appalled and insulted as any Faery possibly could. He drew himself up, looked down his long, straight nose at me and said, "There are rules. We do not cheat."

Hmm.

But then Thea's routine started, and I spun around to watch and focus good thoughts on her. The gym was huge, and my girl looked awfully small out there. But once she started moving, calling out that stupid *Funky chicken, loosey-goosey* chant, it was like she *owned* the place.

There were no nerves. Just a big smile, plenty of confidence and, hey, actual rhythm! She jumped, she whirled, she pumped her fists in the air, and her long hair swirled out around her like a cape in a high wind. She moved fast, every step sure. I noticed that she and Brady had changed a few steps of the routine, just enough so that it was a little different—a little better than the original had been. (Take *that* and stuff it, Elle!) Thea's voice was loud and proud, and just a few seconds after starting she had the crowd behind her, too.

The kids in the bleachers were cheering and clapping. Logan was grinning. Zoe was already doing a victory two-step beside me, and Brady looked like a Tony-winning choreographer, just waiting to accept his trophy. Me? I was happy and nervous and proud and scared and pretty much just holding my breath, waiting for it to be over.

When Thea hit her last cartwheel, then launched into a handspring ending in a split, arms raised and big grin shining, I lost it.

"Woo-hoo!!!!"

My voice was lost in the roar of approval from the crowd, and I took a second to wonder if maybe Mr. Football had filled the bleachers with his pals to ensure that Thea got a standing ovation. But then I figured it didn't matter. All that mattered at that moment was that Thea had done it. She'd gone after something she wanted and had beaten her own fears into submission.

Hell, if she didn't make cheerleader, I wouldn't care. I was so proud of her at that moment, I wanted to find Merciless the Evil and say, "Nyah-nyah-nyah-nyah-nyah!"

Brady swooped me up in a fierce hug, and then Logan pried me out of his arms for another hug, and just for a second I felt like a dried-up wishbone and worried about snapping in two. Then I relaxed into Logan's hug and hugged him back.

"She was awesome!" he said, and dropped me to my feet.

"Was there any doubt?" I countered—hey, come on. I wasn't going to admit to *my* doubts!

Thea raced up and flew into my arms, squeezing me hard. "I did it, Mom. I actually *did* it!"

"You were great, baby girl!" I cupped her face in my palms and knew I'd always remember that look on her face. The shining glory beaming from her eyes. The happy, proud smile.

And when she hugged her dad, and I saw how much it meant to him, I was even gladder Logan had been there to enjoy it.

Maybe I was growing as a person.

"Oh, man," Thea said, turning to me while she blew out a relieved breath. "I'm so glad that's over."

"Me too, baby," I said. Honest to God, I didn't remember being that nervous and scared facing down a demon! Performance anxiety was a real bitch.

Out on the gym floor the cheerleading squad was huddled around the score table, comparing notes, having a whispered conversation while they decided who was going to be their newest member. The kids in the bleachers shifted restively, and the tension in the gym ratcheted up a notch or two. I hoped those girls added up the points fast, because I didn't think Thea could stand the suspense much longer.

She grabbed my hand and threaded her fingers through mine, holding on tight. I squeezed back and held my breath as one of the cheerleaders stood up and walked to the microphone. Everyone in the gym got quiet and waited.

"We've got our new cheerleader," the tiny blonde said, her voice so peppy it almost hurt to listen to it. "She's . . ."

Thea took a breath and closed her eyes.

Logan dropped one hand on her shoulder.

Zoe closed her eyes, too, and started murmuring. Praying?

Brady rocked on his heels, arms crossed over his chest, beaming at all of us like Father Christmas.

Me? I was in a zone, just hoping.

The blonde dragged it out for as long as she could, then shouted, "Thea Burke!"

Applause, applause.

Thea squealed and hugged me, then her father, then Brady, then Zoe, and before she was finished, Ryan Butler had made a leap from the bleachers and swooped in to grab a hug for himself.

And I was so pleased for Thea, I didn't even mind.

Well, not much, anyway.

After that it was sort of a blur of activity. Thea went out to join her new team, Ryan went off to football practice with a herd of testosterone-laden pals, Zoe went up to sit with some friends. The other kids in the gym started milling around, not anxious to go back to class, and Logan grabbed my arm.

"I've gotta go back to work," he said, and flashed a look at his daughter, surrounded by hopping, happy cheerleaders. "Tell Thea I'll see her later, okay?"

"Sure. And, Logan," I said, before I could talk myself out of doing a nice thing, "it means a lot to Thea that you were here."

One corner of his mouth tipped up, and he bent to give me a quick, hard kiss. "That must have stung, telling me that," he said. "But I appreciate it."

"I know." Brady came up behind me. Even if I hadn't felt his presence, I would have known by the way Logan's smile faded and his eyes narrowed. "Look, I'll, uh, bring dinner over tonight, okay? We can celebrate."

"I will be making dinner," Brady said.

"I said I'll *bring* dinner," Logan told him.

Wow. Two gorgeous men threatening to feed me. Could life get much better than that?

"You bring dinner," I told Logan, then looked up at Brady. "You make dessert."

That way I won.

"Fine," Logan muttered, then kissed me again, as if proving to Brady that he could. Then he left, hurrying out of the gym to go and make La Sombra safe again.

When we were alone I looked up at Brady and asked, "So,

what exactly did you do for Thea with that last-minute routine change?"

"You are worried, Cassidy, but you have no need to." He shrugged and smiled. "I gave her only confidence in herself. And a little extra Faery dust to make her shine and sparkle."

I shifted my gaze to Thea standing in the middle of a crowd of laughing girls, and knew that whatever Brady had done, I owed him. Even while I was thinking that, Thea ran toward me and skidded to a stop just inches away.

"Mom, a bunch of us want to go to Tully's for pizza. To, you know, celebrate and everything . . ."

"Who's a 'bunch' of us?" I asked. Hey, still a mom, here. Had to keep up.

"The rest of the squad," she said, hugging a grin close. "And some of the guys from the football team will meet up with us there after practice. . . ."

Here we go.

"Like Ryan?"

"Well . . ."

"You're not allowed to date until you're sixteen," I reminded her, though I had plans to push that off until she was thirty-five.

"It's not a date," she argued. "It's a *group*. And you're the one who said a 'group' is totally fine."

Uh-huh. Hey, I was the master of the glib story. When I was her age—you know, before I was pregnant—I had more moves than *Dancing with the Stars*. So I knew she and Ryan would no doubt be hooking up at Tully's. As long as she knew I knew that she knew, we'd be okay.

"All right," I said, already digging into my black Coach bag for my wallet. I pulled out a twenty and handed it over. "You can go to Tully's and celebrate. But be home for dinner. Your father's coming over and he'll want to see you."

"Fabulous!" Thea grinned huge, leaped up and hugged me,

took an extra minute to hug Brady tight and whisper, "Thank you!" then sprinted back to her new friends.

"She is happy," Brady said.

"She is," I agreed.

"You are happy, too."

"Yeah," I said, looking up at him. "I'm happy, too. Wanna celebrate?"

Ɛ

It wasn't exactly what I'd had in mind, but eating a hot dog and walking along the beach was nice, too. Brady was enjoying himself, and we made sure to walk in the opposite direction from the beach caves where Vanessa was supposedly gathering her army.

Damn. I hadn't wanted to think about the bitch queen of death. Suddenly the hot dog I'd eaten turned to stone, and my stomach was complaining. I slapped one hand to my abdomen, told it to shut the hell up, and concentrated instead on the feel of Brady's arm around my shoulders.

"This is very nice," he said.

"Yeah, it is." But I had a creepy feeling. We were pretty much alone on the sand and prime targets for some demon trouble.

"Not just the beach," Brady said. "Being here with you is nice as well, Cassidy. It has been a long time since I was free to enjoy simple pleasures."

His hand rubbed my upper arm, and spirals of heat started uncoiling inside me. His touch really had a lot of magic in it. When his hand dropped lower to cup my breast, my eyes closed.

"How about we head home now?" I said on a sigh that rippled up from my toes as he tugged at my nipple. Distraction was not a good thing at the moment. Not with that creepy feeling nagging me from the back of my mind.

"I would like that too." Brady turned me around, pulled me in close and kissed me.

More distraction. I didn't know where all of this might have led, because just about then, everything went to shit.

"Duster."

"Damn it." My forehead hit Brady's chest. Then, sliding my bottle of demon spray out of the belt loop where it was hooked, I turned around to face the latest disaster in my life.

Yikes.

He looked like a giant lizard, almost like those velociraptors in *Jurassic Park.* Only without the tiny arms and the weird-ass big feet. Green, pointy head, red glowy eyes and a tail, for chrissakes, poking out of his jeans and swishing back and forth on the sand. (Have I mentioned I don't do reptiles? Snakes, lizards, spiders—yes, I know they're not reptiles, but they're clumped in with the other creepy-crawlies in the world.)

I'd seen some truly ugly-ass demons in the last month, but *this* one was a little too gross for words. I held up my demon spray and readied for the first squirt. Then the damn lizard opened his mouth and a tongue about a mile and a half long shot out of it, wrapped itself around the bottle and tore it from my hand!

"HEY!"

"Oh, CRAP," Brady said, sounding a lot like me.

The lizard guy spit the bottle out, and it lay on the wet sand with the incoming tide pushing at it with every roll of the tiny waves.

"The queen readies for your death," Liz said in a hiss that sounded way too snakelike for me. "But I will kill you first and she will reward me."

"Suck-up." Honest to God, that Web site Vanessa had set up was really starting to piss me off. Wasn't it enough that she had a freaking army? Did she really need to post a reward for me?

"Die, Duster! By my hand, or face the queen!"

To my way of thinking, better the damn queen than a lizard with a tongue that long. That was just too gross for words.

Liz charged, Brady screamed and I leaped straight up. Damn, I was good. When I landed on the sand, Liz had already run past where I'd been, so I was behind him and away from that damned tongue. Worked for me. Before he had time to turn around, I lunged at him and made a grab for his heart. The damn tail ruined that plan.

That hard, scaly tail swept my feet out from under me and sent me sprawling into the water. Icy cold ocean engulfed me for a second while I fought to get my feet under me again. The wet sand sucked me down, and the water tugged at me in an *Outer Limits* kind of way. Liz stalked into the water, splashing sand and spray into the air. The bottle of demon liquid bobbed around on a stray wave like a cork on the end of a fishing line, and I made a grab for it.

Liz screeched loud enough to break eardrums, but I so didn't care. I grabbed that bottle, flopped over onto my back and shot a stream of nasty brownish green liquid right into his glowy red eyes. Then the screeching *really* took off. It lasted only a second or two, though, because while Liz was distracted with all that pain, I reached through his scaly chest and ripped out his nasty heart.

Reptile Boy disintegrated all over me, so I lay back down and let the ocean rinse me off. Cold, but effective. And I only considered floating out with the tide for a moment or two. Then I remembered that fish and other squirmy things lived in that water. As it was, I was probably bathing in fish poop. Well, *that* thought got me moving in a damn hurry.

I scrambled out of the water on all fours and plopped onto dry sand, not even caring about how gross I must look or how all that sand was probably sneaking into all my nooks and crannies.

Then Brady was standing over me. He was wringing his hands, glancing over his shoulder looking for the next attack, and asked, "Is the celebration over? Can we go home now?"

Good idea.

Chapter Nineteen

The day before Halloween arrived and I was out of candy. This happened to me every year. The only thing different this year was how many bags of candy I'd gone through. Six, if you count the M&M's and I don't, really, because they're so damn little they're not really candy at all. They're more candy-light.

Anyway, the upshot was, I had to make a run to the store. Sure, you're thinking Vanessa was going to be attacking on Halloween night, and what were the chances I'd actually have to give out any candy at all to trick-or-treaters? If Vanessa had her way, there wouldn't *be* any kids running around. They'd all be demon chowder.

Oh, God.

I needed candy.

I parked my Bug in front of Von's and ran inside. Candy was probably cheaper over at Target, but at Von's I could get some fried chicken and wine and some cookies. Have I mentioned that I'm a nervous eater? I'm a calm eater, too. Actually, I'm an all-occasion eater. Thank God for the Duster metabolism or I'd be the size of a bus. One of those charter ones with the bathrooms and two stories.

Humming along to the Muzak version of "Like a Virgin," I pushed my cart down the seasonal aisle and grabbed everything I liked. Three Musketeers, Milky Ways and three or four bags of Baby Ruths. No more M&M's. They just weren't worth all the effort.

"Stocking up?"

I spun around so fast I got dizzy and had to hold on to the cart for support. But to be honest, one look into Devlin's eyes and I'd have been dizzy anyway.

"Halloween," I said, and tossed the last of the bags into the cart. "Gotta be ready."

He didn't smile. "I heard about Vanessa."

"Demon grapevine? Impressive." I pushed the cart, headed for the cookie aisle, and Devlin kept pace.

"You're going to face her, aren't you?"

"What? Like I get a choice?"

He grabbed my arm and yanked me to a stop. His grip was tight, his mouth was grim and his eyes briefly flashed red before going dark as night again. "There's always a choice, Cass," he said. "If you face her, she'll kill you."

Gulp. I really didn't want to think about that, because he was right. No way would I be able to win this little contest. Hey, I'd been a Duster for only a month. Vanessa'd been a demon for, like, *ever.*

"You gonna miss me?" I asked, and gave myself points. I didn't sound scared.

"I don't *want* to miss you," he said, and glanced over his shoulder as an old woman tottered down the aisle pushing a cart with a wheel that went WHAPITA, WHAPITA, WHAPITA.

Do they *make* those things broken?

Turning back to me, Devlin lowered his face to mine and said, "I want to help you. Damn it, Cass, you're deliberately shutting me out."

Yeah. I had been. Fine. I can admit it. Devlin had really hurt my feelings when he took Three Boob out for a spin. And I wasn't finished being hurt yet.

"You know," I pointed out as the old woman came a little closer, "I've been pretty busy for the last few weeks. Maybe it's not all about *you*, Devlin. I have a life, you know?"

"The Faery."

"Gaaaahhh . . ." I half shouted, half groaned, and it hurt my throat. "What is it with you and Logan? Leave Brady out of this. This is about *my* life, okay? I've got a daughter, a trainer and a pissed-off demon queen on my ass. Maybe I just don't have time for you to be on it, too."

He let me go and shoved one hand through his hair with enough anger to snatch himself bald, which I totally hoped he didn't do, because Devin has got great hair.

"I don't know what to do for you, Cass," he said as the old woman came up behind him.

"Hello?" she snapped. "Other people need some aisle, you know!"

"Sorry," Devlin muttered, and stepped aside.

"Men shouldn't be let in grocery stores alone. They don't know the rules," she muttered, her purple sneakers squeaking on the linoleum. "Blocking the aisle. Standing there looking stupid. I'm old, you know. I could be dead in a minute."

I rolled my eyes, and Devlin ducked his head to hide a smile. As the crabby old woman moved past me, I reached into my black Coach bag, pulled out my demon spray and gave the back of her head a squirt just for the hell of it.

Smoke lifted off her scalp and twisted in the air-conditioning. *Whoops.*

She stopped and gave me a dirty look. "Duster. Big deal. I've got warts older than you."

"No need to get nasty," I said.

She snorted at me. Old-lady demons and their snorting. She and Jasmine would probably get along great.

"If you're gonna kill me, do it already," she complained. "Otherwise, get outta my way. I need some corn plasters. And some damn fiber. I'm so plugged up, getting dusted would be a vacation."

Ew. "Way too much information."

Devlin kept his head down, but I could see his smile. The old-lady demon paid no attention to either one of us. Just pushed her stupid WHAPITA cart off in a huff.

"Now, why couldn't Vanessa be more like her?"

Devlin's smile faded as he looked at me. "I don't want you to get hurt."

"Me neither." I tore open a bag of Baby Ruths, grabbed one of the little suckers and ripped the paper off. Taking a big bite, I let the caramel and chocolate back me off the emotional ledge.

"You should let me help you."

If I could think of a way for him to help, I would. I'm not an idiot, after all. But when it came down to it, this was going to be mano a mano. Me and Vanessa. She might have an army, but if I could knock off the queen, they might just forget about the whole attacking thing.

Cut me some slack. There is *nothing* wrong with wishful thinking.

"Devlin, if I make it through, we'll talk. Okay? That's the best I've got."

He came up to me, held my face between his hands and gave me a long, hard kiss that had my insides weeping and my outsides going up in flames. When he was finished lighting up my world, he pulled back and said, "Make sure you come through this, then."

"That's the plan." As he walked away, I blindly reached for another candy bar and chewed thoughtfully as I admired the view.

&

"Remember to strike fast," Jasmine said as she took a swing at me in the backyard.

"Really?" I jumped out of the way and landed on the sprinkler. *Ow.* "You mean I shouldn't go really slow?"

Jasmine stopped, took a breath and looked at me for a long, quiet moment. "This will be a dangerous fight, Cassidy."

My hands dropped to my sides and my stomach dropped to my feet. Seeing Jasmine worried and concerned just made me want to drive to Vegas. Or the Grand Canyon. Hell. Anywhere.

"Can I beat her?" I asked, and wanted to bite my own tongue for asking a question I really didn't want the answer to.

"I don't know."

"Well, that's honest, anyway."

"I won't lie to you. . . ."

I just looked at her.

"All right, I *have* lied to you, but not now. This fight is unavoidable. I will help you all I can, but you are the one who must face her. And you must do it at dawn."

Dawn? As in tomorrow morning? Stomach plunging, mouth filling up, brain spinning. So not pretty.

"Her attack will come at sunset," Jasmine said. "Your best hope is to catch her unaware before then."

"Right . . . because if I surprise her, she'll probably just surrender." *Not.*

Jasmine laid one hand on my shoulder. Hell, from the stoic, crabby demon this was almost a hug! "You must win this, Cassidy. For *all* our sakes."

"No pressure, though."

☞

Jasmine was gone, dinner had been eaten, Sugar was in a food coma on the couch and I'd packed Thea off to Zoe's house for a sleepover. Thankfully, Rachel hadn't asked any questions, despite the fact that a school-night sleepover was usually a huge no-no. But if I was getting up at dawn to fight the queen, I wanted Thea safe and far from me, the house and anything that might lead Vanessa right to her.

That was the hardest part of all this: sending my kid off,

not knowing if I'd see her again. I stood at the front window and looked out at the street. Everything was quiet. Logan was home but, thank God, hadn't come over. Lights were on in the Cohen house, and I really hoped that Thea wasn't going to sit up all night worrying.

Like I was.

I couldn't stop thinking about my last fight with Vanessa. How she'd tossed me around like a Frisbee. How she'd beaten me and taken me closer to death than I'd ever been before. And I couldn't help the fear gnawing at my insides.

Nothing had changed. I was still the same brand-new Duster facing off with a demonic wrestler. No way could I win. No way would I come out of this alive.

And no way could I walk away from it, either.

"You are worried," Brady said, coming up behind me.

"Big-time," I agreed, and looked up and over my shoulder at him. "I can't beat her, Brady. She's gonna kick my ass all over the beach, and there's not a damn thing I can do about it. But I have to try. I can't just let her take over the world, can I?"

"No."

"Rhetorical question, but thanks," I said, shaking my head and looking out the window again to my best friend's house—where my daughter was. "But if I die, no one will be here to protect Thea."

"The demons cannot harm her. It is a rule."

"One of 'em tried not too long ago, remember?"

Brady turned me around and wrapped his arms around my waist. "If a demon tries to kill a Duster before her time, the demon dies. The gods will not allow it. Thea will be safe."

"And alone," I said. Sure, she'd have her father, but she wouldn't have *me*.

"You will survive, Cassidy," Brady said.

Oh, God. I wanted to believe him. Seriously. But how could I? No. I needed wine. Or candy. Or . . .

"I will not allow you to be harmed. I will not allow a danger to Thea."

"Nice, but how can you guarantee—"

Brady kissed me. Deep, hungry, tongue-twisting, breath-stealing kissed me. Okay, maybe *this* was what I needed. His arms wrapped tight around me and yanked me in close enough that I felt his Mr. Excitement hard and ready. *Oh, yeah. Orgasm central. Take my mind off dying by lighting up my hoo-hah.*

At the moment? Worked for me.

He scooped his hands up under the hem of my shirt and must have Faery-dusted my bra off, because one moment it was there and the next, gone. I didn't miss it, because Brady's hands were doing its job. And then his mouth.

I've mentioned his mouth before, I know. Brady's a magician with that tongue of his. I stood there swaying, staring up at the living room ceiling and just riding the wahoo of Brady's tongue on my nipples.

"You will survive, Cassidy," he murmured, his breath brushing over my skin, his lips and tongue working me in between words. "You will meet the queen at dawn, as you plan. But tonight you will be here. With me."

"Brady, as good as this feels, maybe . . ." What was I thinking? Was I really going to turn down the comfort, the solace, the *pleasure* he was offering? I felt more alone than I ever had in my life. I was scared, tense and wound so tight I felt as though my insides were nothing more than rubber bands twisted to the point of snapping.

I caught his face in my hands and tipped it up so that I could look into his eyes. What I saw there made me feel better.

He smiled at me, smoothed my hair back and whispered, "We are not meant to be together forever, Cassidy. We both know this. You have love for another and I—" He broke off and shook his head.

Love for another? Did I? Who? Logan? Devlin? Why did Brady know the answers and not me?

"We can give each other tonight, Cassidy. This long night before your battle, you will take all of me."

I looked into his eyes and couldn't think of anywhere else I'd rather be. He was right: We could give each other this one night and worry about tomorrow when it happened. "All right."

I'm not sure how we got to my bedroom, and was it really important? Death by demon in the morning, remember? Didn't I owe myself one last night of happiness? Damn straight.

"Let me touch you," he said, and I was okay with that.

He whooshed my T-shirt off, and there I was, bare boobed for him and hoping *two* would be enough. But in the next instant all of those worries disappeared. Let me just say a focused Faery is a *great* Faery.

Brady buried his face in my chest, moving from one breast to the other in a wild sort of rhythm that had me rocking back and forth on my feet and holding on to his shoulders so I wouldn't fall off the face of the Earth. As it was, it felt as if the floor were wobbling, and I tipped my head back to stare up at my ceiling. Not that I saw it or anything. I slid my hands up and wrapped my fingers in his thick, dark blond hair and held on for all I was worth (meanwhile also managing to hold that mouth to my boobs. I'm no dummy).

But while he nibbled away at me, a voice in the back of my head warned, *You so shouldn't be doing this. You should be training! What are you thinking, getting an orgasm when you have to fight the queen in a few hours?*

Damn it. I didn't want to think, and when Brady ripped my jeans off and covered my hoo-hah with one big hand, I told my mental self to shut the hell up and enjoy the ride. There'd be plenty of time for guilt later—if I survived.

Whoops. No thinking.

Brady pushed two of those magic Faery fingers inside me and I whimpered. (Yes, I'll admit it here. I whimpered and begged for more. There might have been drool.) He smiled against me, nibbled at one of my nipples and then sucked hard while he massaged me on the inside.

Magic fingers, I'm telling you. I felt the buildup inside. There was that coiled tension, that sparkling sense of Happy-land opening the gates. And, boy, was I ready. I rocked my hips on his hand, arched my boob more firmly into his mouth and gave myself up to the goodies awaiting me.

"You're really good at this," I managed to croak. "I mean seriously *good*."

"Your taste fills me and makes me hunger for more." He licked my nipple. "Quiver, Cassidy," he said, pushing his fingers higher, deeper, rubbing that tight little nub with his thumb. "Quiver and come for me. Let me feel you come."

So I did.

I can take direction.

My body imploded, and I'm pretty sure I screeched his name while I shook and trembled and squeezed my thighs around his hand, trapping his touch inside me. Before it was all over, while I was still shaking and sighing, he picked me up and tossed me onto the bed. I landed on the mattress, bounced once, and then Brady was naked and on top of me, pinning me in place.

Good times.

An image of him tied down on Vanessa's bed popped into my head, and I did the quivery thing again. I remembered his lax Mr. Happy, and thinking that, even spent, it was pretty impressive. Let me just say that a hard and ready Brady would have made any woman step back and take a long second to rethink a few things.

"Um . . ." I glanced down at it and thought—briefly—

about changing my mind. *Jesus.* No wonder Vanessa had kept him chained up for a century.

That thing of his deserved its own leash.

"Do not worry, Cassidy," he said, reading my mind, damn it. "All will be wonderful. I will taste you and fill you and make you hunger for me like no other."

Hmm. Already halfway there.

"We will join and our bodies will sing."

Okeydokey.

I was convinced. Okay, I wasn't. Not completely. But I *really* wanted that rock-hard penis inside me. *Badly.*

"Condoms!" I shouted, and held up one hand to keep him and his trained tiger at bay. Hey, give me a point for remembering. Ever since Devlin and I had been seeing each other, I'd been stocking up on the things. *Thank God.*

Brady smiled. "Not necessary, Cassidy. I can protect you."

"Uh-huh." Not that I didn't believe him, but I had more confidence in latex. "They're in the bedside table drawer."

He shrugged, reached over and pulled out a handful. My eyebrows hit my hairline. While I watched he smoothed on a pale green condom, sliding it down the length of him with a slow hand.

My mouth went dry.

"I will have you now," he said, looming over me.

"Promises, promises . . ."

His grin lit up his eyes, and something else occurred to me. "Uh, Brady?"

"Yes?" He stroked his fingertips across my abdomen and everything inside me clutched. *Wow.*

"You're gonna be careful, right? I mean, you won't let my Duster powers slide away from me?"

His easy smile faded as he shook his head. In the pale wash of moonlight streaming through my bedroom window, Brady looked immeasurably disappointed. I hadn't meant to hurt his feelings, but considering whom I had to face in the morning, there was no point in taking chances.

"How could you think I would allow such a thing, Cassidy?"

"I . . . uh . . ." *God.* I sounded like that idiot teenager Elle. "Sorry, but I had to ask. Had to be sure—"

"You have nothing to fear from me," he promised. "I swear this to you with everything I have: You will come to no harm because of me. Never again."

It wasn't just *what* he said; it was *how* he said it. There was a promise in his words, and I accepted it. I reached up for him and took his hand. "I believe you."

"This is good," he said and kissed the palm of my hand before he grinned again and flipped me over onto my stomach. "Now we will have each other."

I lay there, face in the quilt covering my bed, and felt his hands and mouth travel up my spine, then back down again before focusing on my butt. I squirmed a little as sensations started piling up inside me. Greed. Lust. Hunger. And, hey, here came greed again.

I wanted everything he could give me, and I wanted it now. When he grabbed my hips and pulled me up to my knees, I didn't say a word. What could I possibly have said? I just grabbed a couple of handfuls of the quilt and hung on.

He dragged me to the edge of the bed and slid his hands from my hips to my hoo-hah. *Oh, boy.* Both hands rubbed, touched, dipped inside and slid over my wet, slick heat until I was mumbling into the quilt, "Brady, come *on.* Do it. Do it now."

Greed. A very good thing. And I dare you to say you'd have been feeling anything different.

Again and again he stroked me, and when my knees wobbled he steadied me, only to torture me all over again. I was a

woman on the edge. I was ready to jump out of my own skin.
I wanted him, damn it.

And I wanted him *now*.

His fingers opened me, stroking, and I braced myself, taking
a big bite of my quilt. Then he drove into me with one hard
shove that almost pushed me off the bed. I groaned and sucked
in quilt-flavored air. I held on to the bed, bit down harder on
the quilt and backed into him, arching, pushing, swiveling my
hips, driving his body deeper into mine. I wanted to take more
of him, feel him so far inside me that he could wipe away the
last traces of fear still hiding inside me.

He pumped in and out of my body with a rhythm that
sizzled nerve endings and moved my blood so fast and thick, it
was a wonder my heart kept beating. I felt the tension coil and
knew the orgasm I'd been waiting for was almost there. I could
feel it. Taste it. Damn near touch it.

Then he pulled out and flipped me over.

Aaaaarrrrrgggghhhhh!!!!!

"Don't *do* that!" I complained, lifting my hips, demanding
that he get right back to where he left off.

Brady grinned, covered my body and slid his right back
where I wanted it again. "Now we will be one, Cassidy," he
promised, and started moving inside me, setting a new rhythm.
One that rocked my world completely.

Okay, *this* was different.

This was sex like I'd never known before.

It went *way* beyond orgasm time. My eyes glazed over, and
still I could see *his* eyes, glittering wildly. It felt like Brady was
inside me. (Not a pun. I know his penis was inside; this was
more. Try to keep up.) I was trapped in his eyes. Couldn't look
away. Couldn't breathe. Couldn't do anything but lie there and
absorb the magic.

The orgasm crashed down on me, and when my hoo-hah

did the trembly hallelujah thing, I felt something new. Something *amazing*. Something I never could have expected.

My body went wild, erupting with more fire, more sensation than I would have thought existed. I jolted under him, riding an explosion of light and fire and electricity. I held on to him and rode it out, thinking it would never end as wave after wave after wave spilled through me.

Tingles rushed through my bloodstream until it felt as though my veins were in flames, and all around Brady Faery dust shimmered, sparkling in the pale moonlight streaming through my bedroom window. That magical dust fell over me and created a hum of sensation that heated without burning.

Staring up into his eyes, I felt him join me on a much deeper level than penis and hoo-hah. There was so much more. Something rich and strong and damn near miraculous. While I struggled for breath and held his body in mine, my bedroom seemed to glow.

No shit.

Glow.

And the light centered on the two of us. *We* were the light. *We* burned brightly together for a long moment or two, and then slowly that light faded until it was just the moonlight again and Brady was staring down at me.

"What the *hell* just happened?" Points for me just for being able to speak at all after that incredible orgasm.

"We are bonded," Brady said, dipping his head to kiss me long, hard and deep. Deep enough that I'm pretty sure he knew my tonsils better than my doctor did. "I've given you my strength. My power."

Click.

My brain finally caught on. (Not that surprising that it took a minute. Have *you* ever tried to think through an orgasm?

Okay, let me reword that. Lots of us have made grocery lists during sex. But I defy you to do it during Faery sex!)

"The Faery supercharge," I said, idiot savant finally catching on. "The reason Vanessa was holding you captive."

"Yes. I have given that power to you, Cassidy," he said, shifting his hips, making me hungry again as I felt him growing inside me. "After tonight you will be able to defeat Vanessa."

I sucked in air and tried to keep thinking. It wasn't easy. "But . . . how? How do I use the power? How do I defeat—Oh, man . . ."

He sat back and pulled me with him, so our bodies wouldn't disengage. Then he sat me on his lap so I could feel that hard, thick Faery wand all the way through me. "You will know," he promised, cupping his hands over my breasts and flicking my nipples with his thumbs and forefingers.

I squirmed on him like I was settling into a comfy chair—and let me assure you, I was *plenty* comfy.

"For now," Brady said, tugging at my nipples, "we will have the sex. We will merge again and again through the long night, strengthening you for the coming fight."

"We will?" If the next time was anything like the last time, I might not survive the night.

"When the dawn comes," he promised, "you will be ready."

So, if the amazing sex didn't kill me off, I might just stand a shot at taking out Vanessa.

My fogged-up mind reeled when he dropped his hand to the spot where our bodies were joined and gave me a little rub. *Oh, baby.* I swallowed hard and tried for one more lucid thought.

Basically I was looking at a whole night of sex so Brady could fill me with power. Work, work, work. But I was willing to do it . . . for the good of humanity.

Am I a giver or what?

Chapter Twenty

The world was really quiet just before dawn. Who knew? The last time I'd been up this early Thea was eight and she'd been up all night hurling. I remember seeing the first "glorious" rays of dawn through gritty eyes and thinking, *Screw this; I'd rather be asleep.*

I felt the same way now.

Nothing I'd like better than to be back in bed with Brady, pretending that everything was fine and dandy in my little corner of the universe. Instead I was steering my yellow Bug down deserted streets, trying to keep myself from turning around. This whole Duster thing was really turning out to be a huge pain-in-the-ass.

"I soooooooooo don't wanna do this," I whispered, fists clenching around the steering wheel so tightly I felt the hard plastic crack. *Fabulous. Use your Duster power and Faery übercharge to destroy your car.* "Good call, Cass."

Yes, I was talking to myself. Who the hell else was around to talk to? Logan didn't know what I was up to. Devlin had no clue that I was going at dawn. Thea was still asleep at Zoe's house. Jasmine wouldn't be riding in on a white horse like the cavalry. (But that would really be funny, wouldn't it? The picture of Jasmine bouncing around on top of a damn horse actually made me smile—something I wouldn't have thought possible a minute or two ago.) And as for Brady . . . well, he'd done all he could the night before.

He'd given me the Faery equivalent of a nuclear power surge. Power was crackling inside me. I was practically *glowing* with it. I half expected sparks to fly from my fingertips and really hoped they wouldn't. It sounded way too painful.

I stopped at a red light on PCH and tapped my fingers against the wheel while I waited for it to change. You know, this really says a lot about us—people, I mean. If you're ever up at this ungodly hour you'll know what I'm talking about. There was *no one* but me out, and yet there I sat, unwilling to run a red light. So basically we're pretty law-abiding, right? Or maybe it was just that I was in no hurry to meet up with Vanessa and, say, *die.*

My brain was racing; my nerves were jumping. I was terrified, seriously caffeine deprived and a little nauseous. Probably from the no-coffee thing. "So, after you kick Vanessa's ass, you stop for a latte," I promised myself. "Kill a queen, get a doughnut."

My voice seemed to echo in my little car, while the last of the night surrounded me.

I'd never felt so alone in my life.

You are not alone . . . Brady's voice whispered into my mind.

"YOW!" I jolted, nearly strangling myself on the seat belt, and shot a look behind me, half expecting him to pop up out of the backseat.

But he wasn't there. I was still alone. Still on a suicide mission to fight the Bitch Queen of the Universe, and still wishing I were anywhere but where I was. And, hey, fabulous bonus, I was hallucinating, too.

I thought about whistling, but remembered I couldn't. So I flipped on the CD player and let Metallica convince me that I wasn't the only person alive in the world. James Hetfield's voice shouted out and made me feel as if I were connected to something beyond this weird-ass solitary mission.

You are not alone, Brady's voice assured me again. This time I noticed his words were echoing in my mind—not my car. *We are connected, Cassidy. You feel me. Hear me. I will be with you.*

"With me?" I repeated, worried now, because no woman in the world wanted a man in her head all the time. For God's sake, sex with a Faery gave him entry into your thoughts? *That* should have been stenciled on his forehead.

He chuckled, and that seemed even stranger than his talking. *I will be with you during the fight, Cassidy,* he said, his voice no more than a tired whisper.

"Oh. That's okay then, Brady." I answered out loud, pretty much talking to myself when I probably could have just said all this in my mind. But that was the way horror movies always went. The heroine started speaking to people in her mind and pretty soon she was strapped to a bed in the nutso ward and some psycho killer was standing over her with a scalpel.

Didn't I have enough problems without slipping into a B-movie version of *The Fury*? (But wait, wasn't *The Fury* already a B movie anyway? So what was I in? B-minus?)

You are not crazy.

"Says the voice in my head." Okay, nice to have company, but scoring a little high on the creep-o-meter, too.

He laughed, and hearing a disembodied voice laughing through your brain was right up there with ventriloquists— whom I hated even more than I hated clowns.

I made the turn when the light turned green and headed down the Pacific Coast Highway to the cliffs. Not that I was eager to get there or anything. "Mainly because I have *zero* idea what I'm supposed to do."

You will know when the time is right.

"Great, thanks!" Okay, answering the voice in my head. "You said that last night, too. Not a big help. Besides, I think the time's pretty much right, Brady. I'm almost there."

Still time to turn around, Cass. Pick up Thea, head for Canada, maybe. It's nice this time of year, right? "Sure. Late October. Great for visiting all those northern places. Driving a Bug through a blizzard. Good idea." *Hmm.* Demon fight sounding a little better in comparison.

Oh, God.

You will win, Cassidy, Brady insisted, his voice in my head soothing.

I only wished I were as sure about that as he seemed to be. Of course, he was safe at home. Why would *he* be worried?

I am not worried because you have my strength. My power. All I could give you, he whispered, and was it just me, or did he sound more tired than before? Of course, after a night like last night, who could blame him?

"Okay," I said, willing to lie to the voice in my head as well as to myself. Give myself a pep talk. Pull out the mental pom-poms and do a cheer! No, wait, that was Thea. Not me. Oh, crap, I didn't want to do this.

I parked the car on PCH and walked across the strip of grass leading to the cliff edge. There was a fence there to keep idiots from tumbling off the ledge and letting their families sue the city. But it wasn't much of a fence. Just a couple of steel bars that ran the length of the cliffs. I curled my hands over the top rail and let the damp cold of the metal settle into me.

The ocean was gunmetal gray with some frothy whitecaps. There were no surfers out there, though, which worried me a little. Surfers surfed no matter what the weather was like. So what had happened to keep them away today?

Then I noticed a rumble of sound and let my gaze dip from the wide expanse of ocean to the stretch of beach at the bottom of the cliffs.

Yikes.

Okay, now I knew why the surfers were nowhere to be found. They didn't mind cold or rain or choppy seas.

But apparently they drew the line at demon hordes.

My jaw dropped. I looked up and down the narrow strip of beach lined on one side by the ocean and the other by the jagged, dark rocks of the cliff, and all I could see was demons.

The thick crowd of them moved and shifted together in a weird sort of dance. Their skin tones were a rainbow of colors, and the horns, spots, tails and fangs added just the right note of festivity! Not to mention the rumble of their movements and whispered conversations sounded like thunder.

The first pale gold rays of the rising sun winked off the blades of hatchets, axes, machetes and some wicked-looking curved swords.

"Oh, crap." Why the hell hadn't the Faery supercharge Brady had given me come with a damn manual?

I don't mind admitting that in that moment, I came as close as I hoped I ever would to peeing my pants. I've never been that scared and don't expect to be again. Fear was alive and well and grabbing the base of my throat, shutting off my air.

My stomach did a hard pitch, and my hands tightened around the cold metal railing, squeezing until finally the damn thing snapped off in my hands. I glanced down at the short length of pipe I was holding, then threw it to the ground. The sun was rising faster now, and as it climbed in the sky the fear slowly drained right out of me.

Weird? Oh, baby.

But true. All of a sudden, I *felt* Brady's power. The strength that had been humming through me all night came to blistering life inside me. And I felt *him*, too. His presence was so strong, it was like I really wasn't alone anymore, and in that amazing moment I knew *exactly* what to do.

Below me the demons looked up, spotting me at the edge of the cliff. A roar of fury lifted into the air and sent a chill snaking along my spine. But I heard Brady whispering, *Do it now, Cassidy. Feel the strength. Open yourself to it.*

So I did.

Going on pure instinct, I lifted both hands, holding them high enough that the first rays of the sun seemed to balance themselves on my palms. And that was when it got *really* weird.

Electricity pumped through me.

I mean, serious electrical energy.

I felt it blasting its way through my body, spilling into every corner, every inch of me, racing from my legs up through my middle, down my arms, and when it hit my fingertips I remember thinking, *Oh, this is really going to hurt.*

And boy howdy, did it.

Whips of actual lightning shot from my fingertips. White-hot streaks of light and fire spilled from me, arced into the air and then dropped to the demons already trying to rush the base of the cliffs. For a second I felt like I was in the last episode of *Buffy*, with the gazillion ancient vampire things. Then I realized this was different.

Remember that scene in *Raiders of the Lost Ark*? Where all the Nazis got burned up and melted by lightning bolts jumping out of the ark? This was just like that. Only with less melting going on.

The bolts of energy splintered, each of them forking into dozens, hundreds of new lightning bolts. I stood there quivering in my Keds, feeling the power slamming through me and punching out of my body, and watched as those ribbons of fire crashed into the chests of every demon gathered below.

A literal explosion of dust rose up. The demons winked out of existence as the energy ribbons sliced through their numbers as quickly as Thea and I sliced through a chocolate fudge cake. And we left fewer crumbs.

It was awesome.

In seconds clouds of dust were blowing out to sea, but I had only a second or two to hope demons were biodegradable. The lightning shooting out of my fingertips stopped as quickly as it had begun. I wasn't sorry to see it go, either. My fingers still felt like they were on fire. But I was alive, so, good for me.

A shriek of outrage ended my inner celebration, though.

I looked down, and wouldn't you know it? There was *one* demon left standing.

Yep. Vanessa was still there.

Royally pissed off, but all alone.

I shook my right hand and pointed it like a gun, trying to force a spit of lightning out of it. Nothing happened. "Well, for God's sake, don't stop now!"

"You *bitch*!" the queen shouted, her voice booming out around me. "You melded with my Faery! You took the power that was meant to be *mine*!"

"Oh, EW!" I shouted. "Could you just get a grip here?" You know, there's just something nasty about somebody knowing you've had sex. The fact that it was Vanessa only made things worse.

"You've killed my army, Duster, but I remain. I will see you dead and bleeding for this," the queen shouted, and let me tell you, she had no trouble at all making her voice carry over the wind and the ocean and even the hard thumping of my own heartbeat.

End her, Cassidy, Brady's voice whispered through my mind, and I felt his fatigue as if it were my own. Well, hell, helping me shoot lightning had to have been exhausting. But he was right about finishing this with Vanessa. Long past time I sent the bitch queen off to the Dust Bunny Kingdom.

"Damn straight I will."

Okay, I admit it. I was riding a little high on the *whoosh* of dusting, like, a thousand demons all at once! I felt like warrior woman. So, while I was so confident and Ms. Hot Shit, I jumped off the freaking cliff.

I can hardly believe it myself now. But I did. For one little moment I was flying, and then I was just falling and worried about the imminent crash.

I hit the wet sand hard and felt pain zing through my legs. But they weren't broken and neither was I, so big plus. When I stood up I found Vanessa glaring at me through glowing red eyes. Her mouth was pinched, and her tall, regal body was practically vibrating with rage.

Good times.

"This is all your fault. I should have killed you that night in my garden."

"Yeah, well," I said with a shrug, "hindsight's a bitch."

"EEEEEEEEEEIIIIIIIIIKKKKKKKKKKK!!!!!!" She charged, hands outstretched, mouth open, fangs glinting in the morning sunlight. Still riding the Duster high, I rushed her right back. We met in the middle with a thunk that was probably heard around the world.

We bounced off each other like balls banking off the edge of a pool table. Staggering, we both recovered and went at it again. She hit me in the mouth and I stumbled backward, tasting blood and knowing it was mine. *Gross.* She smiled and took another swing, but I held up one hand to block it while kicking out with my right foot.

I hit her belly and she *whoomped* when all her air exploded from her lungs. She was pissed, but so was I. She'd tried to destroy the world. She'd tried to ruin Halloween. And mostly she kept trying to kill *me.*

My fist landed on her nose and I heard the crunch as it folded under my hand. Pink blood spurted. Very pretty. Especially when it was leaking out of *her.* "That damn reward you put on my head really pissed me off!"

"Fool. You've ruined everything," she muttered, swiping one hand under her nose, streaking her own blood across her pale cheek. Then she hit me again under my chin, smacking my jaws together and making me bite my tongue.

"Ekthellent," I said. (My tongue was swollen.) "And it wathn't that hard, either."

Okay, big lie, but why not make her feel even worse?

"That was *my* Faery," Vanessa howled in fury. "For a hundred years he was mine! His power belonged to me!

"He doethn't belong to you, you thtupid cow!"

"Cow!?" She jerked her head back and looked like that one word hurt more than my punches.

"I am a queen!" she shouted, lifting her arms, waving them around like she was waiting for a nonexistent crowd to start applauding.

Well, that ship had sailed. Her demon horde was blowing in the wind and getting snacked on by whatever fishies were out there. Brady'd given *me* his power, and she was just shit out of luck.

"How did you do it?" Her voice sounded like nails on a blackboard.

"You want to *talk* now?" I was staggering. All I wanted was to finish this and get home.

Vanessa stalked closer, the wind pushing at her, whipping her hair into her eyes. "How did you get him to die for you?"

"Huh?" Die? Who died? What the *hell* was she talking about, and *why* wasn't I just dusting her?

"*My* Faery sacrificed himself for *you?*" She was still screeching.

"Thacrifithe?" I scowled at the sound of my stupid voice while trying to get a grip on what she was saying. Brady had *died*? She was talking about *Brady*? Was that why I didn't feel him anymore? Was that the sense of emptiness filling me? No. I wouldn't believe it. Couldn't believe it. She was lying; that was all. Of course she was lying.

She sneered at me, her gaze raking me up and down in dismissal. "When a Faery gives away his power he *dies*. Everyone knows that."

I blinked at her. I didn't know that. Was it true? No. Couldn't be true.

I was tired, bloody, battered and swaying unsteadily on my feet. I'd had *way* too much of this bitch, and all I wanted now was some coffee and a chance to find Brady and thank him for his help.

"I'm done. Thith ith over, Vanettha," I said, trying to sound tough despite my stupid Elmer Fudd accent. Best to just end this now before I had to speak much more.

"Nooooooo!" The wind lifted her long brown hair and twisted it about her head like live snakes. Nasty image. "You will *not* win! I will defeat you in spite of that treacherous Faery! I will have my crown. My legions will cover the face of the earth and you will all bow before—"

I'd had about all I could take. Come on. A demon queen with delusions of grandeur? I slapped my hand into her chest (and thanks to that burst of Faery power, I didn't have a problem this time) and I went through her chest like Sugar went through popcorn.

Her eyes went wide, then she hissed a curse I didn't quite catch, since she dissolved an instant later. The wind carried the last of her out to sea, and I hoped her demon-dust buddies were properly respectful.

"Thcrew you, Vanettha," I said, then winced. Okay. I needed a latte and some ice for my tongue. Hard to be victorious when you sounded like an idiot.

"We did it, Brady," I said.

When he didn't answer, the first tendril of worry spun through me as I remembered what Vanessa had said. Had Brady really died to save me? I rubbed my hands up and down my arms to get rid of the sudden chill I felt and tried again to contact the voice in my head.

When he didn't answer, though, I managed to convince myself he was okay. Probably just as pooped as I was. Vanessa was a lying bitch. But now, at least, she was a *dead* lying bitch. My work here was done. I blew out a satisfied breath. Then I looked up at the cliffside and realized the only way back up was to freaking climb.

⸎

I hit the first drive-through Starbucks I came across, got a cup of ice, a venti latte and a sackful of doughnuts, glazed and chocolate. Then I headed home as La Sombra woke up.

The town would go about its business and never know how close it had come to being overrun by demons. Halloween would kick off tonight, and kids would crowd the streets looking for candy. And I was alive to enjoy it all. Plus, my tongue felt better with all the ice. I'd tried out saying S a few times, and I didn't sound like an idiot anymore.

Everything was good.

Except for the fact that I couldn't feel Brady with me anymore. Ever since just before the queen blew out to sea he'd been silent, which worried me more than I wanted to admit.

I still had the power he'd given me, but the connection to him was gone and I felt empty without it. So I kept chewing on the ice in between latte sips, punched the gas pedal and broke every speed law in town to get home.

The house felt as empty as I did. Sugar was there, of course, but she only lifted her head to look at me and then went back to sleep. I raced around the house like a crazy person, opening closets, looking under beds and behind dressers. "Brady!" I shouted for him, but only silence answered me.

I didn't find him. There was no Faery stretched out on the couch. No Faery making coffee in the kitchen. No Faery waiting to congratulate me on a dusting well done.

There was no Faery in my house at all.

Finally I ran upstairs to my bedroom, threw the door open wide and looked from the empty bed to every corner of the room. I checked the closet and the bathroom before giving up. He was gone, and my chest felt tight. I was shaking harder than I had on the cliff's edge. This was wrong. Brady should be here waiting for me. Helping me celebrate.

But he was gone.

I felt like a kid whose best friend had moved away without saying good-bye. Tears were biting at my eyes when I spotted a glimmer of something shining on the floor beside my bed. I stumbled toward it and tried to concentrate on breathing—in, out, in, out. Then I dropped to the floor, dragged my fingers through the shimmer of what looked like glitter and felt my heart break.

"Oh, God . . ." I remembered Brady telling me once, *At least when Faeries die we leave behind sparkling dust.*

He was dead. Vanessa had been right. Brady had *died* to help me. The first tears streaked down my face. Without him I never would have defeated Vanessa. I'd accepted the gift of his power so easily, never guessing what it was costing him. When that thought hit, something else occurred to me: Had Jasmine known? She'd gone to her "sources" to find out about Faery power. Had she realized that Brady would die if he gave me his power? If she had, why the *hell* hadn't she told me?

I had a few questions for my trainer—but that would have to wait. At the moment I just didn't have the strength for that fight. I felt emptier than I had before, and I hadn't thought that would be possible. "Brady's dead. Gone."

It didn't seem possible, and I lifted my head to look around the room, as if I were hoping to prove myself wrong—that Brady wasn't dead, but hiding behind a chair. Or the dresser. But he wasn't, and I knew it. He was never coming back. He'd sacrificed himself to give me what I needed to defeat Vanessa. He'd given his *life* for me, and I couldn't even say thank-you. I couldn't tell him how much Thea and I would miss him.

"Cassidy . . ."

"Oh, God. Now I'm hearing things."

Brady laughed, and I knew I wasn't hallucinating. He sounded too delighted.

"What the hell is going on here?" I stood up, and my gaze hit the mirror across the room. That was when I saw him. He was there—in the mirror. But when I spun around to look behind me, I was alone in the room. Slowly swiveling back around, I looked into the mirror again and directly into Brady's eyes. "You're inside a mirror."

"Yes. It is odd to me as well." He frowned. "So far it is very strange here on the other side. But I am not in your world anymore, and this is the only way I can speak to you."

"Okay," I said, walking closer to the mirror hanging over my chest of drawers. Seeing him made me feel better somehow. I knew he was dead, yet here he was. Still himself. Still talking. Smiling. Existing.

I saw tear tracks on my own cheeks as I reached out and touched my hand to the glass. On his side of the mirror Brady did the same. I think I felt a tingle, but it might have been wishful thinking. "Weird, but better than nothing."

"You did well, Cassidy," he said.

I gave him a smile. "*We* did well. Thanks to you, the queen's dead."

"I know." He lifted those amazingly broad shoulders in a shrug.

"But you shouldn't have done it," I told him, laying my hand flat against the glass now. "You shouldn't have sacrificed yourself like that."

"As you had no choice in the battle, I had no choice but to help you succeed," he said, then added, his voice coming a little faster now, "I could not allow Vanessa to threaten you and Thea."

"But you died, Brady. How can I repay that? Ever?"

"There is no payment required," he said. "You and Thea gave me much in my time with you. I will always remember."

"We'll miss you," I said simply, because really, what else could I possibly have said?

"Thank you." He smiled, then added, "I do not have much time, Cassidy. I can speak to you this way only once. It is a rule. So you must listen to me."

"One time?" I muttered, and he frowned at me. "Fine," I said. "I'm listening."

"The gift of power I gave you will remain with you. Always."

"Seriously?" *Whoa.*

"A male Faery may give up his powers to anyone he chooses. What you call the supercharge will remain with you. I trust you to use it wisely. But others of my kind may not."

"That doesn't sound good."

Brady glanced over his shoulder into mirrorland. "It is not. Maab, the Faery queen, will not be happy with the gift I've given you."

Oh, man. Just what I needed: A big battle. A friend dying. Now more trouble. My stomach did a quick lurch, and I wished for chocolate. "What do you mean, 'not happy'?"

Brady's smile faltered a little. Then he looked back at me. "Maab will probably try to reclaim the power I've given you. She is very picky about Faery powers remaining in our realm." He shrugged. "There are rules."

"Rules?" My head was spinning—not in a good way. "Brady, you can't just die, dump all of this on me and then disappear into a mirror." Boy, did *that* sound weird.

He flattened his palm against the glass, lining it up with mine. "Have a good life, Cassidy. Say good-bye to Thea for me. Please tell her to be a good cheerleader."

"Good-bye?" *Have a good life? Say bye to Thea?* "Wait a damn minute. You have to explain this. Where is this Maab? What's she like?"

"I must go now. It is a rule."

"Screw the rules!" I shouted as Brady started to fade away. "You can't go—"

"Beware the queen." Even as I watched, his smiling, familiar image grew fainter and fainter and fainter.

I slapped my mirror over and over again, waiting for him to come back. He never did. It didn't stop me from shouting though.

"ANOTHER FREAKING QUEEN?" He was gone and I was still hitting the mirror. "Damn it, Brady," I shouted, "get your Faery ass back here!"

Brady's chuckle floated out around me.

"This isn't funny!" I spun in a tight circle, shouting, "Brady! Brady! BRADY!" until finally I was so dizzy I had to lie down.

Mother of a cheerleader.

Legendary Demon Duster.

New Faery powers.

Another queen after my ass.

Is my life weird or what?

About the Author

Maureen Child is the award-winning author of more than ninety romance novels and often says she has the best job in the world. A five-time RITA nominee, Maureen lives with her family in Southern California.